FATAL FALLOUT
CRIMSON POINT PROTECTORS

KAYLEA CROSS

FATAL FALLOUT
Copyright © 2023 Kaylea Cross

∼

Cover Art: Sweet 'N Spicy Designs
Developmental edits: Kelli Collins
Line Edits: Joan Nichols:
Digital Formatting: LK Campbell

∼

This book is a work of fiction. The names, characters, places, and incidents are products of the writer's imagination or have been used fictitiously and are not to be construed as real. Any resemblance to persons, living or dead, actual events, locales or organizations is entirely coincidental.

All rights reserved. With the exception of quotes used in reviews, this book may not be reproduced or used in whole or in part by any means existing without written permission from the author.

ISBN: 9798393568078

AUTHOR'S NOTE

If you follow me on social media, then you already know I took my eldest son over to the UK last fall to start his studies at Durham University in the northeast of England. It's SUCH a magical place. Visiting there is like stepping back in time or walking into the pages of a storybook. So I had to include it in a book of my own.

I hope you enjoy it.

Kaylea

ONE

Over one hundred innocent Americans dead. Almost three times that many wounded. Every one of them senselessly cut down at an outdoor concert in Washington State two months earlier.

And that was only the latest body count racked up by the monster Walker was about to meet face-to-face for the first time since the interview that had helped lock him away in here. The man might not have been the one to pull the trigger, but he was responsible for those casualties nonetheless.

Walker stared straight ahead as he waited for the automatic steel doors in front of him to open, preparing for the coming confrontation. Throughout his career in intelligence, he had interrogated many prisoners behind bars, but never in a place like this. The ADX Florence "supermax" prison was a max-security facility unlike anything else in the country.

As he stood there, he could feel his former self take over. It had been years since he'd done this. Not since he'd left the intelligence world behind. But life had a funny way of circling back on itself. His background and personal experience with this inmate had landed him here as a consultant for the CIA—

along with the tidbits of intel a little birdie had been feeding him behind the scenes.

Desperate times called for desperate measures.

His security credentials had been checked before he'd been admitted through the front gate, followed by a scan for drugs and weapons. The two heavily armed guards flanking him led him through yet another automatic steel door, their footsteps echoing down the empty hall. Dozens of cameras tracked their every move along the corridor, past a guard station into a different cellblock.

Everything was sterile. Devoid of color and life, the only natural light coming from a few tiny windows embedded in the exterior walls on either end of the hall. The cold, industrial feel and the total silence in every cellblock were almost disorienting.

In here, time had no meaning. Prisoners were completely cut off from the outside world and each other. Once inside, an inmate would never so much as catch a glimpse of the Rocky Mountains that soared into the endless Colorado sky and formed a dramatic backdrop behind the prison.

A series of thick steel doors lined the interior wall. Prisoners sent here—the most violent offenders and most dangerous terrorists in the United States—spent up to twenty-three hours of every day in their cells, in solitary confinement.

There was a reason why this place was called "life after death." That kind of total isolation got to a man eventually, no matter how tough he thought he was. Including Walker's old adversary waiting somewhere within this soulless maze.

"In here, sir," one of the guards said, stepping ahead to slide a key into the lock on the next steel door. Then he swiped an access card into a chip reader, entered a code. A quiet buzz sounded. The door clicked open.

Walker stepped through it into the small windowless room,

steeling himself for the sight of the man he'd hoped never to lay eyes on again, and sat in the chair facing a darkened panel on the opposite wall.

"We'll be right outside the door, sir."

Walker nodded, staring at that panel as the door closed behind him with a quiet steel clang that had a chilling, final ring to it. Being locked up in here must feel a bit like being entombed alive. Yet he questioned whether it was punishment enough for the crimes committed to warrant being sent to this place.

The sound of the second hand on his watch ticking was overly loud in the eerie total silence as he waited. He wouldn't be here unless it was absolutely necessary. And even if he walked out of here with nothing, he'd had to come. Had to try.

Because though the man on the other side of that wall had nothing left to lose, in some ways he was still every bit as dangerous as when he'd been a free man.

The dark screen in front of him suddenly came to life. In spite of himself, a wave of anger punched through him when he saw the familiar figure framed there.

Elliot Fornam. Now fifty-three years old, wearing a bright orange prison jumpsuit and a plain white T-shirt underneath. His cuffed wrists were anchored to the concrete table he sat behind. Shackled feet bound to the concrete floor.

A violent domestic terrorist with extreme anti-government views responsible for the deaths of hundreds of innocent American civilians and countless other people around the world due to attacks carried out by his followers.

Recent chatter said another one was coming. Soon. The CIA was desperate enough to stop it to send Walker here in the hopes of getting even the tiniest clue that might help them crack the case.

He kept absolutely still, maintained a passive expression

even as the eyes staring back at him sent a wave of revulsion through him. Bright blue. Eerie and otherworldly beneath the glare of the sterile white lights that made Fornam look pale as skim milk.

The supermax effect had already begun to take its toll. Fornam looked gaunt, almost shriveled. Frail, his chest and shoulders sunken beneath the jumpsuit. There were hollows under his cheekbones.

But those eyes. They were as bright and sharp as ever, the malicious, unholy gleam in them still present. And that slight curl to his mouth. That fucking evil, smug smirk Walker still dreamed about wiping off Fornam's ugly face with his fists.

A psychopath's smile. He'd seen many in his time, but Fornam's was the stuff of nightmares.

"So. You finally came to visit," Fornam said, eyeing Walker with interest. Probably thrilled by the prospect of a few minutes' reprieve from the isolated monotony that was now his everyday existence. "To what do I owe the pleasure?"

He'd denied having anything to do with the attack on July second. Denied knowing anything about his followers planning it. There was no way he should have been involved with the July attack. And yet Walker would bet everything he owned that Fornam had been *intimately* involved.

And that someone within these walls had helped him communicate his orders to his followers.

He got straight to the point. "Who did you pay off to get word to your network on the outside?" Home Front wasn't just a homegrown American problem anymore. In the past year, Fornam's poison had spread far beyond this country's shores, infecting a whole new generation of disaffected people overseas.

Fornam put on a perplexed expression. "I don't know what you mean."

Walker leaned forward and folded his forearms on the cold surface of the table, never breaking eye contact. Fornam knew him. Knew how he worked.

He also knew that Walker couldn't be intimidated. Not by security or military personnel, rich politicians or heads of state. Not even by the most evil terrorists the world could create.

Certainly not by Fornam.

"I realize you're bored in here," he went on. "That it doesn't matter if you get another consecutive life sentence added on for this latest attack, or five. Your cremated ashes will be dumped into the prison compost heap long before the first one is up anyway."

Walker saw the first indication that he'd gotten under Fornam's skin. The slight tightening of the skin around the mouth and eyes. The subtle tensing in the jaw and shoulders before Fornam caught himself and relaxed again, his smug smirk sliding back into place.

"My memory and the memory of what I've done will live on forever," he said with pride, his expression full of arrogance.

Good to see the time in here hadn't dulled his arrogance any. Walker used it to his advantage. "Until someone better comes along. You know how it is today with how fast things move in the twenty-four-seven news cycle we live in."

The arrogant look faded a little.

He held that eerie stare for several long moments before sliding the verbal blade in deeper. "Because you and I both know that eventually someone bigger and badder than you ever were will come along and erase you from memory. And he's out there right now, Elliot. Maybe you even trained him yourself. Made yourself redundant without realizing it. Wouldn't that be something? Gotta love the irony there."

The barb struck home. Fornam's arrogant smirk turned into

a sneer. "You don't know what you're talking about. You don't know *anything*."

"So who is he?" Walker pressed, refusing to be baited. Fornam hated this. Hated being caged like an animal and subjected to another interrogation, especially by him. Hated being analyzed, insulted and put on the defensive. Hated being talked down to and humiliated more than anything.

Jabbing Fornam's ego was always a good bet. "Hm? Who's going to replace you and take over everything you built now that you're trapped in here for the rest of your life?"

His nostrils flared, lips pinching into a thin line. But Walker caught the flicker of unease in those cold blue eyes. Then raw anger. "You think I'm going to tell you?"

"So someone *has* already taken over. Thanks for confirming that." The intel community had feared another leader had stepped in to fill the void after Fornam was sent here. Now he knew for certain.

Flustered, Fornam consciously relaxed his features, but too late. "How the hell would I know? Like you just said, I'm trapped in here." The smirk was back. He tsked, shook his head, putting on a pathetic display of false bravado that any rookie interrogator would see through. Already faded to a shadow of what he'd once been.

"True. Still, you know *some* things, don't you?" He cocked his head. "No? Already that useless to the others?" He tsked.

Fornam's mouth tightened. "Pretty desperate of you to come down here hoping for answers. You're the one on the outside with all the networking and high-tech resources at your fingertips. And you still can't figure it out? That's pretty pathetic, Walker."

Hearing his name from Fornam's lips disgusted him but he didn't allow a single shift in his expression, gaze or posture. Even this place wasn't punishment enough for this piece of shit.

While Fornam would never breathe free air again, he also got protection, three squares a day and medical treatment for the rest of his existence courtesy of the American taxpayers he'd terrorized.

"Everyone who had contact with you here prior to the second of July attack at The Gorge is gone now. Including the prison employees." He paused, raised his eyebrows. "Having trouble connecting with your network lately?"

A spark of anger flared in Fornam's eyes, the jab igniting his temper. "Locking me up in here didn't stop anything. It *won't* stop anything. Did you really think it would?" He laughed softly. "My organization will continue on no matter what happens to me. You have no idea what's coming. You can't stop it."

"Yes, I can."

The quiet declaration seemed to startle Fornam, who went silent.

"You know I can," Walker continued. "And it's not your organization anymore, as you already confirmed. That's all over. You're nothing now." His quiet words rang with conviction. It was strange, but that had always rattled Fornam. Something about Walker's calm, quiet interrogation method deeply disturbed him. He didn't need to yell or threaten Fornam to get under his skin.

Walker kept staring. Barely even blinked as he let the silence build between them until it was deafening.

Fornam shifted slightly in his chair, betraying his discomfort in spite of his fake bored expression. "I don't know who it is," he finally muttered.

"Yes, you do. And he's in the UK, planning an op right now." According to his sources the chatter there was off the charts. Something big was brewing. Walker was doing his part to help stop whatever it was.

Sudden surprise flared in Fornam's eyes. A recognition that confirmed Walker's worst fear. "Who?" he half-whispered. Testing him. Wanting to see if Walker had figured it out. But no one knew for sure except Fornam.

Walker pushed right back. Baiting him. "You know who."

A slow, skin-crawling grin spread across his face. Then he laughed. A soft, chilling sound. "You see? It's already happening. Like I said, you can't stop it." He shifted again, his growing agitation palpable.

Walker recognized the signs of impending shutdown. He'd gotten everything he was going to get from Fornam. This interview was over.

He stood abruptly, the legs of his chair scraping over the concrete floor. "Thanks for the tips. Enjoy the rest of your sentence," he said, turning for the door.

"Walker," Fornam called.

He kept going as a guard outside opened the door.

"Walker!" The frustration and slight note of panic in his voice was a balm to Walker's soul. Fornam's little reprieve from the endless monotony and segregation had come to an end and now he would be put back in his cage. "Who is it? Say his name! Say it!"

He stepped out into the hallway. The guards escorted him out of the maze of doors and corridors and through security to the outer gate, where his rental car was parked. He got in, closed his eyes and shoved out a breath, releasing all the pent-up tension inside him.

He'd sworn years ago that he'd gotten out of this game for good. Fornam's connection to the July second attack had dragged him back. He wanted to end this as soon as possible and get back to the life he'd rebuilt for himself after Jillian.

He dialed a number as he drove past guarded watchtowers up the long road leading to the turnoff to the prison. Recently "retired" NSA agent Alex Rycroft answered on the second ring, seven hours ahead in London. "Did you see him?" he asked.

They had talked about all of this previously during a joint CIA/NSA brief that Rycroft had been read into. "Just leaving the property now. The new head's one of his. And he's definitely in the UK. Possibly dual US-UK citizenship." It wasn't much, but it was better than nothing and everyone involved could now stop wasting resources chasing their tails here in the States.

"You're sure?"

"Positive." All except the dual citizenship part, but he was pretty certain about that too. At least that narrowed down their list of potential suspects drastically.

"All right. We still on for that pint we talked about?"

"Yeah." In addition to talking about their new suspect, he would finally get answers about the female agent who had been feeding him bits of intel under the radar. "I'll see you Monday night."

∽

WALKER PAUSED in the act of repacking his suitcase in his bedroom the next afternoon when he heard the side door open and close downstairs. Shae back from class at the local community college.

"Dad?" the most wonderful voice in the entire world called out a moment later.

"Up here." He'd barely stepped into the hallway before Shae appeared at the top of the stairs. He held out his arms.

Her face lit up in a big smile. "Hey," she said, and walked right into his embrace. "Didn't expect you to be home."

He hugged her, kissed the top of her head, all thoughts about Fornam disappearing in an instant. Everything was suddenly right in his world. His little girl was all grown up but she still needed Dad hugs and it melted him even more now. "Caught an early flight so I could be home in time to have dinner with my best girl."

"You still flying out to London tomorrow?"

"Yep." He released her and she stepped back. "You cut your hair."

She touched the brown chin-length bob, lips curving upward. "Yeah. Anaya went to the salon with me after we did some baby shopping for the nursery she and Donovan are finishing up."

She adored her new stepmother. "You look like your mom," he murmured, a pang hitting him. Not nearly as strong and painful as the thought of Jillian had once been. Time had faded it to an ache now whenever he thought of her. Shae had Jillian's features and Donovan's green eyes.

"I know. When I saw myself in the mirror at the salon my eyes bugged out." She leaned against the doorjamb and crossed her arms, a slight frown tugging at her eyebrows. "How did it go…wherever you were? You get what you needed?"

He'd kept things vague with her about the purpose of his trip, didn't want her exposed to the darkness of his past work. He'd always done his best to keep his professional and private lives separate, for good reason. "No, but it did my heart good to see this guy locked up tight for the rest of his life."

Shae nodded, expression sober. "Is the London trip connected?"

"In a way. Nothing for you to worry about, though," he said to reassure her. "No danger involved for me." He was glad she didn't know the things he did. Had always done his best to hide and protect her from the darkness he dealt with on a daily basis. She'd had too much trauma and uncertainty in her life already. "Mostly this trip has to do with Ivy." She had to be an operative of some sort. Or a former one. But on paper and in every place he'd looked, she didn't exist. And Walker didn't believe in ghosts.

Shae relaxed, a grin spreading across her face. "Oh, man, I can't wait to find out the details later."

He chuckled because he hadn't told her much about Ivy, only that she was exceptionally skilled and capable. "Something tells me she's not gonna make it easy for me to find out much." He wanted some straight answers from Rycroft about the mysterious, highly trained woman he had only worked with briefly during an op to rescue Anaya's sister in Kabul last summer. "You hungry?"

"Yeah, but I don't feel like cleaning up the kitchen later. Let's go out."

Over dinner in town at a place overlooking the ocean, they talked about Shae's classes and her excitement about becoming a big sister. "You should see Donovan right now. It's hilarious," she said, twirling pasta around her fork like a pro. "He's doting on Anaya like mad and it's driving her crazy. And she's still got four months to go. Imagine what he'll be like close to her due date."

Walker smiled. "Love to see it." Donovan had come a long way since Anaya had walked into his life. And Walker had no doubt that this time around, he was going to be a great dad from day one.

"Yeah, it's actually pretty awesome, I will admit." She tucked her sleek hair behind her ear and kept chattering as she ate. He stayed quiet, letting her talk, enjoying the conversation and her company. When he'd first moved them to Crimson Point, she'd hated it here. Seeing her this happy was everything. In fact, she seemed happier than he'd seen her since Jillian died.

This, he thought with sudden clarity. This was why he'd chosen to walk away from his government intelligence work.

As soon as they'd received Jillian's diagnosis, he'd quit and walked away for good.

Well, until now.

Shae paused, studying him. "Can I ask you something?" She sounded uncharacteristically hesitant.

"You can ask me anything." And he'd give her a straight answer as long as it didn't break any security protocols.

"Do you ever regret it? Leaving your job for Mom and me."

"Never. Not one single day." He didn't even have to think about it.

She blinked at his adamant tone. "Really? I know you miss it sometimes."

"No. Really. Zero regrets about that." The few regrets he did have were related to past failures in his career. Namely Fornam. Never with Jillian and Shae, or his decision to uproot her and move them here for his new job with Crimson Point Security. That change had been good for them both.

"When do you think you'll be back from the UK?"

"I'm not sure yet. Maybe a week or so, just depends on how things go."

"Oh." She visibly relaxed, her shoulders easing. "That's good then."

He didn't want her worrying about him. Ever. "It shouldn't take too long. I—"

"You don't need to explain, Dad. I'll be fine. Just promise me you'll be careful."

"I won't be in any danger, sweetheart," he said with a smile. God, he loved her. Had never known he could feel a love this deep until she and Jillian had turned his world on its head. He just wanted Shae to be happy. "How's Finn?" he asked casually.

She stilled, fork poised partway to her mouth, and flushed. "He's fine," she said, and didn't elaborate.

Walker hid a smile and let it go. He wouldn't pry, but the

people-reading skills he'd honed over the years told him there was definitely something more than friendship brewing between her and his boss's stepson. Finn was a good kid. Walker liked him and was curious to see how this would play out.

In the meantime, he had unfinished business to attend to in London—and it included uncovering the secrets of Ivy's past.

TWO

"Any new leads today?"

Ivy leaned back in her comfy desk chair, watching Amber on her desktop screen. "Nothing of significance. You?"

"No. But something big is coming." Her Valkyrie sister and fellow hacker lived in Montana now but had been helping her monitor online chatter about another possible terrorist attack either here in the UK or in the States.

"I know." They hadn't put the pieces together in time to prevent the July concert massacre in Washington State. Hopefully they could stop this one.

Amber tilted her head slightly. "You okay?"

"Yeah, why?"

"You seem…distracted."

"Just trying to connect the dots, and knowing I'm missing something critical. I'm good though, promise." As good as she'd been in a long time, anyway, since after she'd been Julia Green and "died" in Moscow several years ago. "How are things there?"

Amber eyed her for another moment, then let it go. "Great. Jesse and I are going riding with Megan and Ty later."

Amber and her sister Megan had been separated as young children and secretly funneled into the Valkyrie program. Most orphan girls put into the program had washed out, only a mere fraction making it through to graduation. Of those who had, only a tiny percentage had survived their careers as the most lethal female assassins the United States had ever produced.

Ivy and the eight others had defied all the odds by surviving.

"Nice," she said, glad that Amber and Megan were close again, both settled and happy with men they loved and who loved them. They had defied the odds there as well.

"It's Sunday. You guys having a big roast dinner there tonight?"

"I sure hope so. They're my favorite."

They chatted for a bit longer. "I better get going. If I come across anything promising I'll message you," Ivy finished.

"Sounds good. Say hi to Marcus and Kiyomi for us."

"Will do. Bye." She ended the call and glanced out the tall, deep windows lining the rear wall of the upstairs room she used as her office in the gatehouse.

Up the vast expanse of green lawn bordering either side of the crushed golden gravel driveway, the honey-toned Cotswold limestone exterior of Laidlaw Hall glowed in the mellow autumn sunshine, the ornamental trees dotted around it just beginning to turn shades of orange and rust.

"Mrrreow." Her black and white cat hopped up into her lap and onto her desk, then promptly laid himself across her keyboard to regard her with wise amber eyes.

"You know you're not supposed to do that." She rubbed his soft head, smiled as his eyes half-closed and his inner motor filled the room with the blissful sound of his purring while his little white paws flexed rhythmically on the keyboard. Mr.

Whiskers had been with her since she'd found him as a kitten in a dumpster and he was her baby.

He glanced hopefully toward the window. "Mrrreow."

"No, you can't go outside. Sorry." He didn't like being cooped up in the gatehouse all the time with her, but Ivy didn't dare let him out. There were foxes, coyotes and raccoons everywhere out here in the Cotswold countryside. Not to mention a certain rescue dog up at the main house that would rip him apart if she ever caught him. Karas was a sweetheart with people, if a little standoffish, but her intense prey drive meant she would always be an only pet.

"And I have to leave for dinner now. Sorry, bud."

She took a special catnip ball from her desk drawer, waved it in front of his nose and laughed as his eyes shot open, pupils dilating. "Have fun, buddy," she said, and dropped it on the floor for him.

Mr. Whiskers immediately leapt down from the desk and pounced, sending the ball flying across the old hardwood floors to chase it. Oblivious of Ivy or anything else now that the intoxicating scent of the catnip was making him crazy.

She stepped out of the back door and into the early evening sunshine, a cool edge to the air that promised a mist on the hills later. Her shoes crunched pleasantly on the crushed gravel on the way up to the main house. She drew a deep breath of the crisp autumn air filled with the sweet scents of hay and grass, counting her many blessings. A far cry from the life she'd led before moving here eighteen months ago. Sometimes it still felt surreal.

As soon as she neared the front steps of the manor house, Karas began barking from inside, alerting her humans that someone was approaching. Ivy walked right in and closed the huge, carved oak door behind her, her stomach rumbling at the rich smells wafting from the kitchen at the back of the house.

"Something sure smells good in here," she called out, reaching down to pat Karas, who came to greet her. She liked Karas well enough, but would always be a cat person.

"It better. Marcus has been in here for hours," Kiyomi called back.

The ancient, worn flagstones were cool and smooth beneath her sock-covered feet as she strode down the hallway past Marcus's masculine, wood-paneled study that smelled of wood smoke, leather and old books, past the more feminine library with its pale sage-green walls and painted trim, and into the kitchen where her best friend sat at the island sipping a glass of wine, watching her husband finish dinner.

Kiyomi aimed a warm smile at her. "Hope you're hungry."

Her bestie was stunning. Golden-toned skin and delicate features hinting at her half-Japanese ancestry, her sleek black hair falling to her shoulders. "Starved. What's on the menu tonight, Marcus?"

He stood at the stove with his broad back to her, stirring a pan of gravy. "Roast chicken with gravy and veg," he said in his deep Yorkshire accent.

He might be lord of the manor now, but he'd grown up in a blue-collar, working-class branch of his family and didn't have a privileged bone in his body. He was the latest to inherit this estate and he took his role as custodian seriously, working long hours and doing a lot of physical labor himself to save money. Running a place like this was a ton of work and insanely expensive, even with a minimal amount of staff to help.

"And Yorkshire puds?" she asked.

"Aye, of course."

She whipped out her phone and took a quick video of him doing his thing, plus the pan of Yorkies sitting on the counter. "Wish you were here, but you're not, so I guess I'll have some for you," she said, then stopped recording and pulled up her texting app.

"You're sending that to Chloe?" Kiyomi said dryly.

"Oh yeah." She hit send, then went to stand beside Marcus. He was a big man with features made harsher by the burn scars on the side of his face.

The explosion in Syria and subsequent captivity had almost cost him his life. The scars and the permanent limp would never fade, but Kiyomi had transformed him on the inside, pulling him out of his reclusive shell. This hardened soldier of a man was completely gone over his wife. So adorable.

"Need a hand with anything?" she asked him.

"You could set the table if you want."

"Sure."

"I'll help you," Kiyomi said, standing and going to the cupboards to start pulling down dishes.

Ivy got the glasses and cutlery and followed her into the adjoining dining room. "He's so formal about his Sunday dinners," Ivy whispered with a smile. She ate with them almost every night unless they went into town for a date, but on Sundays it was always in here with the two-hundred-year-old china that had been passed down through the generations.

Kiyomi grinned. "I know. It's endearing."

Once Marcus deemed everything ready, they each carried the finished dishes into the dining room and sat down together. Karas positioned herself under the table at her master's feet, muzzle on her paws as she waited for Marcus to give her a little bit of roasted meat at the end of the meal. There was no grace said over the meal but there was something holy about this weekly ritual nonetheless.

"You guys spoil me," she said.

"We're happy to," Marcus said, his harsh features softening with a fondness for her that she felt all the way to her insides.

Even that slight smile on him was killer. Ivy was slow to trust—all Valkyries were— but he had quickly grown on her and now she adored him. Would take a bullet for him. He and Kiyomi had both been wonderful to her since she'd stepped out of the shadows and finally revealed herself to the others as Ivy.

What an ordeal that had been—for all of them.

Guilt pricked her when Kiyomi reached for the wine bottle with her left hand and then immediately put it down, switching to her right hand instead.

It was her fault Kiyomi had been stabbed and suffered permanent nerve damage in her left arm. She'd been the one to instigate the op that had pitted Kiyomi and the others against Tarasov—as a test.

She wasn't proud of it now. But at the time she'd felt it was necessary to test the surviving Valkyries to find out where their loyalties truly lay and if she could trust them. Because she'd been betrayed by others before and nearly paid for that mistake with her life.

Kiyomi and Marcus could have hated her for it. By all rights they *should* have hated her for it. The others too. Instead, they'd taken her into the fold, along with the other Valkyries. Had taken her into their home and treated her as the family she'd never had. So yeah, she would take a bullet for either of them if it came down to it.

And yet…even though Ivy thanked her lucky stars for them every day, she couldn't deny that she was getting antsy.

Never in a million years would she ever have expected to miss her old life. So much of it had been shitty. Full of isolation and fear and violence. But now she felt oddly bored and restless. Without a purpose and resorting to poking around online and on the dark web to keep tabs on different things while helping Kiyomi with her charitable work to protect vulnerable orphans.

Not exactly saving the world anymore.

The whole point in reinventing herself as Ivy was to start over. A reboot. Except lately it felt like her life was on hold somehow, her unique skill set going to waste. And, even with Kiyomi and Marcus living just a few hundred yards away, even with Mr. Whiskers to keep her company…

She was lonely.

All her remaining Valkyrie sisters had found their One and moved on with their lives. Some even had children now. While Ivy remained alone, a prisoner of her past.

"You and Amber find any more names or details on the new terror threat yet?" Kiyomi asked, using her right hand to help herself to another serving of something Marcus called cauliflower cheese. Basically, cauliflower baked in a smooth cheese sauce until it was bubbly and golden.

Ivy liked watching Kiyomi enjoy her food. For too long her friend had led a life of austere deprivation to maintain a certain body weight and shape to fulfill her deadly role. She looked fantastic now and healthier than ever with the extra weight she'd put on since being with Marcus. The way she looked at him was everything Ivy secretly hoped to find one day.

"Unfortunately, no," she said. "We'll keep digging. Eventually we'll crack it."

"What does Alex say?"

"He's retired, you know," she teased. They all knew Rycroft would never fully retire. It wasn't in him to walk away from the game completely. Not when he might be able to do some good in the world that seemed to be spinning more and more out of control every day. "So he's on a need-to-know basis."

"Yeah, bet he's loving that," Kiyomi muttered.

"What about Walker?" Marcus asked.

Something tensed inside her at the mention of his name. "What about him?" she asked, all nonchalance as she reached for another Yorkie. Marcus made huge ones, crispy and golden brown and perfect for ladling gravy into. Addictive. She didn't care how many calories they were.

"Is he still involved?"

"Yes. On his side of things," she answered evasively. She had taken a vested interest in him during and after the Kabul op to rescue Nadia Bishop. And not just because she was wildly attracted to him.

She admired his capability, his reputation within intelligence circles as a man you wanted at your back when things got tough. She'd seen his steely inner core and the sense of calm he radiated firsthand and was inextricably drawn to both.

It was strange given her background and how deadly she was in her own right, but in her dealings with him, he'd made her feel oddly relaxed and safe. No man had ever made Ivy feel remotely close to either of those things before.

She saw a similar dynamic with Kiyomi and Marcus. The way he acted as a solid, grounding and protective force for Kiyomi when she needed it. How patiently he accepted and supported her through the painful past that came with being a Valkyrie. Especially the seductive femme fatal variety that Kiyomi had been.

"There's been some more chatter here in the UK," she went on. "Nothing concrete so far, but enough that the intel community is on edge." The same group that had carried out a mass shooting at an outdoor concert in the US two months ago were suspected to be closely tied to the assassination attempt on the Prime Minister last June, with a string of alerts and foiled plots since.

This latest buzz in the UK had everyone within the intelligence community bracing for the worst.

Marcus frowned and lowered his silverware. "About an attack?"

"Yes." Her phone beeped twice, signaling she had just received something important. She glanced at the others. "Sorry, I need to check this."

"Yeah, go ahead," Kiyomi said, forking up another bite of chicken.

Looking at the file Amber had just sent, her eyes stopped on a familiar name within the list of possible suspects involved with the latest brewing terror plot in the UK, and her stomach tightened.

"What is it?" Kiyomi asked.

Ivy turned her phone around and held it out for them to read the screen. Both of them stiffened. "How did you get this?" Marcus said.

"GCHQ." She'd been sneaking into a virtual back door and siphoning bits of intel from the Government Communications Headquarters in Cheltenham. The UK's equivalent of the NSA, a mere half-hour drive from here in Stow-on-the-Wold.

Marcus's dark eyebrows lifted. "You've been hacking into the GCHQ for this?"

"Not just me. Amber too. But don't worry, we didn't leave any traces." It was risky, yes, but she was sick and freaking tired of government agencies having the intel and doing sweet fuck-all with it while the danger mounted.

"You need to call Alex," Kiyomi said.

She was right. "Yeah. Excuse me," she murmured and left the table, retreating to Marcus's study where she had total privacy.

She sat on the tufted leather sofa positioned next to the old stone fireplace, a set of logs already laid in the grate in anticipation of the first chilly night of the season. The space was ultra-masculine and Ivy loved it. Sitting in here was like being wrapped up in a cocoon somehow, Marcus's calm, protective presence infusing every inch.

She gathered her thoughts as she waited for Rycroft to answer.

"Ivy, hi. How are things there? Sunday roast night?"

"They were better until the alert I got a minute ago."

He was silent as she explained. Stayed silent after, absorbing everything. "Anything else?" he finally asked in his pragmatic way.

"No. Nothing else relevant, anyway." The name Isaac Grey was enough to set off major alarm bells for anyone who recognized it. "Should I tell Walker?"

"I'm meeting him tomorrow night. I'll tell him then."

"I thought you were still in London."

"I am. If you hear anything else in the meantime, let me know."

Walker was coming to London to meet Rycroft? "What's the meeting about?"

Rycroft chuckled. "Wouldn't you like to know. Talk to you later."

She ended the call, thinking fast. They were likely meeting about the sharp increase in the likelihood of an attack. But she knew they would be talking about her too. It seemed rude not to invite her.

So she would just invite herself and be there tomorrow night to see Walker in person.

A tap on the door pulled her back to the present. "Come in."

Kiyomi opened the door. "Brought you some dessert. Apple crumble with custard sauce."

"Yum. Thanks." She accepted the bowl, moved over to give Kiyomi room to sit next to her.

Kiyomi curled up in the far corner and drew her legs under her. "What did he say?"

"He's meeting Walker in London tomorrow night."

One perfectly arched brow rose. "Is that right?"

"Apparently."

"And you were invited?"

"Not exactly."

Her friend watched her with a knowing look as Ivy scooped up a bite of spiced, baked apple and the crisp, almost toffee-like crumble topping with a bit of the cool, creamy custard. Heaven on a spoon. Marcus was a keeper for his cooking ability alone.

"What is it with this Walker guy?" Kiyomi asked. "Why are you so invested in this?"

Another stab of guilt hit her, threatening to turn the delicious mouthful to ash on her tongue. She swallowed it, avoided Kiyomi's gaze as she scooped up another bite.

"Because I owe him," she said simply.

She loved Kiyomi like a sister. Trusted her implicitly. But she still had her secrets.

They all did.

THREE

The early evening air had a crisp edge to it as Walker strode up the narrow cobbled alley toward the pub nestled in the heart of central London. Faint rosy rays of sunlight slanted along the wall near the opening, quickly fading into shadow.

Around the corner, the ancient pub came into view. Warm yellow lamplight spilled out from its old wooden-sashed windows, the worn front door wedged at an angle into the front of the historic building. The date 1667 was carved into the lintel stone above the entry.

As soon as he opened the door, the yeasty scent of beer and fresh-baked bread wafted out. The interior was dim, the walls, floors and ceiling beams made of old, dark oak. Voices filled the air with a constant buzz. Every table was full, with more people lined up all around the gleaming bar to order a round.

He scanned the dimmer section in the back. Immediately picked out Rycroft seated at a table tucked into the far corner beside the fireplace that was probably older than the United States, a real log fire crackling away inside.

Rycroft glanced up from his phone, saw him on his way over, and stood with a smile. "Walker." He held out a hand.

Walker shook it in a firm grip. Rycroft was an inch or so taller than him and still physically imposing in his fifties, the firelight highlighting the silver in his hair that matched his eyes. Eyes he would bet still noticed every tiny detail going on around him, even though he'd officially retired from the NSA years ago. He was a legend for a reason. "Good to see you."

"You too. Here, sit," Rycroft said, gesturing to the opposite chair. "I already ordered you a pint of proper British ale. You've had a long travel day." He slid the glass toward him.

"Thanks." He sat, a million questions running through his mind as he glanced around. Nobody seemed to be paying any attention to them, and the conversations going on throughout the pub provided enough background noise to cover anything they said.

"You hungry?"

"No, I ate on the plane." He took a sip of the beer. Dark and bitter as hell, definitely an acquired taste.

"So. What do you want to talk about first?"

"Fornam." He was the center of all this. And a recent attack on a government building here in London two weeks ago proved that his web of followers were prepared to continue carrying out his manifesto.

"All right."

"After the July second attack, the DoJ went scorched earth at the supermax. Fornam's network was essentially wiped out and, as far as we know, he hasn't been able to reestablish another one. Yet. But all the chatter says something big is coming, almost certainly a target in the UK—most likely London. And if it's not Fornam, then who is it?"

"It's a depressingly long list of suspects, unfortunately."

Rycroft leaned forward, bracing his forearms on the scarred table. "What are you hearing about the next attack?"

He was in an odd position, being sent here as a contractor to assist UK authorities and report back to his handler at the CIA. "Something softer this time. Likely a civilian target to inflict maximum casualties. You hearing the same?"

"Yes. They've already increased security presence at transit and tourist attractions across the city as a precaution."

Good, but that wouldn't stop the attack. "You heard any names mentioned since you got here?"

"No, but my sources are feeding me bits as they come in."

"What sources?"

Rycroft's gray gaze was steady. "Probably the same ones feeding you intel."

"You mean Ivy? What's her position in all of this?"

"We'll get to her in a bit." Rycroft glanced to the right, did a quick scan of the place before meeting Walker's gaze and continuing. "Specifically, MI6 is looking at anyone with the capability to build bombs like the one used in the most recent attack here."

He nodded. "I've compiled a list of possible suspects too." He paused as a server approached their table carrying two fresh pints of beer. Frowned. "We didn't order—"

"From the lady at the bar, sir," he said with a smile and placed them on the table.

"Ah, hell," Rycroft muttered, looking past Walker toward the bar.

Walker swung around. Went completely still when he saw the woman sitting there watching them. She raised a wineglass in a mocking toast and lifted her eyebrows, a faint smile on her lips.

Ivy.

"Well, this is going to be interesting," Rycroft said in a low, amused voice, and waved her over.

"What's she doing here?"

"I made the mistake of mentioning I was meeting you in London tonight. She must have tailed me here."

Walker sat there frozen as Ivy slid off the stool at the bar and sauntered—there was no other way to describe that confident, sinuous gait—toward them, drawing male attention every step of the way. Including his.

Her now chestnut-brown hair was darker and much longer than the last time he'd seen her, down loose around her shoulders. A pair of dark jeans hugged her thighs, knee-high boots clinging to her calves, and her dark green knit turtleneck sweater molded to her breasts.

The captivating force of her gaze made it impossible for him to look away.

Rycroft rose and pulled out a chair for her. "Ivy. So nice of you to join us." His voice was wry.

She flashed him a smile that was all kinds of mischief. "I'm so glad you're happy to see me. What a coincidence, finding you two here together." She sat and looked at Walker, hazel-green eyes both assessing and full of amusement. "Hi, Walker."

He nodded, still staring. He'd been more than curious about her for over a year now. Seeing her again in the flesh so unexpectedly had thrown him. She was a beautiful, mysterious enigma. Something about her made him itch to peel back all her layers until he discovered every last secret she seemed so determined to keep.

She also smelled good, and it was distracting. Something light and crisp and a little bit tangy. Against his will, his gaze dipped to her mouth and the subtle pink gloss she wore. He'd bet she tasted tangy-sweet too.

The thought came unbidden, catching him off guard as much as her appearance had. He'd been single for five years, hadn't been remotely interested in anyone since Jillian died. But yeah, safe to say he'd been thinking about Ivy more than he wanted to admit.

"So, what were you two boys talking about so intently over here?" she said, crossing one leg over the other.

"Business," Walker said. He absolutely would not allow her to know she threw him. "What are you doing here?"

She gave him a level look, ran a finger around the rim of her wineglass. "I thought it was rude that neither of you invited me when I knew perfectly well you'd be talking about me at some point. Especially when we're friends."

"Are we friends?" Walker asked. Because it sure didn't feel that way to him. No, it seemed more like she was toying with him. Testing him for some reason.

She gave him a surprised look. "Of course. You think I share intel with just anyone?"

Rycroft sighed and leaned back in his chair. "Okay, so now that you're here… Care to save me the trouble and tell Walker what he wants to know?"

"I will when I'm ready."

"When's that gonna be, do you think?" Walker asked, curbing an uncharacteristic rush of irritation. She got under his skin on an intrinsic level that was downright disturbing. And he also got the impression that she knew far more about him than he did about her.

Her smile was every bit as mysterious as the rest of her. "You'll be the first to know."

IVY WAS ENJOYING this little game she'd initiated with Walker over a year ago. Maybe a little too much.

Partly because he intrigued her and she wanted to watch how he handled what she threw at him. But in truth she'd started this because of their past connection he was as yet unaware of.

She was keeping that to herself for now. Because once he found out, everything could go sideways, and there was too much riding on this current investigation to let personal grudges get in the way.

Not only that, but she had eight other women to consider, along with their significant others and children. So before she or anyone else told Walker the truth about her and the others, he needed to prove beyond a doubt that he could be trusted first.

Everything she knew about him so far said he could probably be trusted with the truth about the Valkyrie program. Rycroft trusted him to at least some extent, and his opinion held a lot of sway with her. But she needed to be certain of it herself. She'd almost died placing her hard-earned trust in the wrong people before. People she had thought she could trust with her life.

She wouldn't be blindsided by that kind of betrayal again. Not ever.

He raised a coal-black eyebrow at her, a hint of annoyance in his deep blue eyes. His short, neatly trimmed beard had just a hint of silver in it, matching the natural highlights at his temples. He was a ruggedly masculine, extremely appealing man in his prime who knew exactly who he was and didn't give a shit what anyone else thought about him.

Combined with his trademark self-containment, that was so damn sexy.

"Another test?" he said.

"It's not personal." He just got hotter as the minutes passed. The deep blue collared shirt he wore almost matched his eyes and hugged the muscular contours of his chest and shoulders to perfection. His military bearing was obvious in his posture and the alertness in his gaze.

This man may have spent most of his career working in intelligence, but he was still every inch a trained soldier.

"It kinda feels personal," he said in that same straightforward tone.

"It's not. And I wouldn't have bothered involving you up till now if I had a problem with you."

He held her gaze, a subtle tension building between them that set off a little flutter deep in her belly. Something she hadn't felt in...forever, it seemed like. "Are you an operative?"

She had to at least give him something, and this was harmless enough to confirm when he must have figured it out on his own. "Used to be. Now I'm just a freelance hacker."

"Working for who?"

"Myself, mostly. Although sometimes I do jobs as a consultant of sorts."

"Ivy," Rycroft said in a warning tone.

She held up a hand to stop him, still looking at Walker. She knew his background. Personal details that told her what kind of a man he was. He was solid, both professionally and in his private life as a single dad. He was a thinker. A smart one. Calm. Controlled.

But after five minutes in his presence, she'd known there was more to him than what he projected to the rest of the world.

A *lot* more. And she'd be lying if she said she wasn't dying to find out what lay hidden underneath that composed exterior.

"As a show of good faith, I'm going to share what Amber and I have found on the currently active part of Fornam's network. We're working on more, but this is what we've verified so far." She reached into the inside pocket of her leather jacket and pulled out a tiny flash drive, surreptitiously sliding it across the scarred wooden table toward him.

Walker reached out to meet her part way. Their fingers touched as she relinquished control of the device and an almost electric jolt shot up her arm, sending sparks dancing along her skin. Staring into his dark blue eyes, she was aware of a heightened sense of her femininity along with the shocking rush of arousal.

His long fingers closed around the device. Then he leaned back and folded his deliciously defined, muscular arms, watching her. The gesture would normally indicate defensiveness or boredom. On him, it did just the opposite. And being the sole focus of his full attention for even those few moments sent a secret thrill through her.

"What are your sources?" His tone was level, expression even.

"They're legit, in case you're still skeptical. Anyway, that's why you're here, right? As flattered as I would be if you'd come here just to find out about li'l old me, I'm assuming you're here to gather and share intel about the impending threat with the powers that be."

"If it helps at all, I trust *her*, and she's telling the truth about her sources," Rycroft said to Walker, giving her a censuring look that didn't faze her in the least. She wasn't telling Walker anything about her past until she was damn good and ready.

Walker shifted, angling his body to face her fully, giving her the full impact of his stare. "I'm scheduled to meet with a joint task force here tomorrow morning."

She could see why he'd be good at interrogation. He had an unflappable and patient demeanor that would rattle many nervous prisoners and assets into talking. "You're working as a contractor too?"

He dipped his chin. "Only for this case. But you already knew that."

She did. And she appreciated that he hadn't lied to her or tried to brush her off. It couldn't be easy for a man like him to feel at a disadvantage in this situation with her. "That drive will give you all the details you need before you go in there."

"What makes you think I don't already have them on my own?"

His Boy Scout streak was showing, and she mentally shook her head at him in pity. There was no way he was that naïve. He was too damn smart and experienced. "Because government agencies *always* hide things to protect themselves." *Ask me how I know.*

"Not just government agencies," he said with a pointed look.

She smiled, her attraction to him growing by the second. "No." She downed the rest of her wine, stood. "I'll text you my number. If you have any questions about the drive, let me know. Otherwise, I'll be in touch." She turned and walked away.

"Bye, Ivy," Rycroft called out behind her.

She raised a hand and kept going. Feeling the weight of Walker's stare on her until she stepped outside and the door shut at her back.

Emerging from the shadows of the alley into the purple twilight, she tugged up the collar of her leather jacket, thinking about him. Was she testing him?

Damn right. Too many people's lives hung in the balance for her to risk being careless again.

But mostly… She meant what she'd said to Kiyomi.

She owed Walker. Big time. And seeing that name on the list yesterday…

If it was true he was involved, then she was partly responsible for whatever came next. So she would share everything she thought might help stop this coming attack.

If they could stop it, if they could capture the man she feared was behind it in time, then maybe it would finally wipe all the remaining red from her ledger once and for all.

FOUR

Isaac stood at the kitchen sink window of his rental flat, staring out into the gloom of the tiny courtyard as he sipped his first cup of coffee of the day. And thought about revenge.

Overnight the temperature had dropped, condensing the water droplets in the air. Tendrils of mist floated through the walkways into the courtyard, covering the ground in a low layer of fog, the dew on the turning leaves shimmering like tears in the watery gray light.

He turned away and walked back to the kitchen table where he had his laptop set up. Pulling up an image he'd saved, he studied it carefully. It was the only map he'd found that was detailed enough for what he needed.

His previous targets had been government-related. Before Elliot Fornam's teachings had transformed his way of thinking nine months ago. Now everything was different.

All governments were corrupt. All of them. No one knew that better than him.

He glanced down at his right hand, at the network of scars along the fingers and back of his hand pulling tight as he flexed his stiff fingers. When the cold and damp settled in soon, the ache and stiffness would be twice as bad. Though given what he was facing, that was nothing.

There was a long list of people he'd like to see dead. Including the man who had sold him out in Moscow and destroyed his life.

Walker now worked for a high-end security firm in Oregon. That made him a riskier target. But everyone had a weakness, and Isaac was sure he'd found Walker's. He had an operative over there looking into it now, although Isaac's focus was on something much bigger.

Turning his attention back to the screen, he pushed the bitterness and old grievances to the back of his mind and focused on the task at hand. Working smarter, not harder.

He considered himself a reasonably bright man. But he'd been stupid before. He'd selected his new target on the premise of inflicting maximum civilian casualties with one device. One small, portable device that was easy to transport and less likely to be detected in time, yet powerful enough to do the damage required.

Intelligence services knew an attack was coming. London was one of the most heavily surveilled cities on earth. Here in the UK, they would probably raise the threat level in the coming days. All to give the illusion that they were on top of things and able to protect its citizens.

Lies.

The more people killed and wounded on their way to work and school in the coming attack, the more inept the government would appear. With enough strikes over a condensed period of time, soon the citizens here would realize that the government hadn't kept them safe. That it *couldn't* keep them safe despite its assurances to the contrary and all the taxes they took from people's pockets to fund their corruption.

In time, the people would finally realize the truth and rise up against government corruption and greed. There would be chaos and anarchy at first. But that was the necessary price society had to pay to free itself from the tyranny subjugating it on a daily basis.

The only issue now was the timing. He glanced over at the device sitting in a backpack in the corner. A small but powerful bomb he'd made using various chemicals. His deteriorating coordination meant he was slower than he used to be. It would take longer to finish up, but a few more hours' work and it would be ready. Everything else could be taken care of with a single text message. The courier he'd chosen for this task was ready and waiting for instructions.

Isaac pulled up a physics program on his laptop and quickly did some final calculations. As always, the calculus came as naturally to him as breathing, the rhythm and logic of it flowing like a calm river through his brain. And for those few minutes, he felt invincible.

Until he stopped and the sight of his unsteady hand on the keyboard brought him crashing back to reality.

Certain he'd calibrated everything correctly, he sat back and weighed his options. Technically he could launch the attack as soon as tomorrow, but a couple more days to fine-tune everything was better. He was methodical by nature both in and out of the lab and liked to triple check all his final arrangements before putting them into action to ensure there was no room for error.

After making his final decisions on where and how to plant the device for maximum effect, he stood and went back to the coffeepot to refill his mug. He stirred in two spoonfuls of sugar and took a sip of the hot, sweet liquid. Swallowed. Or tried to.

His throat muscles refused to cooperate.

He choked. Leaned over the sink to spit the coffee out,

racked with coughs as his body tried to eject the small amount of liquid that had gone down the wrong pipe.

His grip on the mug slipped. It crashed to the sink and shattered.

Wheezing, hands splayed on either side of the sink as the spasms finally eased, he wiped his watering eyes with his sleeve. His whole arm shook, muscles weak and unresponsive.

He drew in a ragged breath. Clenched his jaw and looked back out into the misty gloom in the courtyard beyond the kitchen window.

This couldn't wait. His remaining time was running out.

Turning away from the shattered mug in the sink, he took out a burner phone from the backpack in the corner and typed a coded message. Then hit send with an unsteady finger.

The attack would happen tomorrow.

∽

WALKER LEFT the meeting and immediately texted his boss back home as he rode the elevator down to the lobby. Rycroft had made initial introductions for him here at the MI5 headquarters at Thames House on the north side of the river, then promptly left before the joint UK-US taskforce had entered the conference room.

The mood inside had been tense. There wasn't much new intel to go on. He'd known most of what they'd discussed already, and Ivy's thumb drive had provided the rest.

Bottom line was, no one knew for certain when or where the next attack would be, only that it was coming. Soon. Likely in London, and almost certainly an explosive device. Based on MI5's recommendation, the Home Secretary was about to issue a statement raising the threat level in the UK to severe.

Things are getting more complicated here, he typed. *I'm going to be a few days longer than I thought.*

It was midnight back home so he didn't expect a response but Ryder answered within moments. He was no doubt monitoring the unfolding situation through his own channels and would hear about the announcement as soon as it happened.

No problem. Keep me posted and let us know if you need anything.

Thanks. Will do, he answered.

Ryder Locke was a solid guy and a great boss to work for. He cared about his employees and their families. After years of working for the government, that was a refreshing change for Walker and meant a lot.

He texted Shae next, just a quick note to say he was fine but would be a few days longer than he'd initially thought. *Love you*, he finished and hit send.

A message popped up saying that she had silenced her notifications. Hopefully still fast asleep and dreaming about happy things, oblivious of the ominous clouds gathering over London. He'd check in with her later on, because he knew she would check the news about what was going on in London while he was here.

He stepped outside into the cool fog that had blanketed the city overnight. Fifty feet ahead of him, someone pushed away from the wall they'd been leaning against and turned to face him. A blond woman wearing a ball cap and a long trench coat over jeans.

"How'd it go in there?" she asked.

He stopped suddenly, doing a double take. *Ivy*. She looked so different he'd almost walked right past her. "What are you doing here?"

Hands in her coat pockets, she shrugged, the motion making the halves of her coat gap wider and exposing the body-hugging black sweater she wore beneath. "Wanted to check in with you in person and get an update."

Annoyance flared in his gut. She'd followed him here. Had probably tailed him from his hotel and he hadn't noticed a damn thing.

That was twice now she'd shown up out of the clear blue and caught him off guard, and he literally would have walked past her just now if she hadn't announced herself. As a man who prided himself on his situational awareness skills, that bothered him.

Almost as much as his attraction to her did.

There were too many people around and too many security cameras in the area to speak candidly with her. "Not here," he said, and kept walking. She'd taken up too much space in his head over the past year as it was. Now that he'd seen her again, it was only getting worse.

She fell in step with him, stayed silent as they waited at the light to cross the busy road. A gust of wind carried her clean, crisp scent to him.

When the light changed, they joined the knot of other pedestrians across to the center light and waited again. He stayed focused on her without looking, trying to size her up. She was about five-nine or so with a fit, medium build.

As far as their "friendship" was concerned, she had two things going for her. Rycroft had made it clear that he trusted her. And she'd also been an incredibly solid and skilled teammate on the Kabul op last year. Without her, the team might not have been able to get Nadia out.

Whatever her true background was, whatever her past, Ivy could more than handle herself.

Other than those things, she was a blank slate. He wanted to find out what she was hiding, and why. Wanted to solve the mystery because maybe then he could put her out of his mind and stop thinking about her all the damn time.

On the far side of the intersection they headed west down the sidewalk together. "You feel like breakfast?" she asked him suddenly.

He eyed her, wondering what was up with the disguise. She had to be a spy or an undercover officer of some sort, but no one except Rycroft seemed to know anything about her, and, so far, he wasn't talking. "Breakfast?"

She shot him an amused look. "Yeah, the meal people generally eat in the morning? You had an early start. You not hungry?"

He'd only had a muffin and a crappy cup of coffee before the meeting two hours ago. "I could eat." He had nothing else to do until this afternoon's briefing anyway. There were worse things than spending an hour or two in London with a beautiful, intriguing woman in the meantime, and maybe he would finally get some answers out of her.

"Good, because I know a great place in Covent Garden. Come on." She linked her arm through his and turned the corner, heading for the nearest Tube station. "When's the last time you were in London?"

A primal, proprietary part of him liked having her this close. Liked the feel of her hand wrapped around his biceps. "Six years ago."

"That long?"

"Yes."

"Business or pleasure?"

"Both." After he'd finished a job, Jillian and Shae had met him here to spend a week touring the city. None of them had realized it would be their last trip together. Or that their world was about to fall apart. "Do you live in the city?"

"No, but I come into town every so often."

They stopped talking and joined the flow of fellow passengers down a set of steps into the station, tapped their cards and made their way down the long escalators to the platform to catch the next train. There was a noticeable increase in the security presence here, uniformed cops stationed at the entrance and on the platform.

It was hot and noisy down here, the narrow waiting area crowded with commuters on their way to work.

The next train was already nearly full when it arrived a minute later. As soon as its doors opened, the waiting passengers crammed their way inside. Walker automatically moved in behind Ivy in the center of the train and stood close to protect her from being bumped or jostled in the crush, holding onto the same pole as her as the train left the station and rushed along the track.

Six minutes later they arrived at Piccadilly Circus and crossed over the station to another platform to take the Piccadilly Line east toward a place called Cockfosters.

Damned unfortunate name.

This train was even more crowded. According to the map above the window inside the car they squeezed into, Covent Garden was only two stops away. He stood behind Ivy again, so close this time that her back touched his chest, her scent teasing him. That primal part she triggered in him wanted to curl an arm around her waist and pull her in tight.

"The next stop is—Leicester Square," the British woman's recorded voice announced through the speakers, barely audible under the noise of the moving train.

As soon as it came to a stop and the doors opened, Ivy began filing toward the door with the other offloading passengers.

"I thought we were going to Covent Garden?" he said, sticking right behind her.

"Covent Garden station is a nightmare at the best of times, let alone in rush hour," she told him over her shoulder. "It's one of the oldest stations so it only has a few lifts instead of escalators, and a ridiculously long emergency spiral staircase I don't feel like tackling. People will be lined up forever trying to get out of the station, so it'll be way faster if we just walk from here," she said over the noise of tramping feet while everyone exited the platform and took the escalators up to street level.

Outside, the crowd immediately dispersed along the network of streets. He fell in step beside Ivy as they headed east, the street crammed full of shops, restaurants and cafés on either side as far as the eye could see.

"Okay, so, you wanna go first, or should I?" she said when they reached a small park near the actual square itself and had more privacy. Buskers were performing music and dance routines for the tourists already gathering around to watch.

"Why've you been feeding me intel under the radar all this time?" he asked, seeing no point in dancing around it.

"Because of your connection to Fornam. I felt you had a right to know in case the powers that be weren't sharing everything with you."

"Then why all the secrecy?" he said. "Why not just say it was you from the start? You already knew me and we'd already worked together before."

"I don't know you. Not personally. And I wasn't sure I could fully trust you." She met his gaze squarely. The clear interest there surprised him given what she'd just said.

But there was no denying the answering zing of attraction that shot through him. "Fair enough."

"I'm still not sure about that, to be honest," she added, eyeing him again in a way that made his blood pump hotter.

That trust thing went both ways. He didn't trust her fully

either. "I get it." The chemistry between them—or maybe he was confusing it for friction—was totally unexpected.

He hadn't been even remotely interested in or tempted by a woman since Jillian died five years ago and wasn't about to start now, especially with a woman he didn't even know and who had to be an operative.

"Are you CIA?" he finally asked once he was sure no one was close enough to overhear.

She made a disgusted sound. "No."

He'd hit a nerve there. Interesting. "Then who do you work for?"

"Myself. And sometimes my sisters."

Her sisters. He knew next to nothing about them either, or how many there were, except that one ran a charity helping protect vulnerable orphans from being preyed on by traffickers, and the one named Amber was some kind of hacker.

"Did you use to work with Rycroft?" He was the one who had suggested her for the Kabul op when Walker had reached out to him in the first place.

"No. But he helped me out of a jam a while ago and we keep in touch. Now," she said, putting her hands back in the pockets of her trench, "what did they say in the meeting?"

"Exactly what you had on that flash drive. Nothing else relevant."

She nodded, looking straight ahead. He could see the Covent Garden station up ahead on the right at the next block. It had only taken them a few minutes to walk here. Weird that the two Tube stations were this close together. Didn't make any sense.

"What about names," she said, moving onto the sidewalk running along the right side of the street.

"There's a list of suspects they're looking at, but they don't have anything concrete yet. Home Front has gained a lot of traction over here, so it's a long list."

"Yep. I—" At a sharp beep she hastily fished her phone out of her pocket.

He couldn't see what was on the screen but noticed the exact moment she stiffened. And when she looked up at him, the grim set to her expression set off a burst of alarm inside him.

"Surveillance cameras just picked up a man planting a possible device on a train about to arrive in Covent Garden station. We have to stop him."

Before he could say a single word in response she broke into a dead run, racing straight for the station entrance.

Biting back a curse, Walker tore after her.

FIVE

Ivy ran into the station and vaulted the ticket barrier. According to Amber, the suspect had just exited the train at Covent Garden. They might be able to intercept him before he left the station. Had to try.

"Hey!" A security guard shouted to the left, and rushed toward her.

She ignored him and kept going, focused on finding and apprehending the suspect before it was too late. And maybe she could save lives by clearing off the platform.

"Ivy, wait," Walker demanded, right behind her now. Being such a Boy Scout, he'd probably tapped his card and waited for the turnstile to open instead of hopping the barrier.

There were only two possible escape routes for the suspect: the lifts and the stairs. The lifts had just offloaded their passengers and started back down again. She didn't see the suspect in the flow of people leaving them. That left the stairs.

She raced for the spiral staircase, holding onto a picture of the suspect in her mind. If he had planted a device at platform level, they likely had only minutes to intercept him and get people to safety. "Caucasian. Mid-to-late thirties. Jeans, gray jacket. Black beanie and dirty blond hair," she called out to Walker, the top of the stairs in sight.

Their rapid footsteps echoed through the narrow space as they raced down together, Walker on her heels. The spiral staircase twisted counterclockwise on the way down. Several people braving the climb up shrank back and flattened themselves against the wall when they saw her and Walker flying toward them.

"Get up to street level. Quickly," she urged them.

God, these stairs. Hundred-and-ninety-three of them to be exact, assuming she remembered correctly. The equivalent of fifteen stories. Way too many, too far to go before they could reach the bottom and *do* something about this.

Finally, the floor came into view. She whipped around the corner and stopped suddenly, swearing silently. As she'd feared, a crowd of people was packed close together waiting for the lifts up to the station exit, the lines extending along a tiled hallway and disappearing down the short staircase that led down to the platform.

"We have to get them out of here," Walker muttered close behind her. "Do you see him?"

She could dismantle a simple bomb if there was time, but nothing complicated. That was her sister Chloe's department. And as far as she knew, Walker wasn't trained in EOD.

If there *was* a device, the attacker wasn't a suicide bomber. If it was on a timer or pressure plate, they were screwed. The best they could hope for was that the bomber planned to remote detonate and then get to him before he could set it off.

But searching the sea of faces in front of her, she didn't see him. "No." She immediately scanned the whole area, looking at the shape, construction and thinking about blast damage. If there was a device on the platform, the lower staircase and turn in the tunnel would provide some protection for—

A massive explosion detonated from somewhere down below.

The blast wave rushed up the stairs, down the hall and hit them a second later with a punch of hot air that drove the breath from Ivy's lungs. She automatically dropped into a crouch but Walker grabbed her and pulled her tight to his chest, one hand on the back of her head as he turned them to place himself between her and the blast.

"I'm okay," she said, pushing at his chest, her heart racing. Screams rang out from every direction.

He held her tighter. "Don't move. It might not be over."

"Let me up," she insisted, shoving with enough force to make him release her and popping to her feet. The crowd waiting for the elevators was scattering.

A few people cowered on the floor or in the corners, too scared to move. Everyone else was fleeing in panic and rushing for the spiral staircase. Would have knocked her down and run right over top of her if Walker hadn't shoved her flat to the wall and shielded her with his big body.

She searched the panicked crowd for the suspect, but before she could focus on a single face, another, smaller explosion ripped through the air. Closer this time, the concussion hitting her in the chest and ringing in her skull.

Walker pressed her harder to the cold white tile, his body plastered to the back of her. She blinked, coughed as a cloud of dust and debris billowed up to them from the platform.

Ivy pushed at Walker but he wouldn't budge, pinning her to the wall. "Are you okay?" he shouted over the screams and cries.

"I'm fine." Her ears were ringing. She put her forearm across her nose and mouth. Blinked, squinting through the dust that hung in the air as thick as fog as she tried to see past his shoulder and the tide of terrified people fleeing past her and

Walker up the spiral stairs. Was the bomber still here? Or had he managed to already leave the station?

More people were flooding up from the platform below, all of them covered in fine gray dust. Some were wounded. Staggering. Covered in blood. The terror on their faces sending rage whipping through her.

Walker eased up slightly, allowing her to see to the left. There was no time to help the wounded as she quickly scanned the lift area, then looked right up the spiral steps.

Partway up the first turn, her gaze locked on someone shoving his way through the tightly packed crowd. He knocked several people over in his haste, muscling his way upward.

Mid-to-late thirties. Dirty blond hair. Gray jacket, jeans.

Her eyes dropped to his back pocket where the edge of a black beanie stuck out.

A burst of rage detonated inside her. "Walker, it's him," she blurted, twisting in his hold.

"Where?"

"Up there!" She ducked under the arm caging her in and made for the stairs. "Police! Out of the way!" she shouted to the mass of frightened people blocking her path.

Walker was in front of her in a second, his big frame acting as a human icebreaker. "Police! Move, move!" he bellowed, his deep voice cutting through the cries and chaos.

Above them, the suspect disappeared from view around the next turn.

You're not fucking getting away with this, Ivy vowed, prepared to hunt him down like the animal he was.

She and Walker climbed the steps as fast as they could, their progress made frustratingly slow by the sheer volume of shocked, frightened people clogging the narrow staircase.

"Police, let us through!" she shouted, trying to push past

everyone without hurting them. This time barely anyone reacted, too caught up in the need to escape.

She glanced above them. Someone in her upper line of vision stumbled backward and fell into the surging crowd. Sharp cries rang out from around the next turn. A second later, an elderly man pitched backward, his arms scrambling for purchase after being shoved by someone ahead of him—the dirty blond suspect.

Walker surged forward and caught the old man before he could hit the stairs and take out more people with him, quickly righted him and kept going. Ivy was already moving past him, gaze locked on the fleeing suspect, her whole body revved and ready.

"Police! Police!" a loud voice shouted from above. Two uniformed officers appeared, trying to fight their way down through the human tide coming at them. "Clear the stairwell immediately!"

Too little, too late. "Stop him," she shouted, pointing past them in desperation. "Gray jacket and jeans, dirty blond hair. He's the bomber!"

More cries rang out around them. The officers stopped, gaped at her before turning to look behind them. She bit back a curse. The suspect had already reached the top of the stairs.

She shouldered her way between a knot of people blocking the middle of the steps, passing the cops who were clearly torn as to what to do—chase a possible suspect, or go secure the area below and help the wounded.

Ivy was going after him.

She shoved past an elderly couple, lost sight of the suspect for a sickening moment before she reached the top at last, thighs burning. Out of the corner of her eye, she caught a glimpse of the guy past the ticket gates and rushing for the exit.

"Where is he?" Walker yelled over the noise of sirens and the panicked crowd as he caught up.

"Eleven o'clock, just hitting the street," she answered, breathing hard as they reached the ticket barriers.

Walker vaulted one beside her, raced past the police swarming through the entrance and burst out of the station. "Across the street, one o'clock!"

She saw him. Never took her eyes off him as she sprinted for the other side of the road. There was no point trying to alert the police converging on the station. She didn't have time to explain.

It was up to her and Walker to stop him.

Ahead of her, the suspect darted into an alley. She sprinted after him. Burst out the other side and saw a flash of black coming at her.

"Ivy, look out!"

The car braked hard, horn blaring. There was no way to avoid it. She planted her hands on the hood, let her momentum slide her across it and took off again the instant her feet touched the ground on the other side.

A hundred feet ahead, the suspect veered left down another alley. She tore after him, refusing to lose him, aware of Walker speaking urgently to someone on the phone in the background.

Whipping around the corner, a surge of triumph hit her. A large walking tour was blocking off the far end of the alley. Realizing his predicament, the suspect skidded to a stop, had to backtrack a dozen yards to another side street.

Ivy made the turn a few heartbeats later. Up ahead was a dead end.

The suspect whirled to confront her, face grim as he whipped out a knife. "Out of my way, bitch."

She stopped, heard Walker arrive as she whipped out her own knife.

Surprise flared in the asshole's eyes.

"Ivy," Walker said, reaching for her shoulder.

"It's over," she told the man, weight balanced on the balls of her feet. Ready for anything. They'd just cornered this animal. No telling what he'd do.

He lowered the knife. Smiled, sending a prickle of warning through her.

"Drop it." Walker's voice was low. Deadly as it carried along the bricked-in alley.

The suspect laughed. "You're too late. You can't stop it. And there's more coming."

Walker cut in front of her and took a menacing step toward him. "Last chance."

Running feet echoed behind them. The suspect looked past her and Walker, smile fading. He dropped the knife.

Walker and Ivy both rushed at him.

He grinned. Lightning fast, his hand flashed up and put something in his mouth.

Shit. "*No*," Ivy yelled.

Too late. The bastard jerked. Dropped to his knees and began convulsing even before he hit the ground, foam bubbling out of his mouth.

"Son of a bitch," Walker snarled.

Ivy sheathed her knife in disgust. "Coward," she spat, watching his death throes. It was too easy a death after what he'd done.

The running footsteps got closer. "Police! Step back, now!" a male voice rang out behind them.

Ivy and Walker immediately put their hands up to show they were unarmed and turned to face them. "He's dead," she told the three officers. The lack of weapons told her they didn't belong to a specialized unit authorized to carry firearms.

It was almost laughable, police chasing down a terrorist that had just blown up untold number of innocent people in the underground, carrying only a few cans of pepper spray. "Cyanide capsule," she said.

One of them gave her a suspicious look as he edged past and knelt next to the dead man. After a single look he got on his radio. "Request ambulance to our location…"

"What happened? Who are you?" one of the other cops demanded.

Ivy sighed and looked at Walker as more police swarmed the alley, cursing inwardly. Not only did they have a dead end in terms of finding out about the terror plot, but things were about to get really messy for her in a hurry.

SIX

Walker shot to his feet in the small waiting room he'd been left in between interviews when Rycroft stepped inside. "Thanks for coming. Have you seen Ivy yet?" After explaining everything to the police at the scene of the attacker's death, they'd taken him and Ivy here to Thames House in separate vehicles and he hadn't seen her since.

Something wasn't right.

"Just about to. Have you briefed them on what happened?"

"Twice so far. I'm waiting for a meeting with the Home Office. They're not telling me anything about the bomber. Who he was, whether he left some kind of manifesto, or if he's connected to Home Front."

"Looks like he was. Still waiting for official confirmation. Where's Ivy now?"

"Still in the interview room they took her to. I've been sitting in here for over an hour and she hasn't come out of the room. Everyone I ask is tight-lipped about it. It feels like they're treating her more like a suspect than a witness. I don't know if she's asked to contact an attorney or not. What's going on?"

Rycroft shifted his stance and put his hands in his pants pockets. "There are certain…complications with Ivy's background."

"Such as?"

"I can't tell you."

Hearing that was really starting to piss him off. "Is she in trouble?" Some kind of criminal record or something? What the hell else could they be holding her for?

"Not if I can help it."

He was so damn frustrated and sick of being kept out of the loop. "Can I do anything?"

The hint of a smile softened Rycroft's expression. "I'll take care of it. But I appreciate the offer."

"Sure. Will you text me at least and let me know she's okay?"

"Of course. It's going to take a while. I don't know how long, so you might as well go back to your hotel when you're done here instead of hanging around."

Walker eyed him. "You'll let me know as soon as she's released?"

"Yes."

Before he could say anything else, the door opened and a young woman peeked in. "Mr. Walker? They're ready for you now."

Walker nodded and faced Rycroft. "If there's anything I can do, let me know."

"I will." Rycroft clapped him on the upper arm. "Talk to you later."

He strode down the hall to a high-security conference room and was escorted inside, his mind still stuck on Ivy. Were they interrogating her right now?

A hot wave of protectiveness hit him. She had risked her life today to try and stop that bastard. Could easily have been wounded or killed in the attack. Had almost been run over while chasing the suspect. Could have been seriously hurt if the asshole had attacked her with his knife, because the UK gun laws were so strict that only certain police units were allowed to carry weapons.

Although everything he knew about Ivy and the way she'd pulled and expertly handled her own blade—without even looking at it—made him confident she would have held her own.

Not that he would have allowed it. He'd been watching closely, ready to spring. If that son of a bitch had so much as feinted that knife at her, Walker would have come at him like a freight train.

"Mr. Walker?"

He shook himself, focused on the man seated at the head of the table and shook hands before being introduced to everyone in the room. The meeting itself took over an hour, and the Home Office was very careful with the details they eventually divulged near the end.

The suspect hadn't been carrying a phone or any ID. Forensics was running the suspect's prints and DNA now. If he was in the database it wouldn't take long.

As soon as the meeting wrapped up, he was escorted from the building. He tried twice more to get info on Ivy but got nothing. He messaged both Rycroft and Ivy on the way back to his hotel, asking for an update. Neither of them replied, which told him Ivy was probably still being detained.

Up in his room he took a long, hot shower, trying to clear his head. He replayed everything that had happened. Tried to fill in the gaps with the little intel the Home Office had shared. And he thought about his daughter.

He changed and ordered himself a late lunch while

watching the news. The story was the headline on every news station. And the figures coming in were grim.

The initial blast had destroyed two train cars and the second had hit the passengers trying to escape on the platform. More than seventy killed. Twice that many wounded. Dozens of people still reported missing, and the death toll was expected to rise in the coming days due to the nature of some of the injuries sustained.

The shots on screen showed the entrance to Covent Garden station, along with cell phone footage taken inside and below in the elevator area during the blasts.

He saw him and Ivy off to the right of one shot. It was between the blasts, when he'd been holding her. Then the second blast hit. The crowd around them panicked. Fled. He flattened her to the wall to protect her.

He wished he was in the room with her and protecting her now.

Switching off the news, he picked up his phone and responded to messages from Ryder, Callum and Donovan. It was after seven back home now. Shae would be up and getting ready to head to class. He wanted her to hear the news from him, not anyone else.

"Hi, Dad," she said sleepily.

"Did I wake you?"

"No, I was just lying here trying to work up the will to drag myself out of bed."

"One of those days, huh?"

"Yeah, and it's raining like crazy. I'm so cozy in my bed, I don't wanna move." He heard her shifting around. "How are you? And Ivy? Found out anything about her yet that you can share?"

"Not yet. Listen, there was an incident here earlier today. Ivy and I are both fine, but I wanted you to hear it from me instead of the news."

"What happened?" she said, all traces of drowsiness gone from her voice.

He told her with as little detail as possible.

"Oh my God," she whispered. "But you're okay? Really?"

"Yes. I promise. I'll be staying here longer than I thought now, though, to assist with the investigation. Wanted to give you a heads up."

"Is it related to the guy you went to see in prison?"

"We think so. It hasn't been confirmed yet." It felt good just to hear her voice. "You okay?"

"Am I okay? Yeah, I'm fine, just worried about you."

"Hey, don't worry about me, sweetheart. I don't want that. I'm safe, promise, and I'm being careful. I asked Donovan to come over and check on you, so—"

The doorbell sounded in the background. She groaned. "He's here."

"Okay, I'll let you go. I'll text you tonight after class. Have a good day, okay? Love you."

"Love you too," she said, the fear in her voice twisting something in his chest. "Bye."

"Bye." He set his phone down and rubbed at his eyes. They were still stinging from the dust.

A new message popped up. He grabbed his phone, his heart rate jacking up when he saw Ivy's name. *I'm done. You got a few minutes?*

Yes. Call me.

I'm in the lobby.

Even better. *I'll be down in 2 mins.*

He grabbed his jacket and wallet and rushed down the four flights of stairs to the lobby. Ivy rose from the bench along the wall and gave him a tired smile that hit him dead in the heart. Her wig was gone, her sweater and jeans covered in a fine layer of dust. Some of it had gotten into her hair.

He stopped a step away from her, searching her eyes. She'd come straight here from Thames House, not even stopping somewhere to shower. "You okay?"

Something like surprise flared in those hazel-green depths. As if it was strange that someone would be concerned about her. "Yeah, I'm good."

"What happened?"

She glanced around as if to check if anyone was within earshot. And there was.

"Come on," he said, catching her hand in his. She didn't protest. Didn't pull her hand away and curled her fingers around his as they started across the lobby.

Outside in the watery sunlight on the quiet street, they found another bench tucked out of the way and sat on it. "Did Rycroft handle whatever he needed to?"

"Like a champ," she said, finally withdrawing her hand. "I didn't get my phone back until they let me go, but Amber sent me some things about the attacker."

He didn't even care how Amber had gotten the information at this point. The UK government wasn't telling him shit. "Like?"

"Thirty-one. Born and raised in Kent. Computer science engineer who appears to have been radicalized online."

"Did he release a manifesto?"

"Oh yeah. He's definitely drinking Fornam's Kool-Aid. It's dripping with Home Front messaging."

Ivy knew more. He could see it in her eyes. "And?"

"And…there's a possible link to a man named Isaac Grey. A recent one."

Ice trickled down his spine.

She knew about his connection to Grey. But that wasn't the

most disturbing part. "Grey was confirmed dead years ago." A dual UK-US citizen with dual PhDs in chemistry and physics, anarchist views…

With one hell of a personal axe to grind against both governments—and *him*.

"On paper, yes."

Walker stared at her. *Jesus Christ.* "Did Amber find intel proving he's alive?"

"Maybe. She's still trying to verify it. MI5 hasn't verified it yet either apparently. But given what happened today, you have to admit there's a possible similarity here."

He looked out at the street in front of them. At the traffic and pedestrians walking by. People going about their daily lives in spite of today's attack. None of them familiar with the name Isaac Grey, and way better off for it. "How much do you know about my history with him?"

"Most, probably. I know that you were using him as an asset in Russia before he was captured."

His jaw tightened and he turned his head to face her again. "Is that from Amber, MI5, or your own homework?"

"All three."

"So you know all about me and my past, including details about my personal life I'm guessing, and I know nothing at all about you."

"I'm going to tell you."

"When?"

"I—" Her gaze snapped to the left.

Walker glanced over, saw a black minivan pull over and park along the curb. There were two men in the front, both dressed in what looked like suits.

"They're keeping tabs on me. I need to go."

He grabbed her arm and stood with her as she started to get up. She stopped, looked up at him. And for the first time he saw the exhaustion in her eyes.

She might be the strongest, most capable woman he'd ever met, but she was still human. And whether she wanted to admit it or not, today's events had taken a toll on her.

Relinquishing some of his control, he reached up to skim his fingertips along the side of her face and tucked a lock of hair behind her ear. She stilled, her pupils flaring slightly.

And damned if he didn't want to thread his fingers through her dusty hair and kiss her. Kiss away the strain and fatigue. Kiss her until she melted and wrapped around him. Make everything else disappear. Show her she wasn't alone.

"Will you be okay?" he asked.

Her surprise gave way to something softer. Something unguarded and vulnerable that made him ache to wrap her up in his arms and hold her. "Yes." Her voice sounded soft too.

She glanced past him, pulled away almost reluctantly. "I'll call you later," she murmured, then turned and walked away at a brisk pace without looking back.

Leaving him battling the overwhelming urge to go after her.

∽

ISAAC WATCHED the breaking news with a surge of satisfaction. Jack had done it. Carried out the attack and detonated both devices. Then killed himself and given the police and intelligence services nothing to go on except DNA.

They would find Jack's name and background quickly enough. Would see the link between the attack and Home Front in the manifesto Isaac had written for him. Someone high up might even manage to puzzle out that he was still alive and put him back on the intel radar.

His burner mobile beeped with an incoming email. He checked it, surprise punching through him when he read the message from a talented and expensive hacker he'd hired to keep tabs on anything related to him within the UK intelligence services. But tidbits like this made him worth every penny.

Familiar face at MI5 today.

Beneath it was a picture of the intelligence officer he'd worked with in Russia right before his life had become hell on earth. Walker.

"I'll be damned," he murmured into the quiet room.

It was perfect in an eerie way. Fitting to include Walker personally in this op here, as payback.

Which reminded him, he hadn't yet heard back from the operative he'd dispatched in the US. He shot off another message, asking for an update. In light of this latest development, his initial plan would be even more satisfying. To target both Walker *and* his daughter at the same time. Wipe the bastard's lineage from the face of the earth.

He set the mobile down and switched to another news station, glorying in the death and destruction and fear they'd wrought today. The first of a new wave of attacks that was just beginning.

He reached for the glass of water on the coffee table. Swore when his unsteady hand knocked it over clumsily. He rescued the mobile and his laptop before the water could reach them, got up and went to the kitchen to get a tea towel, nearly tripping over his own feet.

Damn. He would have liked more time to plan out his final part in this. Something more epic and spectacular for his final mission. But he was losing more and more function every day and it wouldn't be long now before he was incapacitated and helpless.

A wave of fury whipped through him. No way. He would rather go out in a blaze of glory. One lit by his own failing hands.

He cleaned up. Wiped the place down as best he could, then got in his rental car and headed north out of the city, enacting the first part of the plan he'd already engineered. On the way, he worked out the wording of the cryptic clue he would leave.

If Walker was in London working with MI5, he would definitely be involved in the rest of the investigation that followed. And Isaac's plan wouldn't be quite as much fun without involving a little game.

After all he'd suffered, he deserved to have a little fun with this before he died.

SEVEN

"What are you planning to do after the meeting?" Kiyomi asked.

"Do about what?" Ivy said into her vehicle's hands-free device as she neared Government Communications Headquarters in Cheltenham.

After Rycroft had been forced to show up and run interference to secure her release from interrogation the other day, MI5 and the Home Office had apparently had a change of heart about her. Rather than treating her with suspicion, they had asked her to attend the meeting instead to share intel on the attack and the network that had spawned it.

"About Walker."

She frowned, not liking her bestie's keen perception in this particular instance. "I'll work with him on the investigation as long as I'm needed."

"No. You know I'm not talking about work." She paused. "He doesn't even know who you are."

It was annoying that Kiyomi knew her so well and called her on her bullshit. "If I decide to tell him, would you guys be okay with me bringing him there?"

"Do you want to tell him?"

"Sometimes."

"And the other times?"

She sighed. "The old internal messaging gets in the way."

"You said you looked into him, and he checked out. Amber did too. And Rycroft clearly respects him."

"I know. It's…the past. It's hard to let go of some things." No one understood that better than Kiyomi.

"I get it. You know I do. But what does your gut say?"

"That he's a good guy. A good guy who is still oblivious of what I did." He would blame and hate her for it if he ever found out. "But my gut was wrong before, and we both know how that wound up."

A short silence followed before Kiyomi spoke again. "If you decide to tell him, you're welcome to bring him here. Marcus and I will be happy to have him."

"Thanks. I'll think about it."

"Good. You almost there?"

"Yep. I can see The Doughnut now. Weird to think I'm going to actually walk in there for the first time when I've been hacking into their system for this long."

Kiyomi gave a low laugh. "What they don't know won't hurt 'em. Or you."

She smiled. "Exactly." Same thing applied to Walker. Difference was, she'd never felt an ounce of guilt over hacking into GCHQ or any other government agency. That wasn't the case with Walker. "Talk to you later?"

"Of course, call me when you've made up your mind."

"I will. Bye."

At the security gate, Ivy handed over her British passport—courtesy of some made-up background Rycroft had invented for her and provided paperwork on—and drove to the parking spot she had been allocated. Walker arrived a few minutes later and her nerves eased.

She'd been on edge since the attack and then being hauled in by MI5. If Rycroft hadn't intervened on her behalf, she might still be in custody. Also, having operated alone for almost her entire life, it would be nice to have an ally beside her when she stepped in there.

Surprise flashed across Walker's face when he climbed out of his rental and saw her. "Hey."

She came around the front of her vehicle to meet him. "Hi. How was the drive up from London?" He looked gorgeous as ever in dark charcoal dress pants and a crisp white dress shirt, the weak morning sun fighting through the cloud cover making the silver at his temples glimmer.

"Not bad." He stopped close to her, searched her eyes for a moment. "Everything okay?"

"Yes." Every time she thought about the way he'd touched her the other night it sent a rush of longing through her.

For one crazy second, she'd even wondered if he'd been thinking about kissing her. Because she'd sure been thinking about kissing him.

"Rycroft smoothed the waters with the powers that be, so to speak," she added. "I'm here to share the intel Amber and I gathered."

He nodded. "Shall we?" He gestured toward the entrance.

They crossed the parking lot together. At the doors, he stepped ahead and pulled one open for her. "After you."

"Thanks." She loved his manners almost as much as she loved his Mississippi drawl. And that safe, calm energy she wanted to immerse herself in.

She'd been thinking about him nonstop for the past two days. The way people reacted during a crisis revealed who they truly were at their core.

Walker's immediate instinct after the bomb went off had been to protect and shelter her. No one had ever done that for her before when she was in danger.

While she didn't need anyone to protect her, when Walker did, it made her feel all gooey inside. "This should be enlightening."

All her senses were attuned to him as he followed her through security and up to the third floor. The Doughnut was a huge doughnut-shaped building that housed the British cryptology and intelligence service. He stayed a step behind her the whole way except in the elevator, as if he was guarding her.

Knowing he was watching her back even here where it was safe warmed her insides.

His wife had died more than five years ago. He hadn't remarried and she couldn't help but wonder if he was single. She hadn't done a deep dive into his current personal life beyond checking his marital status. She knew he had a step-daughter living with him in Oregon, but looking into anything more just seemed too great a violation of his privacy, especially when she had already dug so much into his professional background.

An MI5 representative she'd met the other day at Thames House stepped out into the hall. "Ms. Johnson, Mr. Walker. Please come in."

Well, this was already far more pleasant than how they'd treated her last time. She entered the secure room where a dozen other people were already seated around the long table. The director for MI5 rose at the head.

He acknowledged them both with a nod, then held out a hand to indicate the big, dark-haired man seated to his left with a wicked scar running across the side of his right cheek and throat. "This is Warwick James, former SAS and most recently an MI6 intelligence officer. I've asked him here today to share information he gathered on a previous mission."

James nodded at them, dark eyes intense and watchful. Ivy and Walker took their seats across from him and examined the intel packets before them.

"If you'll open to the first page, we'll get started," the director said. "After this week's attack in London, the threat level remains at severe. We are tasked with identifying whoever was involved with the perpetrator and arresting them before any further harm can be done. Let's start with what we know." He gestured to a woman halfway down, who went through a list of talking points about the current intel.

The Underground bomber had planted the devices alone but didn't have the skills or knowledge to build them. Forensic computer analysts had uncovered messages between him and others online using radical rhetoric and talking about the need to attack to make the people "wake up."

"As for the bomb maker, it's a much shorter list of names. And one in particular has now jumped straight to the top. Isaac Grey."

Ivy wasn't the least bit surprised he was the number one suspect. There were, however, major holes that still needed to be filled in. Such as the part about how and why he had been officially declared dead by both the US and UK governments.

"Some of you may not know, but after attaining his PhDs, Grey was recruited by MI6 to act as a bomb maker for certain parties in Russia they were looking at. Including some Bratva members."

In spite of herself, Ivy tensed at the mention of that name, ghostly and nightmarish memories swirling at the back of her mind before she was able to block them and lock them back in the safe she'd put them in.

"Grey was officially declared dead in a fire by the Russians, and we were never able to analyze his remains. Then last June a device was detonated at the Prime Minister's summer home in the Lake District. Four people were killed but the PM avoided injury. Analysis of what remained of the device bore the hallmarks of Grey's work. Online chatter around that period led us to investigate further."

He paused. "It seems our Russian friends lied to us. Grey didn't die in a fire during their custody. He escaped, and they were hell-bent on covering it up." His gaze swept the table. "We don't know where he is, or what identity he's using. But it appears Grey is now back from the dead and seeking retribution for what happened. Previous attacks that may be linked to him have all targeted government officials or buildings up 'til now. Until the recent Tube bombings, that is."

Thanks to Home Front and Elliot Fornam, Ivy thought savagely.

She maintained an impassive expression the entire time, conscious of the uptick in her resting heart rate. She thought about all those people killed and wounded the other day. Their families and the suffering they were going through now.

Partly because of her. It was a hard thing to swallow.

"Mr. Walker, this brings me to you," the director went on. "Please tell us all about your involvement with Isaac Grey."

"He was an asset I'd worked with on several investigations, including Syria. The last one involved a major weapons dealer in Russia. Based on the intelligence he collected, I arranged to have him meet with an informant in Moscow. While on his way to the meeting, Grey was captured and taken into custody."

That was my fault too, Ivy thought, glad Walker didn't know. Or that she had been left for dead that night as well.

"I lost all contact then," Walker continued. "Several weak

attempts were made by both the US and UK governments to secure his freedom, to save face. But the truth is, we left him there."

A sudden thick tension settled over the room at his quiet accusation before he continued. "All of us. Because it was politically inconvenient to extract him or push for a prisoner exchange. So we disavowed him and left him there. It was a relief when they were told he was dead. *That's* the reality. That's why he's doing this."

His words sent a shiver through her. He was dead on. Their sins had come back to haunt them.

Hers included.

After a long, awkward pause that involved a lot of clearing of throats and paper shuffling, the director moved around the table getting everyone else's insight. Ivy went last, sharing only what she and Amber had uncovered, and keeping silent about her personal connection with Grey.

Three hours had passed before they wrapped up the session. Warwick joined her and Walker on the way down to the lobby. "I'd like to talk to you both about Grey more if you're willin'," he said in a strong northern accent.

Sounded Geordie to her. "You from Newcastle?" she asked him.

He flashed a quick smile, his scar pulling the skin taut across his cheek. "Aye."

"Do you know Grey personally?" Walker asked him.

"In a manner of speakin'. Got this and a few other permanent souvenirs from him in the Lake District last summer." He tapped his scar. "I'd say that's pretty personal."

"You were there?" Ivy asked. She remembered looking into the incident with Amber right afterward. Yet Grey hadn't turned up on their or MI5's radar until a few days ago.

"Aye." His phone beeped in his hand. He glanced at it. "Need to go. Speak to you later."

"Sure." Ivy fell back in step with Walker as Warwick hurried away from them down another hallway. "The Lake District attack was egged on by people in Home Front. And so was the concert attack in Washington State."

"Followed by another bombing here, and now this latest."

"Think Grey built all the devices?"

"Probably. And he'll have more attacks planned. The targets will be more refined going forward. More pointed. Things that make a real statement."

"Not if we nail the bastard before he can pull another one off."

Walker nodded and didn't say anything as they neared security at the exit.

They were opposites in so many ways. She was morally gray while Walker was black and white. He was a Boy Scout with unshakable convictions and a strong sense of justice, while she had a vindictive streak when it came to her enemies.

Even ones she had once considered family.

He was stoic and contained. She only appeared to be that way on the outside because she had to. Because it had been trained into her as a child. The real her was adventurous, a bit impetuous, and desperate for real connection with people she could trust.

"So what now?" he asked when they reached the parking lot.

She considered the question for a moment. He had passed every test she'd put him through. There was no reason for her to be suspicious of him. While it was true that she could never be completely certain that he wouldn't betray her, she had come to the conclusion that it was an extremely low, outside risk.

She was ready to tell him the truth. Or at least…part of it.

"You have anywhere you need to be tonight?" she asked.

He cut her a sideways glance. "No. Why?"

She pushed aside the warning voice at the back of her mind. The one that said she was making a mistake.

The one that had been burned permanently into her hardwiring when she'd been placed into the program at age six.

"I want to take you somewhere important. To tell you some things I need to explain."

Surprise flickered in his deep blue eyes. "About you?"

"Yes."

"All right," he said with a nod. "I'll follow you."

∽

CHAD STEPPED through the door juggling three bags of groceries while struggling to get his key out of the old lock. "Damn," he muttered, flinging the key into the dish on the table in the entryway. One of the few things his female flatmate had put in the place that was actually useful.

He slipped off his shoes and carried the groceries through to the kitchen. It was tiny, galley-style, and a tight squeeze for more than one person at a time. He set the bags on the counter along the wall and returned to the entry to slip off his soaked jacket, water dripping all over the floor as he hung it on a hook to dry.

Back in the kitchen, he paused and listened. The rare, blissful quiet meant that his two flatmates were either out or asleep.

He began unpacking. His parents were still paying for his tuition and accommodation. This place was way nicer than what he'd had as a first-year student in halls. He had at least some privacy here, but there were definite drawbacks.

Like having to cook for himself. Which sucked.

He and his flatmates had a system worked out where they each cooked for the three of them twice a week, and either went out or ordered in on Saturday nights. All part of him growing up and "adulting," his parents had told him.

Dinner was hours away yet and he was starving, so he'd make himself a big batch of pasta for lunch and save two portions for his flatmates to eat later. He rummaged through the cupboard and eventually found a pot big enough to boil the noodles. After filling it and turning on the burner to let it heat, he unpacked the rest of what he'd bought, setting aside the macaroni, jar of sauce, the sausage, and the few vegetables he'd decided to chop up and add to the sauce.

Engrossed in his meal prep, the scents and sound of browning sausage and veg filling the air, he didn't hear anything else. Only caught a flash of movement out of the corner of his eye.

He turned, stiffened when he saw the masked man dressed all in black lunging for him.

Chad stepped back and threw out his arms to defend himself. The narrow galley kitchen, being caught off guard, gave him no time to mount a counterattack. He opened his mouth to scream.

The man grabbed him. Wrapped an arm around his throat. Chad let out a garbled yell and fought back, trying to break free.

A gloved hand flashed up. Pressed a sweet-smelling cloth over Chad's nose and mouth.

Chad kicked. Bucked. Thrashed.

It did no good. His muscles turned into warm wax, melting.

His hands fell away from the arm barred across his throat. The room tilted.

He looked up into the man's masked face. Saw cold, pale eyes. Lips compressed into a thin, colorless line.

The weakness spread, pulling his eyelids shut. He slid to the floor. Felt the pressure of the arm release around his throat and the terrible silence that had been wonderful only a few minutes earlier before darkness claimed him.

EIGHT

Where the hell was she taking him? They'd been driving for nearly thirty minutes now, deep into the countryside.

Walker followed Ivy's vehicle up the old Roman road known as the Fosse Way through the heart of the picturesque Cotswolds. Past little villages named Upper and Lower Slaughter and Bourton-on-the-Water.

It was like a different world out here, leaving The Doughnut and the stress of the current case behind. Everything looked like it belonged on a postcard, green rolling hills dotted with farms as far as the eye could see, fields lined with thick green hedgerows and ancient stone walls.

A few miles north, they passed a sign that read Stow-on-the-Wold. At the top of the hill a large village came into view to the east. Ivy signaled right and turned at the traffic lights.

They drove down a sloping road called Sheep Street that cut through the heart of the town, past golden-toned stone cottages and shops with gray slate roofs lining both sides, and down into the valley below. Farmland stretched out in every direction here, covering the landscape in a multicolor patchwork of green.

They were now officially out in the middle of nowhere and his mind was working overtime about Ivy. Why had she brought him way out here to tell him about herself?

A ways up, she turned left off the main road and led him a few miles north up more hills and down more valleys before turning left again down a quiet country road. There was nothing but sheep farms here, so he was even more surprised when, near the bottom of the next hollow, a large manor house rose out of the landscape and Ivy turned into its driveway.

Curious as to why they were here, he watched her climb out of her car, enter the code into the gate, then hop back in and pull around behind a gatehouse made of the same golden stone as every other building in the area. He parked beside her and got out, full of questions.

"Welcome to Laidlaw Hall," she said with a bright smile that made her twice as stunning as usual.

He looked around. "Is it a hotel?"

"No, I live here with friends. Come on in." She opened the back door and stepped inside.

He followed her in, took in the cozy space with a sweeping glance, aware that her bringing him to her home implied a significant level of trust. The worn flagstone floor led into a small country kitchen off the entry.

At a loud meow, he turned around to see Ivy bending to pick up a large, extremely well-fed black and white cat. "Hi, buddy. You miss me? Huh?" She rubbed his head and chin and the cat rubbed his cheek against hers with a rumbling purr, making her laugh.

He stared, the sound and the delight on her face completely transforming her and tugging at something inside him. He'd never heard her laugh before. "Who's this?"

"Mr. Whiskers. Someone threw him in the garbage when he was a kitten. I heard these tiny little mews and found him inside a trash bag in the dumpster. He's been my most devoted companion ever since. Say hi, buddy." She edged closer to Walker, angling the cat toward him while watching him closely.

He couldn't help but feel this was yet another test of sorts. So he rubbed the top of the cat's head and under its chin. Mr. Whiskers half-closed his eyes, a loud rumbling purr coming from him.

"He likes you," Ivy said, and the satisfaction in her voice told her he'd passed.

"He's friendly."

"He is, and it's surprising considering I barely had any interaction with people until I moved here."

He eyed her. "Why's that?"

She set Mr. Whiskers down. "You want anything to drink? Eat?"

"No, I'm good." He only wanted answers at this point.

"Then how about a walk?"

"Sure."

She slipped her shoes back on, did up her coat and stepped out onto the pea gravel drive behind the gatehouse. "Let's head up to the gardens." She started up the sloping emerald lawn that bordered the left side of the manor house.

He wasn't an architectural expert but the exterior looked Georgian, with four small dormer windows set into the bottom of the slate roof. "How long have you lived here?"

"Year and a half. It's my safe space. Where I can let down my guard and completely relax." She nodded toward the manor. "My best friend and her husband own it. Marcus inherited it from a distant relative."

"Your best friend is…?"

"Kiyomi."

He frowned. "I thought she was your sister."

"She is."

Okay. Weird to call her a best friend rather than sister though. "She runs a charity helping to protect orphans, right?"

She flashed him another smile that disarmed him completely. "That's right. Marcus is an SAS veteran. Might know Warwick, I'll have to ask. You'll meet them after."

"After what?"

"After we talk."

Relieved that the suspense was finally about to end, he walked with her in silence up the slope and past the manor house to a formal garden of tightly trimmed boxwood and rose trees.

"There's the stable up there." She pointed up the narrow gravel path that bisected the formal garden. "Marcus is quite an equestrian now. And back there is the spot I want to take you to." She gestured beyond it to the left.

As they crested the top of the rise, a long, honey-toned stone wall came into view. Ivy strode to a spot in the middle and Walker at last spotted the door set into it. She opened it up, stepped through and he followed.

"Wow," he said, looking around. It was like a scene from a storybook, a private sanctuary filled with trees, shrubs and other plants.

"Beautiful, isn't it? It's my sister Eden's favorite spot here." She walked over to a stone bench built into an alcove in the wall and patted the spot beside her.

He sat, listening to the wind rustling the changing leaves and the sound of an unfamiliar bird calling. "So what did you bring me way out here to tell me?"

She gazed out at the garden instead of looking at him.

"What I'm about to tell you is highly classified and needs to stay between us." She looked at him. "You can't tell anyone. Not even Donovan or Shae."

It only made him more curious. But her secret was safe with him. "Okay."

She looked back out at the garden. "You asked what a Valkyrie is. The short answer is, me. And my sisters."

He watched her in silence, noting the slight tension in her shoulders, the way she avoided looking at him. "Go on."

"Years ago, the CIA secretly funneled some young orphan girls with no family to care for them into a classified selection process for the Valkyrie Program."

"I've never heard of it." And he'd been a CIA officer for the better part of a decade.

"No, you wouldn't have. Because no one has except for the people behind it—who are all dead now." She paused, his full attention riveted on her. "They trained us to be the world's deadliest and most elite female assassins. Each of us with a particular specialty."

He stared at her, already not liking where he sensed this might be heading. He'd heard rumors about units like this in other countries from the Cold War. But never in the US.

"They tested us early after arrival and placed us in different streams depending on our aptitudes. We were cross-trained in a lot of different things, but each of us had a primary specialty. Mine was technology and hacking. Some things about the program were good, but a lot of it was harsh. Physical punishment and deprivation. Isolation. Psychological reprogramming. They broke us down and transformed us into lethal weapons."

No, he didn't like the sound of it at all. "It was involuntary?" he said to clarify, appalled. Now he understood why she and Rycroft had been reluctant to tell him any of this before.

"Yes. Girls who washed out were never seen again. Don't know what happened to them and it haunts me to this day. Those of us who made it through to graduation were deployed individually on hunter-killer missions. And we were all proud as hell when we graduated. All of us eager to go out and unleash our skills on targets they had selected." She looked at him again, measuring his reaction.

"What kind of targets?"

She shrugged. "Arms dealers. Drug dealers. Warlords. Politicians. Billionaires. Whoever the CIA wanted eliminated without the hassle of accountability. If we died, it was the price of business. If we were captured, we were disavowed and left to fend for ourselves."

His head was spinning. He'd seen some dark shit during his career. This was abhorrent. "How old were you?"

"Six."

Jesus Christ. He thought of Shae at that age. Felt physically sick at the thought of any of that happening to her. "I don't know what to say," he said finally.

"You don't have to say anything. I wanted you to know, to hear it from me. Thought it would help you...understand me better, I guess." She tucked her hair behind one ear. "There's a lot more to the story, but the one other important bit I wanted to tell you about was an incident that happened several years back."

"What happened?"

"Like I said, we almost always worked alone, but one day out of the blue I was contacted by a couple of Valkyries about doing an op with them. They sold me on it, so I agreed to join them. Long story short, as soon as they got what they wanted from me, they betrayed me and handed me over to the enemy. I almost died. Well, on paper I *did*. Julia Green officially went to her maker that night. I escaped, went off grid, and after a long and extremely painful recovery, transformed into Ivy Johnson."

Her tone and expression were even. As though it was no big deal.

She was good at hiding it, but he could sense the pain buried in her words. Knew she'd left out so many details and couldn't begin to imagine what she'd actually been through. What she'd survived, both in the program she'd described and the attack that had almost killed her.

"What happened after that?" he asked.

"Valkyrie justice." This time there was a savage edge to her tone. "My sisters found out about the betrayal and took care of business for me. But the man responsible for my capture got away with it. So I made it my mission to destroy him."

She was so matter of fact about it. And he realized he was seeing her for the first time. Understanding just how deadly she was. It should have made him uneasy, but it didn't. She wasn't dangerous to anyone who didn't deserve it.

"It took a few years, but I finally saw an opportunity." She shifted on the bench, her discomfort clear. "Problem was, I couldn't go after him alone. And I was…lonely. So damn lonely after being on my own for so many years."

The wistfulness in her voice triggered an ache in his chest at the thought of her being alone for so long with no one to turn to. Living on the run, always looking over her shoulder, never trusting anyone. That wasn't a life. It was a sentence. "What did you do?"

"It wasn't easy, but I eventually found leads on Kiyomi and the others. I wanted to come out of hiding to reconnect with them but wasn't going to risk being betrayed again. So I…set them up. A test to see where their true loyalties lay."

He listened, hanging on her every word. Stunned by everything she'd revealed thus far.

"I fed them bits of intel on the target because I knew they wouldn't be able to resist, then sat back and watched them systematically destroy him and his network. Except it didn't go entirely according to plan. Kiyomi was badly injured in a one-on-one fight with the target. And another sister's boyfriend was nearly killed in a different part of the op."

She released a long breath, kept going. "Anyway, they killed the network and got the target, who will now die behind bars. Then I decided to see if it was safe to reveal myself. Kiyomi recognized me even despite the plastic surgeries."

He frowned, looking more closely at her. "You…?"

She gestured to her face. "I was disfigured in the attack. The private surgeons I paid for later on gave me a new look. But Kiyomi still knew me." She shook her head, a bittersweet smile on my face. "She and the others embraced me even after what I'd done. All of them. They brought Rycroft in to help Ivy Johnson finally step into the light. And that's how I wound up here."

He kept watching her as she fell silent, fighting the urge to pull her into his arms and hold her. He hadn't known anything about the Valkyrie Program. "Is the program still operating?"

"No. That's all over. My sisters took care of the mastermind responsible for the program personally. It's a pretty amazing story. Maybe Kiyomi and I'll tell you about it later if you're interested. But anyway, this is why I've been so cagey about protecting my identity and background. And why you couldn't find out anything or anyone who did." She gave him a wry look. "You could say I have trust issues."

"Yeah, well, I'd be shocked if you didn't." He shook his head, still trying to take it all in. Government-trained elite female assassins. Forced into an involuntary and punitive system that had taken everything away from them. "How many of you are left?"

"Nine of us. Kiyomi and I are the only ones currently based in the UK. The others are all back in the States. And believe it or not, they've all settled down with good, stable men. Which was something none of us expected."

But not her.

He looked down at her slender hand, braced on the bench between them. Slid his over to rest on top of it, not wanting her to feel alone anymore.

She stiffened slightly. "I didn't tell you because I wanted you to feel sorry for me."

"I know." He did feel sorry for her though. For all of them becoming orphans in the first place and then put into such a brutal program sanctioned by their own goddamn federal government to be used on off-the-books hits. How the hell had none of this ever come to light before? "But I'm glad you did tell me. I know that couldn't have been easy, so thank you."

She turned her head toward him, surprise flashing across her face. "You're welcome." Her shoulders relaxed and a tiny smile curved her lips. "Well, you've got the gist of it now. Wanna meet Kiyomi now?"

"God, yes."

She laughed at his curiosity, the happy, carefree sound making him want to pull her close and crush her to him. It in no way could make up for a single fraction of what she'd endured in her painful past, but damn. He was awed that she'd shared so much with him. Was outraged that no one had stepped in to protect her before.

"Come on, then." She stood, pulling her hand free.

Walker followed her back through the secret door and up the rise where the back of the manor house was visible.

"Regretting asking me now?" she said, her gaze measuring him.

"No. I was just thinking about Shae."

"What about her?"

"That I can't wait to tell her I love her again when I call her later."

NINE

Walker's words set off a pang of longing in Ivy. His deep love and devotion to his daughter was so damn pure.

Ivy would give anything to be loved that way. "She's lucky to have you and Donovan."

"We're the lucky ones. He'd be the first to tell you so."

"Oh, he already did in Kabul." She put her hands in her pockets to stem the urge to touch him and kept pace beside him up the slope, filled with a strange mix of relief and apprehension.

While she was glad she'd told him in one sense, she dreaded the fallout later when he learned how she'd interfered with his op in Russia and was ultimately responsible for Grey's capture there.

"What happened to your family?" he asked, pulling her out of her thoughts.

"Died in a hotel fire when they were away on a business trip for my dad. I don't really remember him much. Just a few snapshots in my memory here and there. My mom, I can picture more clearly, but only a few images are left."

"I'm sorry."

She shrugged. "Life's not fair sometimes."

"No." But what she and the others had been put through was unforgivable. "What about the CIA? They should be held accountable—"

"None of us wanted to dredge it all up again. It's better left buried. Everyone else directly involved with the program is dead. We agreed as a group to leave it alone and move on." Also didn't hurt that they were all wealthy women now, having funneled money from criminals they'd hunted into offshore accounts to be divided among them.

"That's admirable of you all, considering what had happened. Not sure I would have been able to do the same."

She made a murmuring sound, her mind already shifting topics. "When you—" She stopped. "Never mind."

He glanced at her. "No, go on. What were you going to ask?"

"Something really personal."

"Only seems fair. Go ahead."

"It's been a long time since your wife died."

His expression tensed, confirming that she was treading on unwelcome ground. "And?"

"Has there been anyone since?"

"No," he said, easing a little.

"No one?" she asked in surprise.

"No. Wasn't interested in anyone else, and I've been too busy with work and wanting to be there for Shae." He glanced over at her. "After the bits that Donovan and Nadia told her about Kabul, she's insanely curious about you, by the way. Huge fan. Keeps asking me to update her with anything I find out—which was nothing, as you know. Though obviously I won't be telling her any of what you just told me."

"No," she said with a grin, believing him. And that felt good. To be able to at least mostly trust a man with her secrets.

Well. Some of them.

He was such a revelation compared with the others from her past. She just hoped she was right in trusting him as much as she did. "Here, let's go in the back." She led the way up the narrow pea gravel path in the center of the formal garden and up to the rear entry of the house.

The dog started barking when they got within fifty feet. "That's Karas. Marcus rescued her in Syria when she was a pup. You like dogs?"

He shrugged. "I like animals."

More points for him. And Mr. Whiskers had certainly given his approval earlier. That carried weight with Ivy.

"Come on in." She opened the door. The white and brown Anatolian dog immediately stopped when she saw the newcomer, sizing him up with an intense stare.

Walker stood still and let her come up to sniff him suspiciously.

"She's got trust issues too, so she fits right in," Ivy said, and called out in the direction of the kitchen. "We're here."

Kiyomi appeared in the hallway a moment later, closely followed by Marcus and the rhythmic tap of his cane. She smiled at Walker. "Hi, it's so nice to meet you. I'm Kiyomi."

Walker shook with her, his warm smile giving Ivy butterflies. His smile was deadly and made her pulse race. "Hello."

Marcus stopped beside his wife. "Marcus Laidlaw. Welcome," he said, shaking with Walker.

"Thank you. Amazing place you have."

"Aye, thanks. It keeps me busy." He lifted a dark eyebrow at Ivy. "So you told him, then?"

"Yes. The meat and potatoes, anyway."

Marcus looked at him, a twinkle in his deep brown eyes. "You fancy a drink?"

"God, yes," Walker said.

Marcus chuckled. "This way." He turned and started back down the hall. "Karas, come." The dog immediately trotted to his side and walked with him, tail wagging.

Kiyomi gave Walker a bland look. "In case there was any doubt who's number one in my husband's life, there's your proof."

"Not true," Marcus said. "You're both tied for first place."

In Marcus's cozy study, Ivy and Walker sat on the tufted leather sofa together while Kiyomi took one of the comfy armchairs across from them and Marcus went to the sideboard along the exterior wall. "Whisky okay?" he asked.

"Fine," Walker answered.

Marcus poured them each a drink and handed them out before easing himself stiffly into the armchair next to Kiyomi.

Walker's gaze slid to Kiyomi, who was watching him with a look Ivy knew all too well. Studying him. Analyzing and assessing in the automatic way they all did.

"How did the meeting go this morning?" she asked them.

"It went," Ivy answered. "Grey's definitely at the top of the list." She opened her mouth to say more but her phone rang with a familiar ringtone. She looked over at Walker, raised her eyebrows. "Can you handle meeting more of my family?"

"Just let me get some of this down first," he said, taking a sip of whisky.

"Fair enough. All right, brace yourself." She answered the video call. "Hi, Amber," she said when her sister's face popped up on screen. "How's it going?"

"Is he there?" Amber craned her neck this way and that, trying to see past Ivy.

"He's here, but he's currently in shock and fortifying himself with a stiff drink, so be nice. Want to say hi?"

"Yes, hang on a sec." Amber glanced away, typed rapidly on one of her keyboards and smiled in satisfaction. "Guys, he's there. Say hi."

Ivy blinked as not just Amber's biological sister Megan, but all six remaining Valkyries appeared in individual boxes on screen.

Poor Walker. Talk about baptism by fire. "Oh my God, you guys—"

"Don't try and hide him from us, Ivy. We know he's there," Briar said.

She shot Walker an apologetic look. "You sure?"

His mouth twitched and he squared his shoulders. "I'm ready."

Smiling, she turned the phone around so everyone could see him. They all started talking at once.

"Ivy, why didn't you tell us he was so hot?" This from Chloe, the most outgoing and outspoken of the group.

To give him credit, Walker maintained his composure and calm, his gaze bouncing from one square to the next as he tried to make sense of the chaos. "Hi, y'all."

Simultaneous grins broke out. "Love the drawl," said Eden from the top right corner. "Hi, back."

"Well, don't just sit there, Ivy, introduce us already," said Trinity, her toddler son perched on her lap.

"All right, here goes. That's Trinity," she said, tapping the corresponding square. "Then there's Briar and Georgia, both kickass snipers. Eden up there is a poisons expert."

"Did you show him the garden?" Eden asked. "You gotta show him the garden."

"I showed him. And this is Megan, Amber's biological sister. She's our resident professional thief if we ever need anything retrieved on short notice. Amber, of course, is a hacker like me. Wave, Amber."

Amber waved. "Hi, Walker."

He lifted a hand, taking it all in stride with good humor. "Hi."

"What, you left me for last?" Chloe asked, pouting. "Why am I last?"

"Only because I wanted to save the best for last. Walker, meet Chloe. She's our explosives expert and the biggest handful of us all. As you can imagine, that's saying something."

Chloe shot her a dirty look before turning a grin on Walker. "Hi, there. I'm really not as bad as they make me out to be, honest."

"That's good to know," he said.

"I'd actually like to bring Chloe in on our current investigation," Ivy said to him. It was damn bizarre to phrase it as if she was asking his permission, but she was learning to be more of a team player. "She'll be able to give us insight about the devices used so far, establish patterns and whatnot."

"Oooh, yeah, bring it," Chloe said, all eagerness as she leaned closer to the camera until her face took up nearly her whole square. "Been way too long since I did anything worthy of my talents."

"I think we can probably…make that happen," Walker said with a straight face.

He was doing great so far. Meeting any one of them was memorable enough. Meeting all of them at once had to be overwhelming as hell.

Chloe beamed at him. "I like him. So, when are you gonna send me the stuff?"

"Soon as he has a minute to catch his breath," Ivy answered.

Briar snorted. "Doesn't look much out of breath to me. In fact, based on what I've seen so far, I'd say it would take a lot to make Walker break a sweat. But I bet you could manage it, Ivy." The others snickered.

Hell. They all knew she was into him. Damn Kiyomi must have blabbed to them. "Okay, well anyway, now that you've all met and traumatized Walker with this firing squad of an introduction, we're gonna go."

"Aww, so soon?" Georgia said in a disappointed tone. "We didn't even get to know him a little yet."

"Lucky for him. Love you guys, but I'm going now. Bye."

A chorus of byes and other teasing parting shots followed before she ended the call with the touch of a button and looked up at Walker. "So. That was my family."

He nodded, humor dancing in his sapphire eyes. And she wished they were alone so she could take his bearded face in her hands and kiss him the way she'd been imagining for way too long. "Colorful group."

"You have no idea."

He tilted his head slightly. "No, I've got some."

She smiled, feeling all off-balance and jittery inside. Part of her was horrified that she'd just opened the door to her most closely guarded secrets and then introduced him to all the others. That she'd just laid herself bare and made herself incredibly vulnerable. She'd needed to get it off her chest, though, to at least partly appease her conscience.

And also because of the tiny seed of hope tucked away deep inside that she might have a chance with him once this was all over. If he could forgive her for interfering in his op in Russia.

She would have to come clean about that at some point and was already dreading it.

"Hey, by the way," she said, turning to Marcus. "We met a former MI6 agent today who is former SAS. Wondered if you knew him. Warwick James."

Marcus swallowed his sip of whisky and lowered his

tumbler to the arm of his chair. "Aye, I know who he is. From Newcastle. Good lad. Never served with him, but everything I heard about him was solid."

No sooner had he said it than a ringtone went off. Walker shifted and pulled out his phone. "Walker," he answered, looking at her. "Hi, Warwick." His expression changed slightly. Turned borderline grim as he listened. "Right. Got it. Thanks for the update."

He ended the call, looked at them all.

"Anything you tell me, you can say in front of them," Ivy said. She would just fill Kiyomi in later anyway.

He hesitated only a moment more before speaking. "News just broke that the former Home Secretary's eldest son was kidnapped from his flat at Oxford this afternoon." His tone was somber. "The same minister who was Home Secretary when Grey was disavowed."

TEN

Warwick's update put a definite damper on Walker's mood, but since there was nothing he could do at this point to help find the missing student, he accepted the invitation to stay and eat. While Kiyomi and Marcus worked together in the kitchen, Ivy gave him a tour of the manor house.

"Each room has its own color theme. My sisters all stayed here for various periods of time before I got here," she said.

He'd worked with her remotely as an operative to get Nadia out of Kabul. Had seen the way she handled herself during and after the bombing the other day before she'd chased down the suspect and been prepared to take him on in a knife fight. Her skills and bravery were commendable. But he liked this version of her the best.

It was so different seeing her with her guard down, made all the more special because he knew she didn't let it down easily, and only for a handful of people on this earth. And she'd chosen him to be one of them.

It humbled him. Made him wish she could feel safe enough outside these gates to be herself all the time.

Dinner was served in the breakfast room where its large

windows overlooked the formal garden out back. At Ivy's request, Kiyomi recounted the story of how she and the other Valkyries had tracked down and eliminated the head of the program, and how it had hit way too close to home for Amber and Megan.

Walker was left mentally shaking his head. He couldn't believe what these women had been put through and that *no* one had put a stop to any of it. It was a goddamn outrage.

"I'm just sorry I wasn't part of it," Ivy said, helping herself to more roast potatoes and gravy. She held the platter of potatoes out to him. "Want some? And if you like Yorkshire pudding, you'd better grab yourself that last one before I steal it."

"I thought Megan was the expert thief?"

She flashed a grin that made her eyes light up. "I can hold my own. Wanna see?" Quick as a striking snake, her hand flashed out to stab the crispy pudding with her fork. She raised an eyebrow. "Last chance before this baby goes on my plate."

"You're as bad as Chloe," Marcus said from across the table.

"How 'bout we split it," Walker said.

Ivy inclined her head. "Deal."

The rest of the meal was relaxed, with Ivy and Kiyomi shooting banter back and forth and the occasional dry remark from Marcus. Afterward, Walker insisted on helping clear the table and doing the dishes with Ivy. They worked together side by side at the kitchen sink while the light outside faded and she chattered away about theories on where Grey might have taken the hostage and why.

She had good insight and instincts, but Walker was focused far more on her than he was on the ongoing investigation, struck by the homey intimacy of the moment. It had been forever since he'd done something this domestic with anyone but Shae.

He and Ivy worked together well. He liked her quick, agile mind. Her focus and dedication. Her willingness to jump in and do whatever was necessary to get the job done.

He imagined her standing next to him in his kitchen back in Crimson Point, chatting away while they tidied up after a meal. And it felt way too right.

"I guess I should hit the road and get going back to London," he said, placing the damp dishtowel over the oven door handle to dry. He needed to go before he gave into the deep yearning she created in him and crossed the line.

"I'll walk you down to the gate," Ivy said.

He still had so many questions about her and her past. But there was one that had been circling his brain for the past few hours. "During the video call, you told me every one of your sisters' specialties except two. Trinity and Kiyomi." The conclusions he'd come to on his own were ugly and bothered him.

She paused a moment, looked away. "I'll tell you now because they gave me permission before. They were intimate assassins. Seductresses. The deadliest of us all, trained to kill up close and personal, and you can read between the lines well enough to understand what that entailed."

He'd guessed right. Wished he hadn't, especially after meeting Kiyomi and seeing the warm, genuine bond between her and Ivy. Damn. "You said you were all cross-trained," he continued, unable to shake the building dread.

"I never had to do what they did," she answered quickly, correctly guessing the direction of his thoughts and easing the restriction in his chest. "And I'm glad. I mean, I used certain common techniques to get close to male informants or targets sometimes, but no. I wasn't subjected to that kind of trauma over and over like they were."

"Good."

She shook her head, jaw tightening. "I don't know how they made it through, to be honest. Their specialty had the highest mortality rate of all, and the highest trauma rate. For obvious reasons."

"I'm glad you were spared that at least." Thank God.

She looked at him, and for a moment he plainly saw the shadows swirling in her eyes. More secrets he wanted to learn. "Me too," she finally said.

Time to change the subject. He surveyed the sprawling grounds surrounding the main house in the fading light. "This really is a gorgeous spot. Do you like living here?"

"Yes, but it's too quiet for me sometimes. I liked the isolation at first, but…"

"Not anymore."

"Not so much, no." She swept her brown curtain of hair over one shoulder, the breeze catching it, the deeply golden rays of the afternoon sun making it gleam. "I lived that way for most of my life, and now that it's finally safe and I don't have to always look over my shoulder anymore, I'm feeling the need to make up for lost time."

"Makes sense." He couldn't imagine living that way. He was pretty introverted, yet he had Shae and Donovan and Callum in his inner circle. People he could count on. She'd had no one before coming here. "I was lucky. No matter what was going on in my job, I always had my family to go home to."

"I think it's really cool how close you are with Shae. That says a lot about you as a person."

"She's the best thing that ever happened to me. She was only little when I came into her life." Around the same age as Ivy had been when orphaned and sent into the Valkyrie

Program. His insides grabbed at the thought. "Within that first month she had me firmly wrapped around her little finger."

Ivy smiled at him. A warm, approving smile that hit him deep in his chest before she looked away. "I'll bet. And it doesn't surprise me in the least."

"No? It surprised me. I had no experience with kids before that and didn't know what the hell I was doing."

"Kids are great judges of character. She obviously felt safe with you, and I can completely see why."

He glanced at her in surprise. "You can?"

She kept looking straight ahead. "You have a way about you. Measured. Calm. Watchful. It makes people feel safe around you. Including me," she murmured.

Something caught in his chest. His fingers flexed with the need to grab her. To spin her around to face him. Slide into the thick, shiny waves of her hair and then kiss those tempting lips.

Today had shifted things between them again. He'd gone from confused about her to surprised, then outraged and protective in the space of a few hours. Her bringing him here into her private world, giving him a glimpse of who she was underneath all the badass, was totally unexpected.

The whole thing felt intimate. But her latest admission, tacked on as if she hadn't wanted to say it aloud, from the most skillful woman he'd ever met… Jesus, she was turning him inside out.

"That's…thank you," he said at last, battling the primal urge she triggered in him. Reminding himself of the reasons he needed to keep his hands off her. They barely knew each other. Were working on a case together, and lived on opposite sides of the world. A fling would be messy and unprofessional, and nothing good could come of it afterward.

She lifted a shoulder. "It's the truth."

They continued the walk down to the gatehouse in silence,

his entire body humming with awareness of her. Wanting her more every minute they spent together until the hunger was a live thing twisting inside him.

When they finally reached his vehicle, she stopped and slid her hands into her pockets. "Well, thanks for coming. I bet you got a lot more than you bargained for when you agreed to follow me here," she said with the hint of a grin.

He stepped closer to her, watched a mask drop into place to conceal her reaction. "I'm really glad you brought me." He looked directly into her eyes. "Thanks for trusting me."

He was watching her face so close he saw the way her pupils dilated, the flare of desire in her eyes.

And his resolve to keep his distance went up in smoke.

His hand came up to cradle the side of her face, his thumb caressing her cheek for a moment before he bent his head to kiss her.

The instant their lips touched, a shockwave ripped through him. Ivy drew in a startled breath, her hands going to his shoulders. Holding on, not pushing away.

The feel of her hands on him sent a burst of pure lust through his system. He slid his fingers into her hair, angled his head to kiss her more fully, on fire at the way her lips softened under his and she leaned into his body.

At the feel of her breasts brushing his chest, he banded an arm around her back and pulled her flush to him, turning her to press her against the side of his vehicle. Her soft moan made his entire body tighten with need, lips parting to allow his tongue inside. Caressing his. Teasing, while every firm curve of her body was imprinted on his.

In three seconds she'd destroyed his control, left him dizzy and hard as a goddamn club. He kissed her deeper, struggling to rein in the brutal lash of hunger and the need to strip her pants and underwear off so he could wind those sexy legs around him and plunge into her warmth.

He pulled back abruptly, breathing fast, shocked at what he'd just done. How quickly and easily she'd destroyed his control.

But he wasn't sorry. Would do it all over again.

And again, until she dragged him to her bed in the gatehouse and begged him to slide inside her.

With effort, he eased his hold. Made the mistake of pausing. Her eyes were heavy with the same kind of need he felt.

His gaze dropped to her lips, a soft groan of mingled frustration and defeat coming from him as he dipped back down to kiss her again. Softer this time. Slower. Full of everything he was feeling and didn't dare say aloud before he managed to release her and step back to pull in a deep breath.

"I'll talk to you soon," he murmured, staring into her eyes. If she asked him to stay, there was no way he could leave.

But she nodded, watching him with an undisguised hunger he felt deep in his gut as she stepped away from his car door, and ran her tongue over her lips. "Drive safely."

She stood at the gate as he drove away. For a moment the sheer longing in his gut almost made him stop and turn back around, visions of them tangled in her bed filling his head until it was hard to breathe.

He tore his gaze away from her in the rearview mirror and focused on the road leading him up the hill. At the heavy, leaden gray clouds gathering to the west, slowly closing in on Laidlaw Hall.

Walker exhaled and pressed down harder on the accelerator. They'd crossed the line, there was no undoing it.

He was already in over his head with Ivy and sinking fast.

LAURA STEPPED onto the sidewalk in front of the Melville Building in the cool night air and drew in a deep breath that smelled of the recent rain showers and damp leaves. It was dusk now, the vast sky arching overhead streaked with purple on the horizon, a cascade of stars already winking in the deep blue above.

It felt good to get out of her hall and be alone for a while. Wednesday was the longest day in her timetable. She'd been in class since nine that morning, attending back-to-back lectures, tutorials and workshops right until six with only an hour break. Now the rest of the evening was hers and the break in the weather meant she could still stick to her routine and get her run in before showering and tackling the latest deluge of assignments she had to get done.

She stuck her earbuds in, turned on her running playlist at low volume and started south up the path at a brisk walk. At the tall wrought-iron gates at the edge of the property, she reached Bow Lane and glanced up the hill where the edge of the cathedral was visible, already lit up and glowing against the darkness.

She turned left, leaving Hatfield College behind and jogging down the stone steps to the top of Kingsgate Bridge. Instead of crossing east to the opposite side, as she did each morning to get to her classes on campus up on the hill, she took the trail to the heavily wooded, narrow footpath that led around the river and started north.

The damp, crisp fall air enveloped her as she began to jog, the rhythmic beat of her runners on the pavement audible beneath the song she was listening to. To her left, the River Wear slid past calmly, barely a ripple in its dark, glassy surface as it flowed toward the northern tip of the peninsula. All around her the dense trees formed looming shadows along the riverbank, the forest filling the air with the rich, sweet scent of damp soil and fallen leaves.

She loved this route and this time she took to clear her head of all the stress and assignments waiting for her back in the room she shared with another international student. Cheryl was Canadian, and nice enough, but they were opposites and had pretty much nothing in common.

Cheryl also spent way more time partying than studying, because she could.

Laura didn't have that luxury. Even half a world away from home, she was always conscious of her parents' expectations of her.

It wasn't enough to pass her classes, she needed to be a model student and athlete. To not only stay out of trouble, but excel in everything she did. Do her father proud and never do anything that might risk tarnishing the family's precious public image or jeopardize her father's political aspirations in case any reporters came checking on her.

This run was exactly what she'd needed. Her breathing grew more labored as the minutes passed, blood pumping, warming her muscles. Up ahead, the path curved right as it followed the shape of the riverbank.

She emerged from the deep shadows cast by the dense canopy of turning leaves overhead and into a puddle of light cast by a lamppost. She could see the point of the peninsula now, less than a hundred yards ahead.

Odd that so far she hadn't passed a single person. This time of night there were usually other people out jogging or walking, and it was a gorgeous night.

She kept going, maintaining her pace past the tip of the peninsula as the path curved again. The distinctive three-stone-arch outline of Prebend's Bridge was silhouetted across the river in front of her.

A pleasant hum started in her quads as she picked up speed. This was the warmup. The real workout would be at the end when she climbed up Silver Street and around the top of the market square to Saddler on the way back up the hill to her college.

Over the song playing in her ears, she thought she heard someone approaching from behind. She automatically moved right to hug the edge of the path and turned her head to glance over her shoulder.

Her heart rocketed into her throat when she saw the shape of a man only a foot behind her.

Before she could react, his arm came out of nowhere and hooked around her ribs, yanking her off her feet. She opened her mouth to release the scream rising in her throat, terror ripping through her.

A hard, gloved hand cut it off, clamping across her mouth.

Help!

She twisted, clawed at the arm and hand holding her captive. Kicked and thrashed, trying to smash his face with the back of her skull. But he'd clapped something over her nose and mouth, making it hard to breathe.

A sickly-sweet scent hit her and instantly the world began to spin. She tried to fight but her muscles were suddenly weak and uncoordinated. Her limbs too heavy.

The man holding her dragged her off the path and into the dense cover of trees. A jagged bolt of fear sent adrenaline screaming through her veins, along with the sickening realization that she was about to be raped and possibly murdered blaring in her mind.

Help me!

It was no use. She couldn't fight back.

Panic and grief ripped through her. Only Cheryl knew

where she was. No one would come looking for her anytime soon. No one would find her until it was too late.

Her head swam, the weakness growing worse. Through her heavy eyelids, she barely made out the silhouette of a masked man dressed all in black just moments before the darkness swept over her.

ELEVEN

Walker's ringing phone woke him from a dead sleep. He rolled over to grab it from the nightstand, squinting against the light coming from the screen. His hotel room was pitch black, meaning it was still the middle of the night. 01:07 hours, according to his phone.

"Warwick," he answered. "What's up?"

"Sorry to wake you. Just got word about another kidnapping possibly linked to the investigation."

"Connected how?" he asked, sitting up and propping his back against the padded headboard.

"A female student was taken tonight from a public footpath at Durham."

"When?"

"Initial intel says it was around six hours ago."

He frowned, trying to think of possible connections between the two kidnappings. Oxford and Durham were both Russell Group universities. Research-focused, high-profile and elite post-secondary institutions. "Any connection with the male student?"

"Aye. She's the eighteen-year-old daughter of former CIA director David Hawes."

If he hadn't quite been fully awake a minute ago, he was now. Both the former Home Secretary and the former CIA director had been at the helm of their organizations during the fiasco after Walker's failed op in Moscow. And both had just had their children abducted from their universities within the space of one afternoon.

His jaw tightened. "Grey?"

"Aye, looks that way so far. Or at least someone actin' on his orders."

He ran a hand through his hair, thinking fast. "What's the prevailing theory?"

"No one's sure yet. There's a massive investigation being launched as I speak, but officials are keeping everything under wraps for now. It's all hands on deck."

"Any surveillance video?"

"So far none have shown anything. It's possible there were two different kidnappers involved. Whoever was in charge of the abductions, they mean business. They sent a sort of ransom note to the FBI and Home Office."

Ballsy. "What's it say?"

"'One has to go back to the beginning periodically. Now the sins of the father are to be laid upon the children.'"

The asshole's meaning could not be any clearer. And it sent a cold wave of foreboding through Walker as he put the inevitable together.

Shae.

His heart thudded hard, fear congealing in his gut. It was possible Grey might try to target her as well.

He had to call Donovan. Make sure she was safe. Out of Grey's reach, and stayed that way until they nailed the bastard.

"Did it give a deadline?" he asked, mind racing.

"No. But somethin' tells me we'll find out soon enough."

Yeah, Walker had that same feeling, and he was frantic to call Donovan and protect their daughter. "Does Ivy know?"

"Not yet."

"I'll call her." Right after her took steps to keep Shae safe. "Let me know if you hear anything else." He ended the call and immediately dialed Donovan.

He sat there for a minute afterward, fighting the impulse to race to the airport and get the first flight back stateside. Donovan would take care of Shae. Walker was needed here.

Pushing aside the worry for his daughter, he called Ivy.

"Hey," she answered, her voice all soft and drowsy. "To what do I owe this pleasure? You can't stop thinking about me and had to call and tell me so at one in the morning?"

"Well, you're impossible to forget." Especially now that he'd kissed her. And hearing the word pleasure in that sleep-drenched voice made it hard not to think of her lying in her bed, possibly naked, which was an incredibly welcome distraction from thoughts about Grey targeting his daughter. "But no, I just got a wakeup call from Warwick." He explained what he'd been told, ending with the ransom note.

"It's Grey." Her voice rang with conviction, all traces of drowsiness gone.

"Considering the targets, has to be. We're not sure how many others are involved. The double kidnappings likely mean he's got others working for or with him on this." As usual.

"He could have acted alone this time."

"It's possible, but not likely." Why would Grey suddenly change his MO so radically and take such significant risk all on his own? In the past, he'd always used other people to supply intel and plant his devices. Kidnapping was a whole new game for him. And both abductions had been close together.

"If that ransom note came from him," he continued, "then

guaranteed there was a lot of thought put into it. The message will be multilayered." Pointed little digs aimed at the government and the people he was targeting personally with this.

"He'll kill those kids."

"I know," he said in a tone as heavy as the lead weight currently sitting in the pit of his stomach. *Donovan's got this. You know he'll take care of her.*

"How long do we have to find them?"

"Not sure. But it won't be long." Days. Maybe less. All depended on how sadistic Grey was feeling and what message he was trying to send.

"No. His ego demanded he take this step to punish the people he holds responsible for what happened to him. Makes me think there's a good chance he's acting alone on this one. He's had a lot of time to plan this out."

"He certainly has. But two flawless, back-to-back kidnappings without a single sighting or tip coming in? He may have had help. Someone within his network whom he considered expendable."

"He's choreographing all of this incredibly carefully."

No doubt, which would make their job all that much harder. He rubbed at his eyes. "Is Chloe on her way over here yet?" Ivy had sent her the details after he left, and booked flights.

"She and Heath are on en route to Heathrow right now. They'll meet me here at the manor and you and I can coordinate then." She paused a moment. "Listen, about the missing uni students…"

"Yeah?" he said, his brain still churning through all the intel he knew about Grey. Where he might be in the UK right now. What his next move might be. What could be done to find him. The hostages wouldn't have much time.

"Grey's already targeted two kids of people he blames for what happened to him. Granted they were both here in the UK, but do you think there's any chance that he might go after more elsewhere? Maybe even in…the US?"

"I already called Donovan. Shae's in class right now." Would likely have her phone silenced and he wasn't going to tell her over the phone anyway. "He's on his way to get her right now."

"Oh, good," she said in clear relief.

"Yeah." But he wouldn't relax until he knew she was safe.

And now the need to bring down Grey burned even hotter inside him.

∼

WHEN THE PROF finished giving out their homework assignment for the week at the end of class, Shae stood and headed for the doors. It had been a long day and she was looking forward to a night curled up on the couch under a blanket in front of her favorite show with a bowl of buttered popcorn for dinner. The fridge and pantry were pretty bare and she didn't feel like having to grocery shop on the way home, let alone go home and cook afterward.

Hitching the strap of her backpack higher up on her shoulder, she funneled out of the lecture hall doorway with the rest of the students and into the hall.

"Shae."

She whirled, her gaze landing on Donovan standing behind her down the hall in his black leather jacket. "Hey. What are you doing here?" A ribbon of alarm wound through her when he didn't smile. He'd never showed up to get her after class before. "Is it Dad? Did something—"

"No, he's fine. Come on." He took her by the elbow and led her quickly through the crowd of students filling the hall, then down the stairs to the lobby of the commerce building.

It was too noisy and crowded to ask questions, but she was worried in spite of his reassurance. She kept pace with him, unable to shake the building anxiety. He wouldn't be doing this if something bad hadn't happened.

In the lobby, they hurried straight for the main doors. Through the wall of glass doors and windows, the sky outside was already deep blue with a wall of black clouds amassing in the west that promised more rain overnight. A gust of cool wind scattered fallen oak and maple leaves when they stepped out of the building.

"What's going on?" she demanded in a low voice when the crowd dispersed enough to give them some privacy.

"Not here," he said, making her glance around. Were they being followed? "I'm parked on the access road just over there." He nodded at the narrow lane across a wide section of lawn bordered by a row of deciduous trees, their leaves glowing gold in the tall lampposts set along the sidewalk.

Shae rushed to the vehicle with him and got in the passenger seat, heart thudding. "Okay, *what*?" she said when he started the engine.

"Walker called me an hour ago. Two students were kidnapped from their universities yesterday in the UK. The chief suspect is someone your dad has a history with. It's possible this guy might want revenge on him too."

Shae stared at him as the SUV drove for the main gate, stomach sinking. "Meaning Dad thinks I might be at risk too?"

"We're just taking precautions."

It was a pretty major precaution. "Why didn't he just call me?"

"You had your phone silenced, and he wanted me to escort you personally anyway."

"I'll call him as soon as I get home—"

"You're not going home."

She blinked. "Your house, then."

He shook his head, jaw tight. And he was being extra vigilant, looking all around them as he drove. "I'm taking you to a safehouse."

Holy shit. This was insane. Her dad must be really damn worried about her safety to ask this of Donovan. "What about Anaya?" She was in her third trimester now.

"She's staying at Nadia and Callum's. And you won't be going back to class until this is all resolved either. You'll have to attend your lectures online in the meantime, and make arrangements for homework."

She swallowed, the threat of tears clogging her throat. "How long will this take?"

"Hopefully not long. But we don't know yet." Once he merged onto the highway, he relaxed enough to reach over and squeeze her shoulder. "I know this is sudden and a little scary, but like I said, it's just a precaution. You're safe, and I'll make sure you *stay* safe."

The tears burned her eyes. She blinked them back, waited until she was certain she had control of her voice. Donovan hadn't always been there for her in the past, but he'd made a point of stepping up big time recently, and was now literally guarding her—away from his heavily pregnant wife. "I know you will."

She trusted him completely, knew he wouldn't let anything happen to her. But this situation triggered a deep-seated fear she carried around every day. She'd already lost her mom to cancer. Couldn't lose her dad too. Either of them. "Is Dad really okay?"

"Yes. He'll call you when things settle down a bit. No need to worry about him. He's with Ivy."

That helped push the tears back. "Really?"

"Yep. She'll look out for him."

From everything she'd heard, Ivy was a total badass. Like,

ninja-level badass, with an insane amount of training. She knew her dad was badass in his own way too, but she felt better knowing he had that kind of backup with him. "Still want to meet her one day."

"Maybe Walker will invite her back here once this is all over."

That was a possible bright spot on the horizon at least. "I'd like that." She glanced at him. "Can I still have contact with my friends?"

He threw her an apologetic look. "No. Sorry. You can send a quick message to them now but don't tell them what's going on. Tell them you're going out of town for a few days. Then you'll have to turn your phone off for the time being. I'll give you a burner to use for emergencies."

It sucked, but she got it. "Okay." She shot off a quick text to Finn to tell him that she was going away for a bit and wouldn't be able to talk for a week or so. He was still technically just a friend but the way things had been going lately, there was a chance he would be more soon. A girl could hope, anyway.

He responded right away. *You okay?*

Yeah, I'm fine! Talk soon. She added a little happy face.

Next, she texted her dad, because she wouldn't be able to relax at all until she did. *I'm with D. Call us when you can.*

Not that he or Donovan would tell her anything else about what was going on. It was frustrating, but she understood why they would keep it from her. And she was probably better off being ignorant about the truth anyhow.

Say hi to Ivy. Stay safe. Love you, she added.

With a heavy heart, she turned off her phone and stared out the window at the passing headlights heading the other way on the highway. Whoever her dad and Ivy were going after, she hoped they got him fast.

TWELVE

The prisoners had to be fed.

Isaac took two sandwiches down the stairs to the cellar in the place he had rented. There were two rooms down here that he could secure from the outside.

He kept his hostages separate. Had gagged and blindfolded them both to disorient them and prevent them from communicating through the wall between them.

Both had refused to eat the last time he'd taken something down to them. But it had been long enough now that hunger had to be winning out over stubbornness.

He stopped at Chad's door first. Used the key to unlock it and swung the door open. The young man was ramrod straight in the chair he was tied to, facing the door. "I brought you a sandwich," Isaac said. "Feel like eating yet?"

No response.

Isaac approached him, went around behind the chair to loosen the gag. "Well?"

"Sod you," the young man spat.

"Suit yourself." Soon enough, the isolation and darkness would break him down.

With a hard tug, he yanked the gag back into place, forcing it between Chad's lips as the lad tried to fight it by twisting his head this way and that. "I'll come back in a few hours, see if you've changed your mind."

He walked out and locked the door behind him, then stepped over to Laura's door. As soon as he unlocked and opened it, the sudden stillness hit him. He stared hard at her where she was tied to a chair in the center of the small room, his gut registering the tension hanging in the air.

The shaft of light entering the room drew his eyes straight to the problem. Shards of gleaming ceramic lying on the floor from the water jug he'd left there earlier.

He strode forward quickly, saw what she'd done. Knocked it over deliberately to break it, had somehow tipped her chair over enough to grasp it even with her hands bound behind her. The nylon cording he'd used to tie them was frayed where she had tried to saw through it.

Annoyance flared—at himself—even as he was impressed. He should have foreseen this. Kidnapping her from the footpath had been more of a challenge than he had anticipated. She was stronger than she looked and had put up more of a fight than Chad. The only reason he'd been able to take her was because of the chloroform.

She was an athlete and an archaeology student. Of course she would have thought to make a tool with the jug, and her strength and athleticism had allowed her to enact her plan.

She didn't know how lucky she was to be young and healthy and have a body that did exactly what she asked of it.

He snatched the shard from her stiff fingers. Felt the keen edge of it along with the slickness of blood on the surface where she'd cut herself whilst trying to saw through her bindings.

"Clever girl," he murmured. "But no more of that." He bent

and collected all the remaining fragments large enough to be any use as a tool, his fingers clumsy. "I brought some food. Do you want it?"

A stony silence answered him.

"Well?" he said in a harsher tone. Receiving a firm shake of her head, he retreated to the door. "You'll change your mind soon enough, believe me," he said before closing and locking her back into her temporary holding cell.

His captives were unused to this kind of treatment. Neither of them knew how to cope with it. And neither had any idea what constant darkness and isolation could do to a person. How it could break you so completely that you would never be whole again. Not even once you gained your freedom back.

Which these two would not.

He had nothing against them. It was all about the message he was sending. Unfortunate but necessary sacrifices to pay back two of the men he held most responsible for his fate.

Walker's time would come. As for his daughter, Isaac hadn't yet heard from the man tasked with finding her.

In truth, he would have preferred not having direct contact with any of them. Contact made this far harder to go through with. He'd already seen Laura and Chad's faces up close. Every time he had to see or move them, it got harder.

Tomorrow he would move them to their final place. He had everything he needed. Everything but time, and as far as he could tell, those who were chasing him weren't putting the pieces together quickly enough.

Idiots. All of them.

He trudged back up the cellar steps, clinging to the handrail along the wall to help steady his clumsy feet. There was nothing for it. He would have to help his enemies along to get them on the right track. Not in such an overt way that it spoiled the game, of course.

Near the top of the stairs, he was forced to pause when a vicious leg cramp seized the muscles in his calf. He gripped the handrail tight, teeth clenched to hold back a groan of pain.

This was going to be his last hurrah, as people back in the country of his birth would say. He had to make every step, every hour count.

The burner phone he'd been using sat on the kitchen table. There was a message from the man he'd sent to Oregon.

She's not at home and I didn't see her leaving the building after her last class.

Isaac clenched his jaw. The incompetent sod had been too slow. *Keep looking*, he commanded.

He wasn't giving up on that yet. But neither was he wasting time and critical focus on a side operation right now when he had so many other things to take care of.

He opened his laptop. Absently took a bite of his own ham sandwich as he waited for his encrypted program to load.

His damn throat spasmed when he tried to swallow. The wad of bread and meat lodged partway down his throat, cutting off his air.

He choked. Shot from his chair, gripping the edge of the table for support as he fought to suck in air. He could feel the blood vessels in his face swelling. Feel the way his eyes bulged as he groped blindly around for the glass of water on the table.

He managed to bring it to his lips and take a gulp. His throat muscles stubbornly resisted for another few agonizing seconds before the water did its job and forced the bolus down his throat.

He collapsed back into his chair and drew in several wheezing breaths, eyes closed, heart still thundering in his ears and his skin slick with sweat. God, he hated this. Hated this goddamn disease as much as he hated those who had left him to die in that inhumane Russian prison.

They had needed him once. Convinced him that he was a hero for serving his countries. Then disavowed him and left him to rot.

It still shook him. Their callous indifference. The sheer inhumanity of it.

When his heart rate had settled and he was able to breathe normally again, he opened his eyes and reached for his laptop with trembling hands to compose another message. Hopefully this time the people on the other end would figure out the clue before the deadline, because he was determined to catch Walker in his trap too.

His fingers clicked the keys as he typed out the message.

Pray for your children, and for mercy. For I will have none.

~

TOO MANY HOURS had passed already, and the taskforce was no closer to figuring out where Grey was or where he had taken the hostages.

When tempers flared and the third argument of the morning broke out between the FBI and MI5 groups in the room, Ivy got up from her seat and left the room before her frustration bubbled over in front of the others.

They now had an entire joint US-UK taskforce working around the clock to find Grey and the hostages. The team was made up of the smartest people in the intelligence world—including her, Amber and Walker—and they were arguing instead of finding answers.

"You okay?"

She turned to face Walker, the sound of his low, deep voice like a soothing hand stroking down her back. He was another reason she was feeling edgy and off her game. A constant temptation she couldn't ignore. That kiss had stirred up longings in the deepest part of her soul.

She wanted more. Everything he had to give her. And she couldn't have it while they were in the midst of all this. "We're moving too slow. Grey's given us what we need to find him in that ransom note. You know it and I know it, and they're in there fucking arguing. We have to figure out the missing pieces."

"We knew he wouldn't make it easy for us."

"No. But it pisses me off that people are bickering like old ladies and he's toying with us while two innocent young adults' lives are at stake. They're not to blame for what their fathers did."

Which was exactly why Grey had used that second line in the note. He didn't care that the students or all his other victims were innocent. They were pawns used to get his message across.

Walker nodded, his deep blue gaze steady on her. He always made her feel seen and heard. And understood on a level that she'd only ever experienced with her fellow Valkyries.

It shook her a little.

"You heard from Donovan yet today?" she asked to change the subject. She was worried about Shae too.

"Yeah, everything's good. He's got Shae at a safehouse a few hours from Crimson Point."

"That's good."

He nodded, eyeing her. "Let's take a walk."

"To where?" The "meeting" was still going on. Not that they were missing anything in there at the moment.

"Outside." He motioned for her to join him and headed for the hallway. "Be good to take a breather and clear our heads for a few minutes."

She didn't believe for a second that he needed to clear his

head, but it couldn't hurt for her to take a short breather and refocus. "Fine."

She went down to the lobby with him. He stopped at a coffee bar, ordered something while she checked her phone for messages from Amber, and pressed a steaming to-go cup into her hands along with a package of biscuits. Glancing at it, she smiled. "Thanks. I love Jammie Dodgers."

He lifted an eyebrow. "What?"

"These." She held out the package so he could see the print on it. "Best British biscuit ever made."

"Yeah? Then I'm having some too." He snagged a pack for himself, then put a hand on the middle of her back to guide her.

She could feel the imprint of every square inch of his big hand through her thin sweater. Her skin turned ultra-sensitive, her mind conjuring up images of his hands stroking all over her naked body.

He was detail oriented and observant. She was convinced he'd be like that in bed too, attentive and picking up on every cue to use it to heart-pounding effect. The sexual frustration might kill her.

"This way." He took her across the building, through another set of secure doors and out into the central courtyard. A green space covered with grass and trees, all surrounded by the ring of steel and glass that lined the doughnut hole.

On the far side, they sat on a bench beneath a tree whose leaves were just beginning to turn orange around the edges in the weak sunshine punching between the clouds. He leaned back next to her and stretched out his long legs while she sipped at her coffee. After a minute, she could feel some of the tension bleeding out of her shoulders.

Walker looked over at her, his steady, calming energy surrounding her, seeping through her pores. "Better?"

"Much." She bit into her first Jammie Dodger, savoring the

crisp biscuit base along with the cream filling and the chewy jam center sprinkled with sugar. Though she'd much rather straddle him right here on the bench and kiss him until neither of them could breathe.

She popped the remainder of the first cookie in her mouth. The breeze kicked up, blowing her hair across her lips. She went to sweep it away but Walker's hand was already there, his fingertips brushing first her lips, then her cheek.

When she looked at him, the quiet intensity in his expression made her mouth so dry she could barely swallow.

Damn. She'd been trying so hard all day to ignore the ache he created inside her, to remain completely focused on the task at hand and be professional. But now that they were alone without anyone watching them—with the notable exception of however many people were monitoring the security cameras posted throughout this space—that heat flared back to life, stronger than ever.

Her heart tripped, her nipples tightening as his warm fingertips caressed the side of her face. What she wouldn't give to feel them gliding all over her. They found and traced the thin, almost invisible surgical scar behind her ear. "Is this from one of the surgeries you told me about?" he asked softly.

She nodded, managed to force the mouthful of cookie down her tight throat. The man was just so edible and gorgeous. She wanted to wrap around him, devour him and absorb him into her body.

"You never told me what happened."

She stilled inside. Her instinct—her training—was to deflect and divert his attention to something else. But for the life of her, she couldn't look away. Didn't want to lie anymore, even though she had to keep lying by omission about most of it for now.

"I was attacked in Moscow during an op," she finally said.

He frowned slightly. "Moscow? By who?"

"Bratva."

He went dead still, shock flaring in his eyes. "Jesus. How?"

"Long story." She looked away from him, out at the calming sea of green in front of her and the far side of the curved inner wall beyond. "That betrayal I told you about by the other Valkyries? They approached me about a job and I turned them down. I suspected something was off so I kept tabs on them and they eventually brought Amber on board instead."

The painful memories flooded back as they always did, breaking through the steel door at the back of her mind where she kept everything ugly about her past locked away.

She kept going. "One of them found out I was sending intel to Kiyomi. In the meantime, I'd made a mistake by getting personally involved with someone close to the leader while I was gathering intel." She shook her head at herself. "It was stupid of me. And I paid for it."

Walker made a low sound, understanding and empathy combined, his fingers now gliding through the back of her hair. "You don't have to talk about it."

"No, I want to." She wanted him to know at least this much. "The Valkyries told him what was happening. In turn he handed me over to his Bratva buddies. They came for me. Worked me over and dumped me in an alley to die." Those fragmented memories, all jagged and sharp as broken glass, still haunted her.

"I shouldn't have made it." She should never have dropped her guard around Luka Tarasov. "Kiyomi found me." She looked at Walker again. "Did I tell you that?"

"No." His fingers kept up with that steady, lulling motion that made her want to climb into his lap and cuddle into him like a child.

"She'd been tracking me leading up to that night. Trying to

find me after recent contact we'd had about the other Valkyries."

That part was fuzzier. Less distinct. By then she'd been hypothermic and lost in a haze of pain from all the broken bones and internal bleeding.

"There was nothing she could do for me and it was too dangerous for her to stay, but she called an ambulance and that saved my life."

She drew in a deep breath and let it out slowly, willing the memories and the tension away. God, she hated not telling Walker the rest of it, not coming clean. She vowed to herself she would once the hostages were safe and Grey was in custody, no matter if it cost their friendship.

If Grey went quietly, that is. And every one of her instincts told her he would not. Whatever was brewing now was bigger and more personal to him than anything that had come before.

"I hate that you went through all that," Walker said with a frown. "And I especially hate that you went through it alone."

"Me too. Anyway, that's the gist of it." The sterilized version without all the gory details of what they'd done to her that night.

Including the tricky little truths that put her squarely to blame for ruining Walker's op and Grey becoming the deadly domestic terrorist they were now hunting.

She pushed that to the back of her mind again. "I made it through and got a new look out of the deal."

"Were you this beautiful before?"

The question threw her so much that she laughed softly. "I don't know. Beauty's subjective."

"Okay, then do you look a lot different now?"

"I think so. Kiyomi doesn't. She recognized me instantly that day I went to see her in Bourton-on-the-Water." It still gave her shivers.

"Then you were beautiful before too," he said.

Her heart squeezed, that lonely, empty space deep inside her that was starving for love and belonging flaring to life. "Thank you," she murmured, not knowing what else to say, her cheeks flushing.

"It's the truth," he answered, his long fingers curving around the back of her neck. Sending a delicious trickle of heat down her spine. "And for the record, you can trust me."

And I haven't been honest with you. A dagger of guilt drove into her chest. "I know." Jesus, she needed to steer this conversation in a different direction—right now. "Why did you leave the game?"

"For my family," he answered without hesitation, his gaze straying back to the green space in front of them. "Jillian had just been given a terminal diagnosis and there was no question about what I needed to do. I never for one second regretted walking away so I could be there for her and Shae for those last thirteen months."

She nodded, struck again by the strength of his character. The values and morals he lived by. "I respect that a lot. But you're good at what you do. Why didn't you go back after?"

"Shae." Again, zero hesitation. "As much as I liked to think my work made the world a safer place, losing Jillian made it crystal clear what was really important." He shrugged. "After that, I couldn't go back."

He had no idea how amazing he was, or how rare. It must be incredible to be loved by a man like him. "You never missed it?"

He thought about it a moment. "No. Honestly, it wasn't just the long hours, all the overseas trips and the secrecy that I didn't miss. I didn't realize it at the time, but I was burned out. Sick of the manipulation and lies I dealt with on a daily basis in my job. It was changing me. I didn't see it until Jillian got sick, but all the negative stuff that came with the job was starting to make me cynical and bleed into my personal life."

"You don't seem cynical, but that comes with the territory in this line of work."

He nodded. "I'm good at compartmentalizing things but I started to notice that I felt numb when I went home. Couldn't connect with my wife and daughter on the level they deserved. It's not what I wanted anymore. And Shae needed me. That was that."

"I hope she knows how lucky she is to have you for a father."

His lips quirked. "I don't think that's always the case, but I'm pretty sure most of the time she does. Not right now, though, since she's essentially on lockdown with Donovan. It's okay, she understands, and she's resilient. And knowing she's safe with him makes it way easier for me to focus on this case." He shook his head, staring up at the inner portion of the building opposite them. "Never thought I'd be pulled back into all this again."

"Until Fornam's network was reactivated."

"Right." He was quiet a moment, a thoughtful frown creasing his forehead.

"What?" she asked.

"I feel partly responsible for all this."

"Why? You didn't do anything wrong." She of all people would know.

"I keep thinking I missed something vital that could have prevented all this. That I should have dug deeper back when Grey's death was announced."

"You're not the only one," she muttered under her breath.

He looked at her sharply. "What do you mean?"

"Nothing." Dammit, the guilt was weighing heavier on her every day, but she couldn't confess yet. They needed to remain a team and keep working together to save those kids and stop Grey. Admitting what she'd done would only add unnecessary friction in the midst of this. And Walker was damn smart. If she said much more, he would put things together on his own and that would be even worse.

"We should probably get back," he said, glancing at his watch.

"Wonder if the others are still arguing about that first line in Grey's note. 'One has to go back to the beginning periodically.' Does he mean a location or a past event he's referring to?"

"I think it's probably both."

She started at the top of her list. "Newcastle, where he was born? Moscow, where he was captured?"

Walker shook his head. "I think he's going for something deeper. Something significant for him—" He stopped suddenly, his gaze snapping to her. "Durham."

Her heart rate shot up at the intensity on his face. Grey had done his undergrad and master's there. It was where he'd laid the foundation for the career that had led to him being recruited by the government. "You think?"

"Yeah, has to be. Come on." He shot off the bench, pulled her up after him and together they ran for the doors on the other side of the courtyard.

THIRTEEN

It felt surreal to be back here again.

Warwick exited the train station and made his way down the hill toward the center of Durham under a heavy iron-gray sky that promised a cold, soaking rain later. From up here the soaring towers of the cathedral were visible in the center of the medieval bailey on the peninsula jutting out into the River Wear. Its steep banks were thickly covered in trees turning different shades of gold and rust in the cool October air.

As a lad he'd come down to Durham often enough on school trips to visit the cathedral and castle. Hadn't thought much of it back then, except for being bored by the tour guides and teachers and far more interested in running around pretending to be a medieval knight in battle with his mates. Slaying dragons.

Now he was here to slay a different sort of monster.

He hadn't been back to the northeast in years. Not even his hometown of Newcastle, just a fifteen-minute train ride north on the LNER. Why would he when there was nothing to come back to? Any semblance of family he'd known was long dead and buried. Much like the rest of his life.

Being here now, he couldn't deny the pang of nostalgia he felt at walking around the familiar surroundings and hearing the comforting sound of his childhood accent spoken all around him. Or the irony that it had taken all this to make it happen.

Against all odds, Isaac Grey had brought him back to his roots. Now Warwick would end him.

As people around him went about their business he was all too aware of the mental clock ticking at the back of his mind. Grey had initiated the countdown yesterday with the delivery of another note specifying the deadline.

Only two days remained until he killed the hostages. They were running out of time to find the hostages and stop him. He bloody well hoped they were right about him being here.

His phone buzzed as he neared the foot of Old Elvet Bridge, the crenellated walls of the octagonal castle keep just visible over the treetops above the town. A message from Walker.

We're here. Meet you up at campus in twenty.

Warwick responded and kept walking up Church Street while a steady stream of traffic passed by on the two-lane road. He continued past Kingsgate footbridge that led to the medieval bailey holding the castle, cathedral and some of the colleges, including Hatfield where Laura Hawes lived in halls. Past ancient St. Oswald's Church with its rows of tilting headstones filling the graveyard.

A renewed urgency to find Grey gripped him. His new teammates were interesting additions to this taskforce. He didn't know much about their backgrounds except that Ivy was American but based in the UK now, and Walker was former intelligence and lived somewhere on the Oregon Coast.

Before he'd stopped periodically keeping tabs on her from afar, last he'd heard, Marley had been talking about moving to that area.

For a brief moment, he let his mind drift back in time to

what felt like another life. A fleeting moment when he'd stupidly thought he could leave all this behind and start fresh with the woman he'd fallen for.

After all the things he'd seen and done in his military and while working as an undercover intelligence officer all over the world, one would have thought it was impossible for him to be that naïve. But he had. Only to find that Fate had other plans for him.

Just as he'd thought he'd made it to the place where he could call the shots, just when he'd been about to hand in his resignation and look to the future, it had all been taken away. In one brief, blinding explosion that had ripped apart his body—and his world.

Nothing had been the same since. He was a ghost, not truly dead but not really alive either. Still had gaps in his memory from around the time of the bombing.

But one thing he could *never* forget was Marley.

They'd told her he was dead. He'd let her believe it. Had let her go to protect her. Keep her safe from the specters of his past that he still sometimes sensed were following him.

But even now not a single day went by that he didn't miss her down to the marrow of his bones. Not a single day passed when his chest didn't ache at the thought of her and the reminder of all he'd lost.

He pulled his hand from his jacket pocket to rub at the scar bisecting his right cheek. The scar itself was numb, but the healing area around it was tender. He knew it was better this way. Best for her, and far safer. While he…went through the motions of living.

Finding Grey and putting him behind bars was all that kept him going these days. An inextinguishable fire that burned in his soul.

Once that fire was extinguished, once Grey was either

locked away or dead, maybe then Warwick could finally find some peace in this world.

The main campus finally came into view ahead, perched on the top of the hill. He waited outside the Palatine Center for Ivy and Walker, spotted them the instant they came around the corner and nodded at them. "You made good time."

"Not bad," Walker said, dressed in a navy blue peacoat buttoned up against the autumn chill. "The others all here?"

"Waiting for us inside." He waved them into the bright, modern interior of the building drenched in natural light, down the ground-floor hallway to a private office on the left. Inside they were introduced to university officials and the lead local Durham DCI in charge of Laura Hawes's file. Both MI5 officials present they already knew from the meetings at GCHQ, and there were US agents present as well.

Once everyone was settled, the male MI5 official started a PowerPoint on the screen set up on the far wall. "I'm going to quickly run through both abductions, focusing on Laura Hawes. What we know so far and what we're still working on."

Everyone listened in silence, absorbing all the details. But there wasn't much new.

"That brings me to Grey's motive," the man continued.

"Revenge," Ivy said flatly, seated between Warwick and Walker.

He nodded. "Exactly. Although he could be targeting more than just the former Home Secretary and the former CIA director by doing this. At the very least we know he's not bluffing. And we know he'll try to detonate another bomb. We just don't know when or where, or who his accomplices are this time around."

"My team has already searched and secured the university, including the campus buildings and colleges both on the hill and the bailey," the middle-aged DCI said. "Nothing suspicious or out of the ordinary found."

"If you're looking for a bombing target, best start with the cathedral," Warwick said, and the others nodded. "The second clue Grey sent points there, and it's also a UNESCO heritage site. Blowin' it up would make a bloody big statement."

"There was a suspected sighting of Grey near Edinburgh this morning," the MI5 official said, taking him and apparently everyone else in the room by surprise. Warwick hadn't heard a word of it until now. "We're checking it out now, but still looking here in Durham just in case. A bulletin will be announced in the media and online within the hour."

"Not including anything about the missing students," a university official added. "It's imperative that we not cause panic amongst the staff, students, and people of Durham. We still don't know that he's here."

"Right, well," the MI5 official went on, "the cathedral has been shut for the afternoon under the pretense of a maintenance emergency and was thoroughly searched earlier with no sign of Grey or any suspicious activity. So it looks as if we can rule the cathedral out as a target. Now, if there's nothing else to add for the moment, let's—"

"I've got something to share."

All eyes turned to Ivy.

"Since our last meeting, I've identified four different aliases Grey appears to have used since his escape from Russia." She named them, gave a brief rundown of when and where he'd used them while the MI5 people stared at her in astonishment.

"How did you get this information?" the male agent asked.

She gave him a cool look. "You asked me to be part of this taskforce because I'm a research expert. So I researched. And I want to make it clear that Grey has only used these identities sparingly since leaving Russia," she added. "He's not stupid. He's covered his tracks well."

More's the pity. Warwick could do with some stupidity on Grey's part right now.

A low buzz of conversation filled the room after Ivy's announcement as the MI5 guy stepped into a corner and pulled out his phone to presumably call his boss and inform him about what Ivy had just said.

"Right," the DCI said, shooting a sideways look at the male agent who was now talking fast in a low voice in the corner. "Let's keep going and study a detailed map of the area."

When someone put up a map of Durham on the wall screen and the DCI began giving them a virtual tour of the town, presumably thinking he was being helpful, Warwick barely stopped himself from rolling his eyes. They were wasting precious time when they should all be splitting up to follow leads and tips coming in. If anyone in this room had come here without studying a damn map of the area and learning the lay of the land, they had no business being on this taskforce.

Next to him, Ivy pulled her phone from her pocket. "Gotta take this," she murmured to Walker. "It's Amber." She got up and quickly left the room.

Warwick met Walker's gaze. He didn't know who Amber was, but he was betting she had something to do with uncovering Grey's aliases.

Five minutes later, Ivy came back in and the room went silent, everyone watching her. "We found another alias Grey's been using," she announced.

"And?" the male agent said.

"And it looks like he's not going to be a problem for much longer," she answered.

"Why?" the second MI5 official asked.

"Tell you in a second. But the bad news is, he's definitely

going to kill those students, and anyone else he can—including himself."

Warwick frowned, a chill sliding through him. "Suicide?" That didn't fit with what he knew of Grey. Grey was many things, but a coward wasn't one of them.

"Yes." She looked from him to Walker, then to the MI5 guy. "Apparently Grey was diagnosed with ALS seven months ago. And based on the evidence I've just seen in a medical report, it's progressed fast. Doesn't look like he'll be able to function physically for much longer. He knows this. So he'll be acting fast, and that might work in our favor if he's so rushed that he gets sloppy."

Warwick absorbed the magnitude of the news in silence. It meant Grey was more dangerous and unpredictable than he had ever been. Already on his way out with nothing left to lose. In fact, dying in this final act would save him months more of suffering and a slow, agonizing and degrading death while entombed in a paralyzed body.

"How did you find this out?" MI5 guy asked, his face flushing a dull red, giving away that this was news to him.

"Same source as all my other intel, which I'm sure your agency has now verified," Ivy said, her gaze sweeping around the room. "Grey has months left at most, maybe less. But he's not going to wait that long. He'll take himself out long before he's incapacitated."

"So he means for this to be his swan song and plans to go out with a bang. Literally," Warwick said, his gut tightening. Taking on a fanatical enemy who had no fear of death upped the danger tenfold.

Ivy nodded at him in the stunned silence that followed. "Unfortunately, that's exactly what it looks like. So if we're going to stop this, we have to find him well before the deadline."

A prickling sensation swept over Warwick's skin, the buzzing at the back of his brain growing louder. Ruling out the cathedral was premature. Grey worshipped science as much as he hated religion. Now neither of them could save him.

What better act of revenge and symbolism than to kill himself and his hostages in a priceless and irreplaceable ancient house of God with a device built by the scientific expertise he'd gained within sight of its very towers.

~

WALKER'S BRAIN was still trying to process everything after the meeting ended. Ivy had dropped one hell of a bombshell in there earlier. The urgency to catch Grey was higher than ever.

"So the ALS diagnosis was the new intel you and Amber were trying to verify?" he asked as they left the building just after five. She'd mentioned something about it on the drive up to Durham this morning but had been vague about details.

"Yep. I was waiting for her to button everything up before I said anything."

"Talk about a bombshell. The MI5 guy looked like he was going to have a stroke." He shot her a sideways glance, his concern for her growing. "They're going to have people all over you to find out who your source is now." Even with the extra manpower assigned to the search for Grey, they had the resources to put others on her and Amber if they identified her.

She gave an unconcerned shrug. "Let them try. Amber and I've both survived way worse than them."

Maybe, but he would contact Rycroft tonight to alert him and try to head off any trouble for Ivy and the other Valkyries, just in case. She and Amber were both using all their expertise to help them stop Grey. That had to count for something, and Walker would do everything in his power to protect her.

They crossed the road at the intersection and turned down Church Street, leaving the campus behind as a cold, light rain began to fall. The sidewalk was narrow here. Narrow enough that it forced them to walk one behind the other. He reached for her hand, tugged her into his side and curled his arm around her waist.

She flashed him a startled smile, inhaled sharply when he stopped them to lean in and run his nose up the side of her neck because he couldn't help himself. He'd been sitting next to her for hours without being able to touch her, her presence making his entire body hum with awareness.

He kissed her soft skin, the edge of her jaw, then hovered over the corner of her mouth. She turned to face him, grabbed the back of his neck and brought their lips together in a kiss that sent all the blood in his brain rushing to his groin.

He made a rough sound and nipped at her lower lip, soothed the slight sting with his tongue before kissing her full on the mouth one last time and lifting his head. They were out in the open in plain view of anyone who came along, including anyone from the taskforce.

He didn't want an audience. Wished they were alone in their rental so he could show her exactly how much he wanted her. "Been wanting to do that all damn day."

"Then why'd you stop?"

"Because if I do it again there's no way we're making it down to meet Chloe and Heath at the restaurant." They had arrived in town partway through the meeting. Ivy had told them to tee up a place for dinner so they could meet in person.

He wished the whole Grey thing was behind them so he could spend the rest of the night alone with Ivy. But with Grey still at large and Chloe here to offer assistance as an explosives expert, this dinner was happening.

Her low laugh didn't reduce the sudden tightness in his pants. "Hmm, decisions, decisions."

"Come on, before I change my mind," he muttered, setting her in front of him this time as they continued down the narrow sidewalk. The rain was falling steadily now, coating everything in a thin layer of water. "Let's go this way."

He turned them onto Kingsgate footbridge and crossed the river rippling with raindrops, and up the steps to the end of Bow Lane, its misted cobbles shimmering in the changing light.

"There's Hatfield up there on the right," Ivy said, linking her fingers through his as he drew alongside her and continued up the hill.

Walker eyed the tall, open wrought-iron gates that marked the southern entrance to the college grounds. He could hear students talking and laughing on a pathway inside, all of them oblivious to what had happened to their classmate days ago or the possible threat hanging over the city.

At the top of the lane, Ivy stopped. For a few moments they stood looking up at the intricate rose window set into the tracery work on the eastern edge of the cathedral. "I've been all over the UK since moving here and been to dozens of places," she said in an awed voice, rain slicking her hood. "But seeing a thousand-year-old building like this will never get old."

It was damn impressive, he had to admit. It seemed so solid, too solid for Grey to bring it down with a few bombs. "We'll be seeing it up close and personal tomorrow." He intended to look inside for himself, no matter what security services said about there being no evidence.

Glancing up a little street called Dun Cow Lane on the way back down, he got a good look at the long, northern side of the cathedral. It was scheduled to open as normal in the morning. An additional search of the campus, castle and cathedral completed two hours ago while they'd still been in the meeting had turned up nothing. Security inside had been increased as a precaution until Grey was found.

Ivy hooked her arm through his, leaned her head on his shoulder as they walked down the hill past the west entrance to Hatfield College where shops, cafés and restaurants lined either side of curving, cobblestoned Saddler Street. "This place is like stepping back in time. Too bad we couldn't visit under nicer circumstances and play tourist for the day."

He agreed, and wished he could stop the clock to make the most of his time alone with her. "Maybe we'll come back after this is all over and spend a few days together."

She glanced up at him, gave him a soft, unguarded smile that punched him square in the heart. "I'd love that."

"Me too." When they reached the top of Old Elvet, he glanced down the bridge toward the area where their rental was, picturing Ivy naked in the double bed in his room, and continued around past the marketplace to Silver Street. He could wait a few more hours to have her all to himself. Probably.

Up ahead on the right he spotted the green wooden restaurant sign with gold lettering on the ground floor of a three-story timber and plaster building that looked like it was from the Tudor era. "There's the place." One of many Italian joints in town. Guess college kids in the UK loved pizza and pasta just as much as they did back home.

"Oh, I see her," Ivy said in excitement, her face lighting up at someone waving at them through the window.

As soon as they entered, Walker saw Chloe skirting the table and holding out her arms to Ivy, her long blond hair pulled back in a ponytail. "Hey, you."

"Hi," Ivy gushed, wrapping her up in a hug. "Oh my God, it's so good to see you."

"I know, it's been way too long." Her deep brown eyes lingered on him curiously over Ivy's shoulder. "Hi, Walker."

"Hi." They shook hands. She had a strong grip for a woman, and after only five seconds in her presence he could tell she was a live wire, a palpable energy radiating from her. Then he looked at the tall guy standing behind her.

"I'm Heath, by the way," he said after hugging Ivy in turn, and offered his hand. "Good to meet you."

Walker shook with him. "Same."

"I hear you live in Crimson Point?" Heath said as they sat down at their table against the wall as Ivy and Chloe chattered away to each other.

"That's right."

"I know some PJs based there. Travis, Brandon and Grady. Do you know any of them? We served together overseas."

Walker looked at him with interest. "Not well, but yeah. You're a PJ?"

"Was. Now I mostly follow this one around doing damage control," he said fondly, jerking his thumb at Chloe.

Yep, he could imagine she needed someone to keep an eye on her. "Small world."

"Isn't it?" Chloe said, beaming at them. "Okay, now catch us up on everything about the investigation. I've got a bottle of wine all ready to go." She began pouring everyone a glass.

"Patience, Chlo," Ivy said, casting a glance around the packed restaurant. It was tiny, all the tables crammed close together. Too much chance of someone overhearing them, so they couldn't talk about anything pertaining to the investigation. "We'll eat and then jump right into it at your place."

Chloe pouted. "Fine." Then her face brightened and she set the empty bottle down. "Can I at least talk about what I've found out on my end so far?"

"No."

"But it's really cool! I'll whisper."

"No." Ivy reached out to ruffle Chloe's bangs affectionately. "Later."

Chloe sighed. "Have you guys checked out the cathedral yet? Amazing. We only saw it from the outside, of course, but based on the architecture and what I've studied about the interior, I can already tell you where I'd plant charges if I wanted t—"

"What are the specials today?" Ivy said, pretending to ignore that.

Chloe snickered and winked at Walker. "I love giving her a hard time."

"You love giving everyone a hard time," Heath said as he perused his menu.

"True. Well, if we can't talk shop, then what should we talk about?" Chloe set her chin in her hands and looked between Walker and Ivy with pointed interest. "Hm? Maybe whether he's seen your tat yet or not?"

"What tat?" Walker asked with interest.

"Never mind," Ivy said, shooting Chloe a censoring look. "Maybe we could tell him about the time you avenged Karas after what happened on Bonfire Night instead."

Chloe smiled, her expression turning fond. "Oh, yeah, that was a good one."

"What happened to Karas?" Walker asked.

Her honey-blond brows snapped together in a forbidding frown. "Some local asshole teenagers threw a firecracker at her and burned her. So I taught them a lesson. Someone had to."

He got the feeling it hadn't been a regular ol' run-of-the-mill lesson, either. But he wouldn't forget about Ivy's tat she'd mentioned, and looked forward to finding it himself later when he explored her naked body at his leisure. "How?"

"Well, I don't want to give too many details," Chloe said.

Heath set down his menu to look at him. "She waited in a tree to jump on them in the middle of the night, then stripped them to their undies and left them tied to the trunk in almost freezing conditions with a note insulting their characters and ah…junk."

Walker's eyebrows shot up and he looked at Chloe. "For real?"

"Oh, it wasn't for very long," she said with a dismissive wave. "Those little buggers had it coming."

"They're probably still in counseling," Heath said, back to looking at the menu.

"Where I come from, that's called gettin' a whoopin'. And from where I'm sitting, it sounds like they deserved it," Walker said with a healthy respect for the way Chloe operated. She looked so sweet and innocent, but she was every bit as skilled and deadly as the others.

Chloe beamed at him. "See? Walker gets it. I like him."

"Another exciting event I missed back at the ranch, because it happened long before I arrived," Ivy said with a dramatic sigh, then reached across the table to pat Chloe's cheek. "See what I mean? How can I not love her, her being an animal defender on top of everything else."

"Among all the other stellar personality traits that make me awesome," Chloe added, finally looking at her own menu.

"Just imagine if anyone hurt Mr. Whiskers," Ivy said to him.

Chloe lowered her menu to look at them over the top of it, a menacing scowl on her face. "I would kill for Mr. Whiskers."

Walker picked up his own menu, suppressing a smile. They wouldn't get around to talking business for another hour or two, but he could already tell the rest of the night was going to be anything but boring.

FOURTEEN

"Chloe and Heath in town yet?" Amber asked her.

"Yes, we just left their rental," Ivy said into her phone as she and Walker made their way back across the river to their own place. There was no one else around to overhear but she kept her voice pitched low anyway. "The taskforce is following up on two more leads that came in on Grey, but they'll be dead ends. He's here somewhere."

"What kind of manpower do they have out looking for him?"

"Police, undercover units and some from MI5."

"What about the FBI?"

"They've got representatives here but just a handful of field agents. Everyone else is out doing a search except us, because we're just contractors." She couldn't keep the resentment out of her voice.

"You and I found those aliases that led to finding the ALS diagnosis. Not MI5 *or* the FBI."

"I know it. This is bureaucracy at its finest. I can't believe there hasn't been a confirmed sighting of him yet on camera somewhere."

"Did Chloe have any good insight into Grey's methods?"

"Yes. She's full of ideas and hunches. We're meeting up with them first thing in the morning, but she's going to send you some files she's been working on tonight."

"Chloe made *files*?"

"Yeah, encrypted ones. Heath forced her."

"He's so good for her."

"I know. He's a great guy." A stabilizing force in Chloe's brand of chaos.

Speaking of great guys, an incredibly sexy one was next to her right now. His nearness, knowing they were about to share a roof had butterflies fluttering around in her stomach. The quiet, absorbed way he'd watched her all evening had made her entire body tingle and now they were about to be alone together all night.

The building anticipation was killing her in the most delicious way.

"He is," Amber agreed. "Listen, I've sent you a few encrypted docs of the medical info for you to review when you get time. You could forward one or two to your MI5 contact as a show of good faith, but by now they should have tracked down most of it on their own."

"Thanks, I'll check it in a few minutes when I get to my laptop." She'd hidden it under some blankets at the bottom of the upstairs hall closet because the safe was too obvious a spot and it took nothing to unscramble a code.

"I'll let you know if anything else relevant turns up. And hey, Ivy?"

"Yeah?"

"Have a *great* night. You deserve it." There was a definite nonverbal wink in Amber's voice as she ended the call.

"All okay?" Walker asked as she slid her phone back in her pocket. She was starting to think the others had some kind of bet going on to see when she and Walker would get together. Or get it on.

Nosy bitches. They were lucky she loved them all to death.

"Yes, I just hate being benched, and that's what this feels like. The lack of evidence here is eating at me, especially given how many boots on the ground and all the tech they have looking around the city for him. It's not that big a place, and now we're down to just over a day left before the deadline. Why haven't they found anything solid yet?"

"We'll find him."

But would they find him in time?

"Anyway, there's nothing more either of us can do tonight. Not unless a juicy new tip comes in. Hopefully there'll be a big break in the case overnight."

She made a humming sound, aware that the stalled Grey investigation wasn't the only thing weighing on her. The closer they got to their rental, the more her mind turned to Walker and the nerves buzzing inside got louder.

It had been a damn long time since she'd been with anyone, and Walker meant more to her than any of them. She didn't want to mess up this chance, even though she knew withholding the truth from him would bite her when all was said and done.

Then there was the tiny warning voice at the back of her mind that she couldn't shake. The one that begged her to be careful. To protect herself and not risk letting him in any further than she already had.

He was so quiet beside her as they crossed the main road leading away from the old town, the silence heightening all her senses until all she could think about was him and what it would be like to have that long, powerful body pressing her into the bed while he delivered the pleasure she'd been fantasizing about for almost a damn year.

She exhaled quietly, trying to rein in the surge of desire and anticipation. Their rental cottage was a two-story, brick row house set back off a narrow lane a block off Old Elvet.

To give herself room to breathe and a little more time to settle her mind, as soon as they got inside she took off her coat and took her laptop into the kitchen to look at what Amber had sent. Work was what she needed right now. Focus.

"Here are Grey's medical reports," she said, fully in work mode as she angled the screen for Walker to see. "You can see the date of birth given here doesn't match his real one but everything else does. Amber said this alias is also linked to a credit card used to purchase medication and other medical supplies in north London last month. Two of his other aliases were living in and around London within four months of that same time period."

Walker leaned over her shoulder and reached out a hand to close the laptop.

In the second of shock that followed, the tension in the room turned thick.

She opened her mouth to protest but stilled when he swept her hair aside and nuzzled the back of her neck. "Leave this for now," he murmured in a deep, quiet voice that sent goosebumps flashing across her skin. "There's nothing more either of us can do tonight."

Her eyes fell closed at the feel of his lips on a sensitive spot near her shoulder, the slight prickle of his beard magnifying everything. A torrent of heat rushed through her, settling between her legs in a relentless pulse.

He grasped her right wrist. Tugged, urging her to stand. "It's late. You need to sleep."

"I can't sleep now." With her strung taut and wanting him this badly? Forget it.

"Bet you can if I help. Come here."

Her heart thudded hard as he turned her to face him and slid those big, powerful arms around her. Forming a delicious cage she had zero desire to escape from.

They locked gazes for a long, breathless moment, then he enfolded her in a bone-melting hug. One hand cradled the back of her head, pressing her cheek to his chest.

Something twisted deep in her chest. *Oh, Walker, don't do this to me…*

Raw lust she could handle. But not this level of tenderness.

"Close your eyes a minute and let your mind be still." His voice was a dark, velvet caress along her quivering nerve endings.

Her pulse was beating too fast. Her eyes were already closed because he had a terrifying drugging effect on her, and her mind had stopped functioning the instant he'd touched her.

Now she felt like she was floating. Drifting in a warm current.

She slid her hands up his broad back, hungry to explore the feel of him. Breathed in his clean, masculine scent. Absorbed the warmth of his body. The steady beat of his heart thudding beneath her cheek.

"Better now?" he murmured against her hair.

Better, yet worse. So much worse, the building ache spreading outward from her chest. He'd barely touched her and he already had her more aroused than she'd been in forever.

In that moment, she decided that even if things turned to shit later, once she confessed everything, she still couldn't say no to this. Didn't *want* to.

When she nodded, the hand at the back of her head slid into her hair and tipped it backward. Ivy stared up into the deep blue pools of his eyes, felt an answering echo deep inside.

She was lost. Utterly incapable of stopping this as his hold tightened and his mouth came down on hers.

Molten need punched through her, intensified by the way he

held her in place, refusing to let her rush as he slowly deepened the kiss. He made it clear he was in charge, the erotic seduction of his lips and tongue making her belly flip as though she'd just plunged six floors in a runaway elevator.

A soft, breathless moan wrenched from her throat before she could stop it. Walker answered with a low sound and backed her up against the nearest wall. Pinning her with his solid weight, giving her counter pressure in all the right places.

Her arms locked around his neck as her tongue twined with his, need flooding her. She wanted him desperately and the way he refused to rush made it far worse. He kissed and licked and nipped and teased, one hand cradling her nape while the other slid up to find her breast.

Hot currents of pleasure sizzled outward from where his thumb stroked across her aching nipple. She kissed him harder, impatience riding her hard, and grabbed the muscled curve of his ass to pull him closer. His erection was rock hard against her abdomen. She rubbed against it shamelessly, ready to combust. She wanted them both naked and horizontal. Now.

Walker touched his tongue to hers and sucked gently at her lower lip. "Wrap around me."

The low command had her obeying instantly, curling her arms and legs around him. His arms came around her, lifted her and held her close as he strode for the bedroom on the ground floor, his mouth on the side of her neck. "Gonna enjoy unraveling you, sweetness."

Her heart squeezed even as a shiver sped through her. Sweetness, in that deep Southern drawl, was about the sexiest thing she'd ever heard.

The bedroom was dim, the only light coming from the kitchen down the hall. Walker yanked the covers back and laid her down. She tried to pull him down on top of her but he shrugged free and straightened, that deep blue gaze steady on her.

Ivy watched, breathless, as his long fingers went to the top button of his shirt and slowly undid it. Then the second. And the third, revealing the deep indent beneath. One after the other until the shirt finally came undone, revealing a tantalizing strip of his bare chest.

She sat up, reached out to push the rest of it off his shoulders, but he caught her wrists and held them in one hand while he shrugged first out of one arm, then the other. Ivy stared at the unbelievably sexy display before her. A landscape of sculpted muscle sprinkled with dark hair.

He dropped the shirt on the floor. Brought her wrists to his lips. Pressed a kiss to the inside of each, his tongue stroking across her racing pulse. "Take off your sweater."

The instant he released her, she grabbed the hem of her sweater and peeled it upward. He helped her, tugging it over her head, his eyes fastened on the sheer black lace bra she wore underneath. "Now the jeans." His voice was pure sin.

She complied, hungry for the feel of skin on skin, quickly shimmying out of her jeans and panties. Her fingers had just unhooked her bra behind her back when he dropped to one knee beside the bed and pulled it from her, his heated stare locked on her tight nipples.

"So damn sexy, Ivy," he whispered, his palm cupping the side of one breast as he bent his head toward her.

She grabbed hold of his muscled shoulder with one hand, the other sinking into his hair as his mouth closed over the rigid tip. She whimpered, arching her back as pleasure pulsed through her, every tug of his mouth, every flick of his tongue setting her on fire.

Walker pressed her backward, following her down and switching to her other breast, his hands gliding over her skin, mapping her curves with his fingers and palms. She did the same to him, following the hollows and contours of hard muscle across his shoulders and back, over his chest.

He caught her hands. Pressed them flat to the bed at her hips as his mouth moved lower. "Spread your legs for me, sweetness. I wanna see how wet you are for me."

Oh, God… He was so quiet all the time, she'd never imagined he was a sexy talker. Her fingers fisted around the sheet as she complied, parting her thighs to reveal the slick, sensitive folds within.

His stare all but burned her flesh, a low sound of raw hunger and male approval coming from his chest. "Don't move," he warned, his lips inches from where she was dying for them. His fingers tightened around her wrists and he lowered his head…

She made a high-pitched, needy sound as his mouth found her, his warm, soft tongue gliding over every sizzling nerve ending. He anticipated the roll of her hips. Controlled it with his forearms, his hands holding her exactly where he wanted her while he took her apart with every decadent stroke and caress of lips and tongue.

Within minutes he'd found the exact spot and pressure she wanted. Licking, swirling until she was trembling, tiny cries of need coming between each panted breath.

Just as she was climbing the crest, just as her thighs and belly pulled taut and the orgasm shimmered before her, he stopped.

Her eyes flew open, her body trembling. "Walker—"

"Watch me," he said in a low, dark voice. "Watch me make you come."

She stared down at him through heavy-lidded eyes, swallowing hard. His dark head dipped back down.

The tip of his tongue touched her clit. Traced it gently while her spine flexed like a bow, tremors rippling through her spread thighs.

She was drowning. Barely clinging to her sanity while he took her apart with each slow, seductive stroke, finally releasing one wrist to slide two fingers into her aching core.

"Oh, God," she cried. She grabbed a fistful of his hair, rocked her hips as his fingers gave her the exact friction she needed, the firm strokes contrasting with the melting caress of his tongue.

The orgasm suddenly intensified, a looming wave ready to crash over her. Walker stayed exactly where he was, refusing to speed up, forcing her to feel every second of the delicious climb to ecstasy while he stared up at her with molten blue eyes.

Her eyes slammed shut and a long, liquid cry of release filled her ears as the pleasure finally detonated, wave after wave rolling through her.

She lay limp and gasping in the aftermath when his mouth moved up to her belly, the fingers around her right wrist releasing to slide into her hair. "So hot, sweetness," he whispered against her skin, the reverence in his tone making her heart squeeze.

"I want to touch you all over," she demanded, her hands moving greedily over his smooth, hot skin. "Take off your pants."

His lips found hers in a languid, sensual kiss that sent more heat pouring through her as he came up on his knees and stripped off his jeans. She helped him shove them down his hips, her hands finding the thick, rigid shaft of his erection and fisting him tight. He sucked in a breath and pressed his forehead to hers.

Power surged through her. She stroked him slowly, exploring him as leisurely as he had her. Reveling in the way his face tightened and his breathing shortened. She kissed her way across his jaw, down the side of his neck to nip at the sensitive spot where it joined his shoulder. "Want to suck you."

She smiled at the shudder she got, got on her knees and kissed and licked her way down his sculpted torso. Enjoying every ridge of muscle along the way until her lips finally closed around the wide head of his cock.

His fingers clenched in her hair. "Ivy."

"Yes," she whispered, loving the sound of her name in that pleasure-roughened voice. Loving the slight sting across her scalp as his fist tightened.

She slowly licked around the sensitive underside. Wetting him before taking him in her mouth. Flicking her tongue against the taut skin while she sucked, her hand pumping him.

Walker made a low, rough sound, the muscles in his thighs and six-pack flexing. The hand in her hair squeezed tighter, tighter yet as she pushed him.

A heartbeat later, she found herself flat on her back with more than two-hundred pounds of aroused, hungry male on top of her.

"I want inside you," he said in a rough voice a heartbeat before his mouth came down on hers, the thick ridge of his erection trapped between them.

She wrapped her legs around his thighs and tilted her hips, one hand palming his ass to guide him into her.

He came up on his forearms, his breathing uneven as he stared down at her. "Are you sure?"

He hadn't been with anyone since his wife died, and it had been almost as long for her. "Yes, I can't get pregnant," she whispered. Surgeons had done an emergency hysterectomy to stop the internal bleeding when she'd been brought in by ambulance that night in Moscow. But being here with Walker made all that seem a million miles away.

He kissed the bridge of her nose. Her cheeks and eyelids,

his tenderness in spite of his lust turning her inside out. She cupped the side of his face, feeling her heart give way into free fall.

He slid a hand between them. She gasped when the smooth, hot length of his cock nestled between her folds. But not inside her.

Instead, he angled himself to press flat against her and began gliding it up and down her slick, sensitive flesh that was beginning to tingle and throb all over again. Finding the swelling bud of her clit with each controlled glide. Watching her face the whole time.

Oh, shit…

She drew in a startled breath, floored. She wasn't like this. Her body had never done this before, but Christ he was good, and the way his hips moved, stroking her in exactly the right spot… "I—ohhh, God…"

His hand found her hip, gripped tight to keep her exactly where he wanted her while he slowly undid her all over again. She could feel his gaze on her, felt a flash of intense vulnerability before the building pleasure obliterated it.

Then there was nothing but need. Her fingers digging into the bunching muscles of his back. His mouth on hers, tongues tangling, his deep, velvety voice whispering praise and commands.

The pleasure sharpened suddenly. She hitched in a breath, felt him shift and then the smooth, heated slide as he finally penetrated her.

Pressure. Fullness. His cock stroking every aching nerve ending hidden inside her.

She made an incoherent sound and clung tighter, automatically tightening her thighs and rubbing her clit against his body with each rocking glide.

"So good," he groaned against her lips. "So goddamn good, *Ivy*..."

She couldn't respond, too lost in sensation. Stunned at what her body was capable of.

His fingers found her nipple. Rolled it. Squeezing gently. Heightening everything until it was too much. She moaned into his mouth as another orgasm tore through her, holding on for dear life.

Walker growled low in his throat and pumped harder, his tempo increasing. She had barely stopped shuddering when he went rigid and plunged deep, throwing his head back with a deep groan.

Ivy drank in every detail of him in that moment, his face contorted with ecstasy he'd found within her body, and felt a soul-deep satisfaction she'd never experienced before. She smoothed her hands up and down the slick skin of his back, over his shoulders, gathering her to him and holding him close when he finally relaxed and melted into her.

She held him, absorbed the astounding sense of peace and rightness. Along with a fierce possessiveness that was also new.

She would kill for this man. Defend him with her life.

Walker sighed, his lips finding the side of her neck. "You all right, sweetness?"

God, she loved the way he called her that. "Yes. You?"

His rough chuckle gusted against her neck. "Yeah." He kissed the spot beneath her ear, levered up on his arms to stroke his fingertips down the side of her face, his expression impossibly tender. "Damn, I knew it'd be like that with you."

Her heart slipped another notch. "I need to clean up," she murmured.

He shifted, easing out of her. "I'll bring you a cloth."

"No, I'll do it." She rolled from the bed and strode for the en suite, needing a few minutes to herself. In the bathroom, she quickly cleaned up and splashed water on her flushed face, shaken by the depth of what Walker made her feel.

When she came back out, he was lying on his back watching her with the covers around his waist, one muscular arm tucked behind his head. His gaze swept over her naked body from head to foot and back again. He shook his head, almost in wonder. "You're stunning."

She felt her cheeks get hot as she slid in next to him. Walker immediately curled his arms around her and pulled her to his chest, where she pressed her cheek into the solid slab of muscle resting over his heart. "Tired yet?" he murmured, fingers gliding up and down her spine.

Her body felt warm and languid. Safe. "A bit."

He kept up with that lulling motion, the quiet and peace settling around them. "Why me, by the way?" he finally asked.

She opened her eyes. "What?"

"At the start of all this. Why the vested interest in helping me specifically? You could have passed your intel off to anyone at the CIA, or just Rycroft."

Ivy tensed, her stomach grabbing tight. She hesitated, thinking fast. Trying to come up with some excuse that would seem plausible.

Tell him the truth.

His hand stilled. "Ivy? Come on, tell me."

She squeezed her eyes shut, her mind rebelling. Not wanting to admit what she'd done. But he would find out, and after what they'd just done…

No. It had to come from her. Face to face, no wimping out, and she'd just have to take whatever consequences came. Walker was a logical, reasonable man. Once he heard her out, he would understand.

And hopefully forgive her. Because if he didn't…

"Hey." He leaned back a little, cupping her jaw in his hand and turning her face toward him. "What's wrong?"

The concern on his face twisted her insides. She took a deep breath, braced for his reaction and told him her guilty secret.

"Because I was the one who burned Grey on your op in Moscow."

FIFTEEN

Walker went dead still as his brain struggled to process that, convinced he'd heard her wrong. Or at least misunderstood.

Prayed he had.

"Say again?" he said in a low voice, dread coiling in the pit of his stomach. He'd never wanted to be more wrong about anything in his life.

Ivy stayed silent and rigid against him, confirming his fears.

He pulled away from her enough to come up on one elbow and look down at her, the faint light coming from down the hallway showing her face. The stricken, guilt-ridden look on it made his guts clench. She'd blown his op? "It was *you*?" How?

"I...yes," she admitted miserably.

He jerked away from her as if she'd burned him and sat up fast, staring at her. "Explain." His voice was low. Hard.

She pushed out a breath and sat up too, tugged the sheets up to cover her breasts and ran a hand through her tousled hair. "I had infiltrated Tarasov's inner circle to find out what his boss was up to. He was Yuri Stanislav's 2IC, and Stanislav's lover was one of the Valkyries who approached me initially about the hacking job I told you about."

Stanislav was a straight-up killer. His second-in-command would have been no different. He didn't want to think about Ivy getting tangled up with a man like Tarasov, no matter how skilled and deadly she was. Everything about this was horrifying. "And?"

"They were involved in a major deal with a top-level Russian arms dealer. They wanted me to hack into his various offshore bank accounts and move money around to sanitize it. Found out later it was because they'd planned to steal it from him. I turned them down because I sensed something was off, but stayed on the periphery with Tarasov to monitor the situation and pass bits of intel to Kiyomi. I didn't realize they had already brought Amber in to take my place."

"Who was the arms dealer?" he said in a flat voice. Though he was pretty sure he already knew.

She was quiet a moment before answering. "Viktor Nikolaev."

Fuck.

He looked away from her, raked a hand through his hair. He'd spent the better part of five months putting everything in place to get an asset close to Nikolaev. He'd chosen Grey personally. And he had a sick feeling he already knew where the rest of this was going. "How did you find out about Grey?"

To her credit, she was calm as she answered. "I came across his name during my initial investigation, and then kept tabs on him off and on after that, just in case."

He swung around to stare at her. "You hacked my intel?"

"Yes," she said quietly, holding his gaze.

Jesus Christ. He hadn't known. Neither had anyone else on the team. Not a fucking clue that Ivy had been monitoring any of it. "And then?"

"And then, I knew Stanislav was getting ready to make his move on Nikolaev. I found out about the meeting you'd set up between him and Grey. I had to act fast to stop Stanislav from getting the money, so I...intervened and passed certain details to someone in the Russian Federal Security Service and they took it from there."

"What details," he demanded, wanting to hear it spelled out.

"The meeting time and location." She paused a moment. "And that Grey was a CIA asset."

Christ. He shot off the bed to snatch up his underwear from the floor and yanked them on, disgusted. Enraged. Blindsided. "What the *fuck*, Ivy?"

"I'm sorry," she said quietly. "I wanted them all brought down and didn't think it would happen unless I stepped in."

He dragged his jeans on, wanting to punch something. "You're *sorry*? Two of my best men were killed that night when Grey was taken! They had young families. I was at their fucking funerals. And now Grey is—"

"I know. I'm so sorry."

His heart was racing. Slamming into his ribs, his brain screaming in denial. He couldn't believe what she'd done.

He jerked his shirt on. Buttoned it as he stormed to the doorway and stopped there a second, his chest constricting. He couldn't look at her. Couldn't face her after what he'd just heard. Definitely not after what they'd just shared in that bed.

"You're good," he said with a shake of his head, feeling sick to his soul. "Really good."

"What?"

She'd lied to him. Had hidden this from him from day one and drawn him in bit by bit anyway. Had just had mind-blowing sex with him. All the while knowing exactly what she'd done and concealing it.

"Walker, hey. I didn't even know you then. I saw Stanislav and Nikolaev as the greater threats and acted. Grey was—"

"Collateral damage. Along with my men," he finished in disgust. "And then you saw me as—what? A means to an end? You wanted to get close to me and involved in this op to ease your conscience?"

"I...no. Okay, yes, I wanted to make amends, but me burning your op wasn't personal—"

"Not personal?" He let out a humorless laugh. Because the joke was on him. "I was buried inside you ten minutes ago, so excuse me for feeling like it's *real* fucking personal."

She'd used him to soothe her guilty conscience, because she knew she was to blame for what happened with Grey. Plain and simple. And he was a fucking idiot for not seeing it.

"Stop it," she snapped in a hard voice. "What happened back then has nothing to do with now, or us. I did what I had to do, what I thought was right."

"Yeah, and you've been manipulating me ever since. Hiding everything, covering your tracks while knowing you've been lying to me from day one. For what? You thought I'd step in to help protect you once the truth came out? Because you knew it was going to come out eventually."

"That's not fair. I...lied by omission, yes, but I was planning to tell you all of this after we stopped Grey."

"Yeah? Well, too little, too late." He stalked out of the room, furious with her—and himself.

Goddamn it, he should have known. Should have put the pieces together before now and realized she couldn't be trusted. Shouldn't have ever let her in or slept with her.

Bedding rustled behind him, then her rapid footsteps followed him into the hall. "Walker, stop."

Nope.

He ignored the pain in her voice and kept going. She was a

liar and a manipulator. Was probably still playing him right now, acting all contrite and apologetic when she actually didn't feel one iota of guilt over what she'd done. Didn't give a shit that she'd cost the lives of two good men and personally had a hand in transforming Grey into the monster he'd become through his captivity.

"Wait," she said in clear exasperation. "Will you stop and listen?"

"I don't want to hear it," he bit out, heading through the small kitchen. There was nothing she could say that would make this situation at all better.

"Well, too bad," she fired back, coming after him.

Nope. He grabbed his coat from the hook on the wall next to the front door, picked up his bag.

"Where are you going?" she demanded.

"Out," he said, turning the deadbolt. He wasn't staying here with her for another second. He'd find somewhere else to sleep tonight, even if it was the fucking car.

"No, *wait*." She grabbed his arm as he reached for the doorknob, wrenched his hand off it.

He tensed, set his jaw and forced himself to take a breath before turning around, the wave of anger riding him hard. Only to stare.

She was naked. Still trying to manipulate him with her body. "Put some clothes on," he bit out.

"No." She raised her chin, stood there stark naked staring him down. "You might not like what I have to say, but you at least need to hear me out."

"I've heard *more* than enough."

She kept her gaze locked with his. "I said I'm sorry, and I meant it."

"For which part? The lying? Getting my men killed? Destroying Grey's life and turning him into what he is today? Or for playing me like a damn violin for the past year?"

She sucked in a breath at the last part, eyes widening. It was dim in the room but her face seemed to pale. "You don't mean that," she said in a stricken voice.

"I mean every goddamn word."

She shook her head, covered her breasts with her arms. "I took a big risk in telling you the truth. Because I owed it to you, and because I trust you."

"Well, I don't trust you. Not anymore." He knew about her background now. What else was she capable of? What else was she hiding?

The look in her eyes chilled. "I was captured the same night as Grey," she said in a flat voice, "so believe me, I've already paid for my part in all of this. You don't think it bothers me that Grey turned into this because I burned his cover? Knowing that I'm partly to blame for the deaths of all his victims? And you can't really believe that I've been using or manipulating you this entire time. Not after we just—"

"Yeah, I sure as hell can. That was a huge mistake on my part, and it won't happen again." He was too much of a professional to let this get in the way while they were forced to work together in this investigation, much less one where lives were at stake. And she knew it. "There is no *we* here. We're done."

Her face tightened, the hurt and distress there making him feel like a monster for a second before the cold knot of anger in his gut forced it away. She'd proven that he couldn't trust her.

"What about the inve—"

"I'll see you at the briefing in the morning," he said in a hard voice.

What the hell was he supposed to do with what she'd confessed? She could be prosecuted for what she'd done, and then even Rycroft wouldn't be able to save her.

Fuck. "As soon as this is over, we go our separate ways back to London." After this was finished, he never wanted to lay eyes on her again.

With that, he shoved open the door and strode out into the cold night air, the pain of her betrayal twisting in his chest a physical reminder of just how stupid he'd been to ever trust her.

∾

THE DARK SKY outside the living room window was beginning to lighten to a pearly gray at the bottom when Ivy's phone buzzed with an incoming call early the next morning. She rolled onto her side on the couch to snatch it from the coffee table, stupidly hoping it might be Walker.

Disappointment crashed over her when she saw Kiyomi's number instead.

For a moment she considered not answering. She didn't feel like talking. To anyone. But she hadn't been this miserable in a long, long time, and desperately needed to vent to her best friend. If anyone would understand, it was Kiyomi.

"Hey." Her voice sounded hoarse.

"You don't sound good. Rough night? Or are you coming down with something?"

"Rough night." Roughest she'd had in years.

"Why, what happened?"

"It's Walker. He— Well, we…" She trailed off, feeling awkward. What she and Walker had shared last night had been magical to her. Too intimate and precious to say out loud.

"Okay," Kiyomi said slowly, accurately putting it together on her own. "And it was bad?"

"No." She rubbed at her tired, gritty eyes, her throat thickening. She had to swallow several times to get the lump to go down. "No, it was amazing," she whispered, her voice catching.

"Completely amazing." On a whole other level she hadn't known existed before him.

Only to have everything come crashing down on her minutes later because she'd opened her stupid mouth and confessed everything. Although, better it had happened now than later, when she'd fallen even harder for him.

"Great. So what's the problem?" Kiyomi asked.

"I came clean to him afterward. About Grey and everything else in Moscow." Partly because her conscience had been pricking at her like knives. But mostly because she didn't want it standing between them anymore.

"Oh." Kiyomi fell silent. "That's some pillow talk, Ivy."

She sighed. God, she'd handled this so badly. Ruined everything. "I wasn't going to tell him until this was all finished, but he started asking me things when we were lying there together after, and I just couldn't keep it from him anymore. I…wanted to come clean and not hide it anymore."

"And he didn't take it well, I'm guessing."

"No." She scrubbed a hand over her face, a leaden pressure in her chest that she couldn't shake. Somewhere between dread and loss, or maybe a mix of both. "He was livid. Apparently two of his men were killed trying to stop Grey from being captured."

"Oh, hell."

"And on top of that, he's convinced that I've been duping him for the past year. Leading him on to help cover my tracks or some shit. Including last night." That's what hurt the most. That he thought she'd been manipulating him while they'd been intimate.

"Oh, shit, hon. I'm sorry."

The sympathy in her bestie's voice made tears sting the backs of her eyes. She drew in a breath, forced them back. She'd already cried once in the past six hours over him and it shamed her even though the logical part of her knew she no longer had to be ashamed of that sort of thing. "I've been thinking about what happened in Moscow. I tried to explain to Walker that from where I was sitting at the time, burning Grey was a necessary evil. Taking down Stanislav and Nikolaev was paramount.

"Ending them meant saving countless lives in war zones by stopping the flow of weapons to militant groups, and preventing God knows how many women from being trafficked. I didn't know the US and UK would disavow Grey. I didn't know what he'd become."

"No, you couldn't have known any of that. And you don't have to defend yourself to me. Tough calls like that are made every day on intelligence and military ops. Walker should know that better than anyone."

She'd also been jumped by Tarasov's goons that same night and had her own nightmare to contend with. It had taken every bit of her strength and stubbornness just to survive and claw her way back into the world of the living.

"I don't know what he'll do now that I've told him. He was too upset to see that there was no benefit for me in telling him. That I made myself vulnerable by doing it. Now I'm wondering if he'll even turn me in."

"Would he do that?" Kiyomi sounded alarmed.

"I don't know. I don't know what to think anymore." She stopped, pressed her lips together hard. Shit, what a mess.

She'd been trained to never get emotional. To always have control over her emotions and not the other way around. Had literally had that lesson beaten into her, repeatedly, until she could master her reactions and conceal her feelings. "It's my fault. I waited too long to tell him because I was a coward." And she'd fumbled all of it when she had told him.

"He didn't know you back then. If you'd told him before, he

would definitely have turned you in because he does things by the book."

Ivy shook her head, unable to make this bereft feeling go away and getting even more worried. Would he turn her in? In the middle of the hunt for Grey? "You should have seen the way he looked at me. Like the sight of me suddenly disgusted him." It twisted her insides to remember it.

"He's angry right now, and I get why. But he's an intelligent guy with a lot of experience behind him. Give him a chance to calm down and think things over, and then—"

"There's no time for any personal shit right now. We've got a briefing with the taskforce in an hour, and then we're meeting up with Chloe and Heath right after at the cathedral to start our own search."

"He's a professional. He won't let this get in the way of the investigation."

"I know. But seeing him so cold after last night is like having a knife shoved in my heart." Walker wouldn't make a scene, but there were only two ways this could go now if he didn't decide to let this slide.

Either FBI agents would be waiting to take her in for questioning, or Walker would bury it all for now and act the polite colleague while they focused on finding Grey. Then drop the hammer on her after.

The second option was almost worse in some ways. She would much rather face his anger than his indifference.

"Oh, hon. Do you love him?"

"I..." She opened her mouth to deny it. Stopped.

This was Kiyomi she was talking to. The only person who really knew her, the good and the bad, and loved her anyway. She sometimes thought Kiyomi knew her better than Ivy knew herself.

"I think I might," she whispered, something close to panic lighting up in her chest.

She didn't know the first thing about what real love was. Wasn't sure she'd recognize it even if it hit her between the eyes. But she'd thought maybe, with Walker…

Kiyomi made an understanding sound. "Then let him be mad right now, and get the job done together as a team. Use this time to focus everything you're feeling on what you need to do to stop Grey and rescue the hostages."

"He made it clear we're not anything anymore."

"He might feel that way right now, but based on everything I know about him, he's going to move forward as if nothing happened, and he's *not* going to turn you in. He wants Grey captured as bad as anyone, and he'll do whatever it takes to make it happen. After that, you can deal with everything else. There's still time, Ivy. It's not over unless you want it to be."

She'd never known hope could hurt. "I don't think he'll listen."

"So make him. You're a Valkyrie, for Christ's sake."

The fierceness of Kiyomi's tone made her smile a little. "Yeah, you're right."

"I know. And take it from someone else who's still got training wheels on when it comes to matters of the heart—don't sell him short. He's smart. After this is over, don't hold back out of pride or fear of rejection. If you care about him as much as I think you do, then fight like hell for him. Don't let him go."

She could fight all she wanted. It didn't mean he would give her another chance. She couldn't force him to. Still, she was grateful to have gotten all this off her chest with someone she trusted with her life. "I'm glad you called."

"Me too. My bestie-sixth-sense must've been burning."

"Must've. How's Mr. Whiskers?"

"Spoiled and pampered as usual. Don't worry, I go hang out

with him a couple times a day when I feed him and clean out his litter."

"Do you play fetch like I asked? He prefers the fluffy blue ball to the green one. Or sometimes he likes his little white mouse—"

"Yes, Ivy, I'm aware. He's fine, I swear. I'll send you more pictures this morning."

"Okay. Thanks. I know he's in good hands. It's just that he's my baby." She missed him so much right now. Wished he was curled up on her purring away. At least then something would be right in her world.

"I know."

"Okay, I'd better hit the shower and get to the meeting." She was dreading seeing Walker again. And she really hoped Kiyomi was right about Walker not turning her in. She didn't feel like being arrested when she needed to be helping stop Grey.

"Sure. Call me if you need more moral support. Or a kick in the ass. And let me know what happens with Grey."

"I will."

In the shower a few minutes later, she washed her face and let the hot water soothe her sore eyelids, thinking about what Kiyomi had said.

She knew how to fight like hell. But she didn't have a clue how to fix what had happened with Walker.

And she was afraid that it might already be broken beyond repair.

SIXTEEN

This was it. After a whirlwind of activity over the past few weeks, everything was finally in place. And in a matter of moments, the final countdown would begin.

Isaac made his way back up the tunnel to the underground room to check the wiring on the main devices one last time. He was having a good day so far, his hands steadier than they'd been in weeks, his muscle control good, but he was short on sleep and that kind of fatigue always made his symptoms worsen as the hours passed. He worked quickly just in case.

Next, he checked the fail-safe. It might not come into play depending on how things went, but he'd readied it just in case. He had seen Walker yesterday here in Durham with a woman.

The government must have brought him in to work with whatever taskforce was in charge of hunting him. Isaac was still hoping Walker would be the one to find him. His moment of revenge would be so much sweeter if he could take Walker out with him.

He heard a stirring behind him, then a slurred voice spoke. "What are you doing? Where have you taken us?"

Straightening, the muscles in his spine stiffening in protest,

Isaac turned to peer across the space, dimly lit by a battery-powered lantern. Laura was finally awake again.

A fierce frown pulled her eyebrows together as she twisted against the bindings that held her chair to one of the support columns holding up the vaulted ceiling.

"Under the cathedral," he answered, because she had a right to know.

"You sick bastard, let us go!" Her voice echoed off the curved ceiling. Not tall and grand as it was tens of meters above them. But impressive nonetheless, considering the technology available when it had been built centuries ago. Of course, Durham County was famous for its miners. Men here had always been experts at working underground.

"Can't do that." He went back to checking the last item on the fail-safe, reluctant to put it on yet. Delaying it until the last possible moment.

Laura continued to struggle in vain.

"Whaas…goin' on," Chad slurred from the other side of the room.

"The psycho's got us tied up under the cathedral," Laura said, still trying to get free. There was no point. Neither of them was walking away from this.

None of them were. And he wasn't a psycho.

"He's going to kill us," Laura said, fear raising the pitch of her voice to an irritating level.

Chad began to thrash, his grunts and groans mixing in the background. Isaac tuned them both out and made one final adjustment, then walked over to where he'd left the timer. He stood there looking at it for a long moment, running through all aspects of his design in his head. Wanting to make sure he hadn't missed any details in his haste to get everything done in time.

But no, he couldn't see any mistakes. He was ready.

Time to end this, one way or the other. The people looking for him were close. It was only a matter of time before they found him. But by then, it would be far too late.

He reached out a forefinger and pressed the button, aware of the way his pulse thudded in his neck. A quiet beep sounded and the digital timer began running backward.

A soothing rush of relief washed over him as he straightened and looked up at the vaulted ceiling above him. The uncertainty and stress of getting it all done had been the hardest part. It was fitting that it would all end here. He would finally get the justice that had been denied him, and peace all at once.

Laura's soft sob brought him back to the present. He spun around. She was crying, the fear and grief on her face touching something deep inside him.

He went to her. Ignored the way she recoiled when he crouched beside her and lifted a hand to push the hair back from her forehead. The last touch she would ever receive, and he wanted it to be full of kindness. He'd considered keeping both her and Chad drugged right up till the end, but hadn't wanted to risk giving them too much and killing them too soon.

"It's all right," he told her gently. "It's not going to hurt. It'll be so quick you won't feel a thing, I promise." He'd rigged everything in here carefully to ensure none of them would suffer when the bombs detonated.

"Don't touch me," she spat, wrenching her head away and squeezing her eyes shut as if repulsed by him, her face streaked with tears.

Isaac rose, met Chad's shattered gaze for a moment before he turned away and crossed over to sink into the chair he'd placed for himself next to the timer. The seconds continued to tick down on the digital display, marking the last few hours of his time on this earth. The end of his suffering was near.

He closed his eyes, forced away the memories of the darkened cell he'd been kept in. The torture they'd inflicted. His hands flexed, the scar tissue pulling at the stiff joints.

He'd done all he could to prepare for what was coming. Whether Walker and the others put the clues he'd left together in time remained to be seen.

Nothing left for him to do now but wait.

∽

WALKER HAD BEEN STEELING himself for the sight of Ivy all morning. Yet the moment she came through the meeting room door, it felt like he'd been punched in the heart.

She met his gaze briefly before looking away and crossing to the other end of the table to sit next to Warwick as though nothing had ever happened between them. He kept his expression impassive and body language neutral so no one else would guess that anything was wrong.

It should have been a relief that she wasn't going to try to talk to him about last night or make things awkward in front of everyone.

Instead, her dismissal only made him feel more hollow inside.

Her betrayal had cut him to the quick, made unbearable because of what they'd shared before that. She was the first woman he'd been with since Jillian. The first one he'd risked opening his heart to. Only to get it smashed.

After walking the quiet, winding streets of Durham for several hours last night, he'd checked into a hotel room where he'd gotten only a few hours of sleep. Most of his time in that narrow bed had been spent tossing and turning, staring at the darkened ceiling while dissecting every part of what Ivy had said before he'd stormed out.

In the end, he'd given up on sleep and called Donovan and

Shae to check in. She was doing well, all things considered. Donovan had wanted details about the investigation. Walker had kept it brief and to the point without giving away anything sensitive.

Too brief, because as soon as he'd finished, Donovan said, "Something going on with Ivy?"

Yeah, something was going on with her.

The time alone last night had given him a chance to calm down and think things through better. He was still angry with her and about what she'd done, but his head was clearer.

When she'd made the call to burn Grey, she'd seen it as the lesser of two evils when weighed against destroying Nikolaev, and by extension, Stanislav as well. She had made the call to sacrifice Grey, not realizing the lingering ripple effects that fateful decision would hold, or that her decision would result in the deaths of two decorated CIA officers.

And she was right, she'd taken a big risk in confessing everything to him. By doing so she'd essentially put her fate in his hands.

He could easily turn her in to the FBI or CIA. Not that there would be any hard evidence against her. All of it would have been carefully scrubbed by her and maybe Amber a long time ago.

But he didn't want to do that. Couldn't. No matter how angry he was or how badly she'd messed up.

After analyzing it from every angle he could think of, he'd come to the conclusion that she'd told him because she trusted him. It was like a knife in his guts.

"Hiya, everyone," the female MI5 agent said to the room from the head of the table. "Let's quiet down and get started. We've got a lot to cover this morning."

She reviewed the most pertinent intel from yesterday, including the fresh leads that had been tracked down and gone nowhere. "I can also confirm that what Ms. Johnson said yesterday is true. Isaac Grey was diagnosed with an aggressive form of ALS by the NHS early this year, under an alias. And an additional search of the cathedral last night resulted in no further leads. Also, Mr. James led a new search of the campus and university facilities." She nodded at Warwick. "Please detail your findings."

"All buildings connected with the university were thoroughly searched, both on and off campus, as well as the colleges," he said, leaning back in his chair. "We found no evidence of the hostages or Grey."

"All indications point to Grey being somewhere in Durham," the woman continued. "MI5 has teams looking across the city, along with local police. There have been no further communications from Grey, and I don't have to remind any of you that the deadline mentioned in the last note is coming up in less than nine hours."

There wasn't a single piece of good news in the remainder of the briefing, except a list of places the authorities had ruled out as possible targets or hiding spots. Everywhere they'd looked, everywhere they turned, was another dead end.

The meeting concluded with a discussion about various theories and hunches that needed to be addressed. When that ended, Walker stepped out into the hall to take a breather, needing a few minutes to clear his head.

Grey was here in Durham. Walker just had to find a new angle, figure out what he'd missed and put the pieces together in time.

Ivy walked out a moment later with Warwick. She stopped, faced Walker, the impact of her hazel gaze hitting him deep inside.

He remembered how she'd felt under him. Surrounding him. How she'd tasted. How she'd come apart for him and given him mind-blowing pleasure. How he'd never be the same because of it.

He blocked out all the personal shit between them, shelved it for a later date when Grey was behind bars and people's lives were no longer under threat by him. "Anything new from Amber?"

"No. But we've all missed something. He's here somewhere. He has to be."

"Aye," said Warwick. "I say we have a look on our own."

"Agreed," Walker said. "I'll let MI5 know what we're doing." He called the agent in charge to let him know, then looked at Ivy and Warwick. "Where should we start?"

"The castle," Warwick said. "I want to check an access point I remember to a 'secret' passageway."

"Okay. Let's go."

The three of them left campus and started down the hill at a brisk pace. There was no point in using a car for this. They would get there faster on foot. "I want to bring Chloe and Heath in for this," Ivy said to Walker. "We'll cover more ground with them."

It was a bit of a security risk. As a former PJ, Heath would have military records on file. Chloe not so much. But they needed all the help they could get, and couldn't pass up two skilled, trained operators to assist in the search. He would deal with any fallout later if necessary.

"Have them meet us in the dining hall."

He could see the top of the central cathedral tower over the line of trees bordering the riverbank. The castle was just north of it. They hurried over Kingsgate Bridge and walked up Bow Lane to the cathedral, then crossed Palace Green and went through the stone gates guarding the entrance to the castle.

Chloe and Heath met them in the huge centuries-old great hall, which served as the students' dining hall. Chloe was a far different person with her game face on. Still a bundle of coiled energy as she chomped away on her gum, but subdued and focused now.

Walker divided up the floor plan and split them into three groups. Chloe and Heath took the north side, Warwick the east, and Walker and Ivy searched the west and southern parts. He'd partnered with her deliberately.

His personal feelings for her aside, Ivy was by far the most skilled operative he'd ever met. She was a pro at what she did, and they needed her expertise if they were going to have a prayer at finding Grey. He also wanted to keep her close to him. Still felt protective and dammit, territorial of her in a primal way he had no hope of fighting.

The two of them worked mostly in silence, speaking only when necessary while a security guard dutifully unlocked doors and passageways for them as they went. Walker wasn't surprised when none of the others reported anything when they met back in the great hall after.

"Cathedral next," he said. It had been searched over plenty of times in the past forty-eight hours, but maybe they'd missed something Walker and the others might spot.

A security guard met them at the door and checked their IDs on a list. Saturdays were always a busy day for the tourist spots in the city, and the cathedral was once again open for visitors, albeit with extra security on hand to keep an eye out.

Walker stepped inside, getting his first view of the interior in person. It was cool and dim in here, the massive stone building echoing the murmur of voices throughout.

"Good morning, how may I help you?" a smiling female volunteer said as she approached them.

"When's the next service?" Walker asked, showing his government ID. His, Ivy's and Warwick's names would all be on an approved list with security.

"Choral evensong is at half-five," she said, sobering. "Will you all be attending?"

"No, but we'd like to talk to the head of security immediately."

"Of course. Right this way." She took them across to the reception desk. "Wait here, please, and I'll get him." She hurried through a door marked private.

"The pictures of this place don't do it justice," Chloe breathed, gazing down the length of the central nave lined by massive carved sandstone pillars that held up the towering vaulted stone ceiling above.

It was incredible, Walker had to admit. Unfortunately, there was no time to stop and appreciate the architecture and craftsmanship.

The volunteer returned with a tall man somewhere in his thirties. "I'm Ted Coffrey, head of cathedral security," he said. "You're part of the taskforce?"

"That's right." Walker introduced himself and showed his ID. "We'd like to take a look around ourselves."

"Of course. I'll get the keys and meet you at the cloisters," Coffrey said, and disappeared through the door again.

"Shame you can't come back for evensong," the female volunteer said as she led them past a towering, ornately carved font hood made of dark wood. "It's a beautiful service and the choir today is from Durham's very own Hatfield College—Oh." She stopped, her smile slipping as her gaze fixed on something across the nave. "That's strange."

Walker and the others looked over. "Something wrong?" He didn't see anything suspicious. Just people wandering around taking in the sights.

"Well, that," she said, gesturing to whatever she was looking at. "The hymnal board."

"What about it?" Warwick asked. The wooden sandwich board displayed several rows of numbers.

"We don't have one," the lady said, marching across the aisle and between the wooden pews.

Walker exchanged a look with the others and quickly followed her. This couldn't be a clue. Could it? "What do you mean," he pressed.

"I mean, the cathedral doesn't use hymnal boards. All the hymn selections for each service are printed out on service sheets and handed out before they begin," she said in annoyance, gesturing to the hymnal board set up near the north wall of the nave.

"Wait." He put a hand on her arm to stop her, his gut tingling. "Leave it," he said when she looked at him in surprise. "Get Coffrey, now. We need to see the security video and find out who put this here."

She gave him a startled look before nodding and hurrying back the way they'd come.

"Is this it?" Ivy asked him, frowning. "Another clue?"

"Might be." He took out his phone and took some pictures, trying to make sense of it. Was the board itself the message? The numbers on it? The placement?

The volunteer reappeared in the doorway behind them, panting as though she'd run back. "He says to come straight up."

Within minutes, Walker and the others were gathered around the bank of monitors in the security room, where Coffrey was reviewing the video feeds. "Here," he said, pointing to the second monitor from the left. "A volunteer places it just after the staff arrived this morning."

The feed showed a middle-aged man with his back to the camera, dressed in a volunteer jacket and black pants as he carried the sandwich board over and placed it near the wall. It was impossible to see his face or tell his exact age. He was a bit stooped over, his gait slightly awkward, possibly due to carrying the board. And he kept his face averted the entire time.

Walker stared hard. Was it Grey? He would know to disguise himself as a volunteer so as not to draw suspicion. Would know exactly where the cameras were located and angle his face accordingly. And the stooped posture might indicate the effects of ALS.

"Zoom in on him," Ivy said, leaning forward and placing a hand on the desk. "Try every angle you have and follow him."

Coffrey did. Four different cameras, each from a different vantage point around the entrance and nave. "I can't get a clear shot of his face," he said in frustration.

It resembled Grey. Could definitely be him. "Where does he go after this?" Walker said.

"Umm, let's see..." Coffrey advanced the feed. The suspect retraced his steps to the entrance, walked back out the north doors and disappeared. All the while managing to keep his face away from every single camera.

"Check to see if he comes back," Walker said, his heart rate kicking up. They'd been chasing shadows for days, assuming Grey was hiding. Finding out that he'd had the balls to just walk in here in broad daylight in front of everyone was surreal.

Ivy took over control of two of the feeds, Chloe the third, while Coffrey checked the fourth. He shook his head. "I'm up to the present time now, and I don't see him come back inside."

"Same," Ivy muttered.

"Ditto," Chloe said, straightening.

"Send all footage of him to GCHQ immediately," Walker told Coffrey.

"Got it," he said, quickly typing away.

"Ivy, can you send one of these to Amber?"

"Yes." She immediately started recording some footage on her phone.

"Have your people evacuate the cathedral immediately," he said to Coffrey. "You need to lock it down right now."

Coffrey stopped, stared at him in alarm. "I can't believe we missed this. We were told there was no further threat—"

"*Now*, mate," Warwick said, then shared a loaded look with Walker before nodding at the ancient wooden door behind them. "We need to get under the floor."

"There's nothing underneath but the burial vaults, and they've all been checked several times already," Coffrey said. "I was with the MI5 agents when they did the last search."

"What about the undercroft?" Warwick said.

"It's on the other side of the cloisters, and it's used as our café," Coffrey said, shaking his head, his eyes bouncing back and forth between them all. "No one's hiding in there, believe me."

"There's nothing else? No catacombs or ancient burial vaults underneath that he could have accessed?" Walker said, desperation beating at him.

"No. A team of architects was called in just last year to do a survey for restoration work. If there was anything down there, they would have found it."

There had to be something everyone else had missed. Why would Grey risk coming in here and leaving a clue if the cathedral wasn't the target? "Let's go," he said to the others.

Back in the nave, the female volunteer was talking to more security guards. She saw Walker and the others come through the glass doors and quickly waved them over, her expression urgent.

"I just noticed something else strange," she said, pointing over at the suspect hymnal board. "The hymn numbers are all wrong. Look." She showed him the printed service sheets in her hands. "These are all the hymns listed for today's services. The ones on the board don't match any of them."

A warning buzz started at the base of Walker's neck. The numbers on the board weren't even close.

He looked at Ivy, saw the verification on her face. The suspect on the security video was definitely Grey. He'd left them another clue. "You said evensong is at five-thirty?" he said to the volunteer.

"Yes." She nodded, eyes full of worry. "The Saturday service is always very popular with locals and tourists alike."

"How many people usually attend?"

"I don't know—a few hundred at least."

A nice-size target for a terrorist looking to make a statement. And the deadline was at eighteen-hundred hours.

Putting it right smack in the middle of the evensong service when the cathedral would be full of people. Not only that, the choir was from Hatfield, the same college Laura Hawes belonged to—and Grey was an alumnus.

Walker's jaw flexed. Goddammit, they were probably standing on top of him right now.

"Get everyone out of here," he said to the woman and security members. "*Now.*"

SEVENTEEN

Ivy studied the picture of the hymnal board on her phone while Warwick, Chloe and Heath looked at it over her shoulder, thinking hard. It had to be a sign from Grey.

"What's he telling us?" Walker said.

"Not sure." They'd just completed their own sweep of the cathedral and found nothing else suspicious. Now they were standing in the middle of the large lawn known as Palace Green.

All around them, security personnel were madly trying to evacuate the cathedral, Palace Green Library, the nearby humanities buildings, as well as the castle. Students living in the castle were already streaming out of the gates looking bewildered.

From a public safety standpoint, the situation was less than ideal. Considering how few access streets there were in this area for people to use and how narrow they were, gridlock was imminent.

Walker pulled his phone from his pocket, glanced at the screen. "GCHQ says it's a ninety-plus percent chance the suspect in the video is Grey."

She didn't respond, busy looking up things on her own phone. "I'm looking at the hymn titles listed. Nothing's jumping out at me." Nothing that made sense or seemed significant enough to be a message from Grey. "Want me to check the lyrics?"

"I thought you said he's not religious," Chloe said, chewing her gum rapidly.

"He's not. He's a scientist. Physics and chem are his altars of worship—" She stopped, looked sharply at Walker as an idea hit her. "All the numbers on the hymnal board are double digits, and he used the word 'periodically' in his first message. What if they represent elements? They could be atomic numbers from the periodic table."

Surprise flickered over Walker's face for an instant, then he started typing rapidly into his phone. "My chem's rusty. Anyone up on the periodic table?"

"Me," Chloe said, snatching Ivy's phone. "Twenty-four is chromium. Thirty-nine…yttrium. Fifteen is phosphorus, and twenty-two is titanium."

Ivy quickly scrawled it all down on a small notepad she'd had in her pocket and the others gathered around to study the list. Grey was sending them a message with this. They were close. Had to be.

"Chromium, yttrium, phosphorus, and titanium," Walker repeated, then glanced around the tight circle they'd made around Ivy. Everyone was deep in concentration.

"That…doesn't help us," Heath said, frowning at the names and numbers she'd written. "Does it?" He looked at Chloe.

"Not really," she said. "Damn, I really thought we were on to something."

"Is he listing the materials he's used in a new bomb?" Warwick asked her.

"The phosphorus and titanium, possibly. The other two, not

so much, and the titanium is expensive because it's a pretty rare metal compared to a lot of others. And yttrium's *really* rare. But Grey's got a double PhD, so maybe he got his hands on some and figured out a way to use them all in a custom device." She shrugged, looking as puzzled as everyone else. "Why would he give us an ingredient list though?"

Ivy bit back an irritated growl. Shit, *another* dead end when she'd been certain they were about to crack this thing. "It has to mean something," she said, her brain working overtime, madly trying to pick it all apart and make sense of it.

Grey had buried a pointed message in here, she was sure of it. And the hostages' lives depended on figuring it out —quickly.

Grey wouldn't have made the clue so hard that they wouldn't decipher it. What would be the point in that? Her gut said they were still on the right track. So close to cracking this. They just weren't looking at it the right way.

Maybe there was another angle. Maybe… "Wait, what if he meant us to use the elemental symbols?"

Walker looked at Chloe. "Can you—"

She was already nodding as she grabbed the pad from Ivy and started writing them down next to what Ivy already had there. "Cr. Y. P. Ti."

The hair on Ivy's arms stood on end. *Bingo*. "Crypt," she blurted, looking up at Walker as an electric flash of excitement shot through her. For an instant, she saw pure admiration in his eyes before his professional mask dropped back in place. "He's gone underground. Literally."

"But they already told us there isn't a crypt," Chloe said.

"There has to be, and he's there waiting," Ivy insisted. "Or it's…"

"A trap," Chloe finished.

Didn't matter. Either way, they had to get down there.

"I'm calling it in," Walker said, putting his phone to his ear. "In the meantime, we need to figure out how the hell to get to him."

~

FORTY MINUTES later they'd updated the MI5, US officials and local police about what they'd discovered. Ivy was growing more agitated by the minute.

The whole manhunt had taken on a new urgency, but no one seemed to have any clue how Grey had gotten under the cathedral. Adding to the confusion, evacuations of the cathedral and surrounding buildings continued, all the lanes and access points now clogged with people and emergency vehicles blocking off the area.

"We have to get under the cathedral," Walker said to the female MI5 officer, having already argued his point to everyone with any clout. The Durham DCI was with them too, but hadn't offered any helpful insight so far.

The woman shook her head. "There's no way to access beneath the cathedral. We've searched everywhere for an entrance. And there is no crypt. The closest thing is the undercroft, which is—"

"A café," Ivy finished impatiently. "Yeah, we know."

"There has to be," Walker argued. "A tunnel, or an access chute for maintenance somewhere. Maybe one that hasn't been used in a long time, possibly centuries. Wherever it is, Grey found it."

The woman shook her head again and opened her mouth to argue some more, but Warwick interrupted. "What about the old legend of the tunnel running under the peninsula from here down to the mayor's office in Market Square?" he said to the Durham DCI.

"What legend?" Ivy demanded, heart beating faster.

The DCI blinked. "It's just that, legend. From way back in medieval times. Many people have searched for it over the centuries but the only thing that ever came of it was…" He trailed off, his expression shifting as though he'd just hit on something significant.

"What?" Walker pressed.

"Well, there were rumors years ago that someone found an opening behind a painting in the town hall. It had been walled up and covered with a bit of paneling to disguise it. But according to the story, when they opened it all up, the passage was completely sealed off after a few dozen yards. If there's a tunnel under there, no one found it."

Walker's jaw tightened. "Take us there. Fast."

"Follow me." Warwick took the lead.

They pushed their way through the crowd of students and tourists clogging short Owengate Street, then raced down the middle of Saddler Street and around the corner to the open square of the marketplace. The old stone buildings that made up the town hall were situated on the northwest corner, right next to St. Nicholas's Church.

At the door they quickly explained what was going on to security, who let them in and immediately locked up to prevent anyone else from entering before ushering them upstairs to a series of ornate rooms. "This is the old mayor's chambers in here," the guard said.

"Which painting is it?" Ivy asked.

"I don't know." The guard hurried to the closest one and eased the frame away from the wall to peek behind it. Everyone else fanned out to check behind the other paintings in the room.

Behind a portrait of a man from the 1600s dressed in a fur mantle with a chain of office looped around his shoulders, Ivy saw a seam cut into the wood paneling. "Think I've got something."

In seconds, Walker was next to her, lifting the massive painting off its hanger. Ivy ran her fingers along one of the seams behind it where a large rectangle had been cut into the wood. Maybe from an old repair job. When she knocked on it, it made a hollow sound.

"This side sticks out a bit. Like it's been opened recently," she said.

"Need you to check the security video for the past twenty-four hours," Walker told the guard, who rushed out of the room.

"That's definitely big enough for someone to fit through," Chloe said, feeling along with Ivy to try and find a way to open it.

"Step back," Walker said. He and Heath examined the slightly raised seam, started pushing on the opposite side. It gave a fraction of an inch. "It's hinged." He put both hands on the edge and shoved hard. When it didn't budge, Heath joined in.

"Must be locked from the inside," Heath said, straining his full strength with Walker.

"I'll find a tool." Ivy raced downstairs and came back with a crowbar from the security guard. "Here, try this." She handed it to Walker.

He wedged the forked end of it into the seam and leaned back, pulling hard, his face set. The wood panel flexed, nails creaking as he slowly pried at it.

Heath and Warwick both grabbed hold of Walker's end to lend their muscle. "On three," Warwick muttered. "One. Two. Three."

The three of them hauled backward with all their might, faces red, muscles straining. There was a metallic groan, as if whatever bolt or lock inside was protesting the invasion. The panel began to give slowly, then all at once there was a sharp snapping sound and the doorway popped open.

They stumbled backward with the force. Walker dropped the crowbar and together they muscled the doorway open.

"Is there a tunnel?" Ivy asked anxiously, marching over to see for herself. Heath moved aside and Chloe came up behind her to peer through the wall...where Warwick was shining a flashlight into what appeared to be an ancient stone passageway.

"I'll be damned," he muttered.

Ivy stared at the stone steps leading down toward ground level. The opening was narrow, would be a tight squeeze for the guys. "Let's see if this goes anywhere." She took the flashlight from Warwick and stepped through the opening.

"Wait up." Walker came after her.

She kept going. The rough stone steps curved left as they wound downward out of view. The temperature dropped noticeably as she descended. At the bottom, she found another door that stood partly ajar, a damp, dusty scent coming from whatever lay on the other side. She checked all around for any sign of a booby-trap. Pushed on it.

It stuck after opening only a handful of inches.

"Is it stuck?" Walker asked.

"Yeah." She put her shoulder to it. Managed to force it open a bit more. Just enough for her to squeeze through. She aimed the flashlight ahead to look for any other signs of danger.

"What do you see?" Walker called through the opening, the door squeaking as he tried to force it open.

Her heart skipped a beat. "It's a tunnel. But it's partly blocked by debris."

She stepped farther inside, heard him shoving at the door again as she squeezed past the obstruction someone had partially removed. Grey? "Oh, wow."

The tunnel widened ahead, the roughly carved stone floor sloping downward slightly. Could this thing really go right under the peninsula all the way up to the castle and cathedral?

"I'm through," she called back and kept moving forward, aiming the flashlight ahead to light her way. It was noticeably colder here, damp and chilly.

"Ivy, wait," Walker called from behind her. Still behind the door. "Let me call it in."

"I'm just taking a look to see how far it goes. Looks like it keeps going under the marketplace toward the castle." She followed the tunnel as it suddenly angled left.

The door behind her finally gave with a scraping groan. "I'm through," Walker said.

Squinting in the gloom ahead, she saw something imprinted in the dust on the ground. "I see footprints." Fresh ones. And were those thin tire marks as well?

She slowed, took a cautious step around the corner and over a low pile of rock as she aimed the flashlight ahead of her. The tunnel appeared to continue—

Something caught on her ankle on the other side of the obstruction.

Her gaze snapped down, insides freezing as the quiet, telltale click filled the confined space and she saw the thin wire she'd just tripped.

Oh, shit... "Get back!" she yelled.

She barely got the warning out before an explosion ripped through the air behind her.

A blinding light pierced her eyes, the small blast wave knocking her to her knees and shaking the floor. Dust and rubble tumbled down, filling the air with a choking cloud of dust.

Coughing, she fumbled around for the flashlight.

"Ivy!" Walker's voice penetrated the gloom, sounding muffled and far away compared to moments before.

She crawled forward, ears and head ringing. Reached out blindly in the direction she'd come from. Her groping hand met a wall of jagged rock and debris that blocked the passage right up to the ceiling. "I'm okay," she called back, searching for a way through the blockage. She had no idea how much rock had come down between them.

"Don't move," Walker commanded, voice still muffled but closer now. "Stay where you are, we'll get you out."

"I'm—" She whirled as a hand clapped something over her nose and mouth.

A cloth. Caught the vague impression of a man's silhouette outlined by the beam of her flashlight and felt the steely strength in the arm around her neck.

She drove her elbow up and back, going for his head as she turned hard, trying to use her momentum to throw him off. But there was no room to move and it was already too late. She'd already sucked in a breath, the sweet, distinctive scent of ether.

Or chloroform.

The man grunted when her elbow struck but didn't release his hold. Ivy held her breath, tried to rip free of his grip but the chemical she'd inhaled was already stealing through her bloodstream. Weakness stole through her at alarming speed, sapping her muscles.

In desperation, she dropped onto her side and swept a leg out, knocking his feet from under him. The man released her. A heartbeat later his weight slammed down on her, knocking the precious remaining air from her lungs.

Ivy couldn't move. Couldn't fight back or even draw breath to scream a warning to Walker on the other side of the wall separating them.

Her attacker's shadowy face appeared above her as her

eyelids began to fall. A bolt of fear shot through her when she saw that unmistakable hard smile.

"So you managed to figure it out after all. I'm so glad," Isaac Grey said, his words registering only distantly before blackness engulfed her.

EIGHTEEN

"Son of a *bitch*," Walker snarled, rushing forward to rip some of the rubble away from the top of the tunnel. The explosion had completely blocked the tunnel, the ceiling caved in on the other side.

He couldn't see a damn thing, his flashlight useless with all the dust filling the air, and now he couldn't hear her either. "Ivy!"

No answer.

"Ivy, can you hear me?" he yelled. His heart thundered in his ears as he tried to claw his way through to her. Was she hurt? She'd answered him initially. Christ, he never should have let her go first. Should have hauled her back before she'd squeezed through that fucking door.

As he dug, all he could picture was her lying buried under the rubble on the other side of the blockage. It made him crazy that he couldn't get to her. Crazy that he didn't know how thick this was. If she was hurt and trapped, she could run out of air.

He worked frantically, his shoulders almost touching the narrow walls. There'd barely been room to move around in the tunnel before the explosion. Clearing all this rock out of the way was costing time they didn't have.

"Ivy, say something!" He broke off, coughing as the dust clogged his lungs and throwing an arm over his face to help block out more.

"Can you hear her?" Chloe called out from behind him up the tunnel.

He finally caught his breath enough to answer. "No, and the whole damn tunnel is blocked with a wall of rock. Have Warwick call it in and request backup. I need help to clear the blockage. And get a firearms team here too." It would take time to get a specialized unit assembled and deployed.

"On it!"

Walker kept working frantically. Grey had done this. Had set this trap deliberately. Might even be on the other side of this wall right now with Ivy.

He still couldn't hear anything from the other side, and the dust was too damn thick. He couldn't breathe or see.

He wrenched off his jacket and button-down and folded it into a bandana to cover his nose and mouth, leaving him in just a T-shirt as he attacked the mound of rubble again.

Warwick and Heath both appeared at his back moments later, quickly reached past him to grab chunks of rock and toss them behind them down the tunnel to spread out the layer of debris and give them room to move.

"We'll get her," Warwick said to him. "No worries, mate."

Walker didn't answer, focused on ripping through this fucking wall so he could at least see her. Fear swelled in his chest, guilt crushing his dust-filled lungs. He'd left her last night in anger without a backward glance. Stormed out on her after cutting her loose because of what she'd confessed.

None of that mattered now. She was in trouble. She needed him. He wouldn't fail her.

He felt sick about last night, the stricken look on her face before he'd left seared into his memory.

"Shit, how much of the tunnel collapsed?" Heath said, working fast.

"Dunno." Each chunk of rock they cleared away revealed more behind it. With the three of them working so quickly, Walker had hoped to punch through enough to make a partial opening and get a visual on Ivy. But the charge that had brought all this down must have been bigger than he realized.

"Fire team is being deployed," Chloe called down. Her voice seemed closer now, as if she was heading down the tunnel toward them. "Made any headway yet?"

"No," Walker bit out, sweat breaking out across his skin.

"Need another hand?" she asked, her voice floating toward them.

"Yeah. Have someone get me a goddamn weapon," he snapped, his heart in his throat.

He was going to get Ivy out of there, no matter what it took. And if his gut was right and Grey was on the other side waiting somewhere…

Walker would end him personally.

∼

IVY WAS VAGUELY aware of sounds around her as she slowly came back to consciousness. Her head was heavy, her eyelids glued shut.

She tried to lift her head and peel her eyes open. Her mouth was dry and there was a dull throbbing in her skull.

It took all her will to pry her eyelids apart a fraction of an inch. It was dim in the room. Someone close by was crying. Softly. A broken, defeated sound that echoed off the walls and ceiling.

She shivered, her eyes slowly focusing on her surroundings. Her mind was fuzzy. She remembered being in the tunnel. An explosion.

Grey.

A rush of adrenaline obliterated the remnants of whatever he'd drugged her with. Her spine snapped taut and she immediately tried to raise her hands—only to find that they were tied down to the arms of a chair.

Her feet were bound too, and there was something pressing on her chest. Something hard and restrictive.

She could see the silhouettes of two other people close by. Both also on chairs, the position of their arms suggesting they were tied up the same way.

She squinted at the first one. More resolve punched through her when she saw the young woman's face. Laura Hawes. That meant the other figure must be Chad. Grey had secured them all to different support columns holding up the vaulted ceiling.

Laura was crying. Her shoulders jerked, soft gasps marking each ragged sob she was trying so hard to smother. She met Ivy's gaze across the dim space, started crying harder.

At a movement in her peripheral vision, Ivy's gaze snapped left.

Grey. It was too dim to see well but she could see him clearly enough to identify him as he crouched to the left and slightly behind her. Tinkering with something. There appeared to be a kind of wagon beside him full of supplies.

That explained the tire marks she'd seen in the tunnel earlier. He'd probably transported her and the others here in it. Given his ALS, there was no way he could have dragged them all down the length of the tunnel otherwise.

"Where are we?" she demanded, her raspy voice carrying across the vaulted room.

He turned to look at her in mild surprise. "You're awake."

"Where. *Are* we?"

"The crypt under the cathedral. But you already guessed that."

She pictured a map of the Durham peninsula. The cathedral was a good seven-hundred meters or so in a straight line from the town hall. Grey had ambushed her close to the marketplace. Had he been waiting close to the tripwire, hoping someone would trigger it?

"How did you get to me so fast from here?" she demanded.

"Sensor I buried in the wall near the start of the tunnel."

Shit, she'd missed that too, along with the damn tripwire.

He set down whatever he'd been working on and turned to face her, blocking her view of what was behind him. She was guessing a bomb. "I was beginning to worry no one would put the clues together in time to find the tunnel. I'm glad you did."

Psycho. "Let Laura and Chad go. They're not responsible for what happened to you."

"Can't. Too late for that now. Too late for any of us."

Chad shifted in his chair and Laura made a heartbreaking sound.

"No, it's not," Ivy said, reining in her anger. "You can stop this right now."

"No. The timer's already started. See?" He reached out and flicked a switch on a portable lantern she hadn't seen, the beam of light slicing through the darkness.

She glanced down at herself. Her heart lurched when she saw what was causing the restriction around her ribs.

An explosive vest. She could see the wires sticking out of it. From the shape of what was tucked inside the various pockets on the exterior, she was guessing plastic explosives.

Laura and Chad each wore one as well. From the way they

were all tied to the columns, it looked as though Grey's plan was to collapse the ceiling when the devices detonated and bring down at least part of the great cathedral with it.

She looked up at Grey, the shock and anger turning to hatred that hardened inside her like steel. "So this is it? You plan to blow us all up and try to bring down part of the cathedral?"

"In part. But Walker will be coming for you. He'll try, anyway."

A wave of cold sluiced through her. "You did this to target him?"

He shrugged. "No. But he's a very welcome and fitting addition to my retirement party, seeing as he's the one who landed me in a Russian prison."

"Walker isn't responsible for what happened to you in Moscow," she told him flatly. "I am."

Grey whirled to confront her, his eerie stare boring into her. "What?" he asked in a low, deadly voice. In the shadows cast by the lantern light he looked almost cadaverous, the hollows under his sunken cheeks and eyes nearly black.

"I tipped the Russians off about your meeting with Nikolaev."

He straightened, the muscles in his thin face beginning to quiver. "Do you know what I went through there? What they did to me because of you?" He stalked over to her, holding up the backs of his hands to show her the web-like scars tracking over his skin and fingers.

"Yes."

His breathing was shallow as he stared down at her, rage popping off him in a toxic cloud she could practically smell. His hand flashed out, the crack of his palm against her cheek loud in the vaulted room. She covered a wince, used the pain to center her as she met his lethal gaze once more, tasting blood on her tongue.

"You don't know," he spat. "You have no *idea* what I went through! What you and their fathers sentenced me to by disavowing me and abandoning me to my fate." He thrust a finger at Laura and Chad.

"Laura and Chad had nothing to do with any of it. They're innocent, and you know it. You've got me now. Let them go."

He stood there glaring down at her for several endless moments while his shallow breathing filled the air. Allowing her to see the epic struggle he was waging to get control of himself.

"You need to let them go," she repeated.

"Shut up," he snapped. "Don't say another bloody word or I'll take out your punishment on them." He nodded at Laura and Chad.

Ivy clamped her jaw shut, loathing him. Before, she'd had empathy for what he'd gone through. But not now. Nothing could ever justify what he was doing to these kids.

Grey spun on his heel, staggered a bit before he caught himself and went back to whatever he'd been working on. The main device, she was guessing. Wired into everything else and holding the largest amount of explosive power.

She kept her gaze pinned on him as she planned her next move. He didn't know who she was. Had no clue that she was trained, let alone to what level.

Didn't realize his life was in danger because he'd made the fatal error of leaving her hands bound in front of her.

Arrogant asshole.

He still wasn't looking at her. She shifted her right leg slightly, testing to see if her blade was still there. Felt the reassuring outline of the sheath still strapped to the inside of her calf beneath her pant leg.

With her hands zap-strapped to the arms of the chair, she couldn't reach it. Yet. But she could move her hips, and that was all the room she needed.

Walker and the others would come for her. If she could get free and subdue Grey before they got here, she could help secure the room and buy the others time to get through the rubble the explosion had dumped into the tunnel.

Watching Grey to ensure she didn't get caught in the act, she braced her feet flat on the ground and shifted her hips up and to the right. She moved slowly, careful not to make any sound, ready to freeze at the slightest indication that Grey was going to glance her way.

Inch by excruciating inch she strained, contorting her body until her straining fingertips brushed the edge of her belt buckle. A little more maneuvering and she managed to grasp the end of the leather tab sticking through it.

Her muscles strained as she carefully undid the buckle and slid the belt free of the belt loops, then threaded the strip of leather between the left chair arm and the plastic strap binding her wrist.

Grey muttered and moved as though he was about to turn around. She froze, heart stuttering. If he caught her like this there was no way to hide it.

But he didn't turn toward her. Still seemed oblivious that she had moved at all.

Exhaling silently, working as quickly as she could without making any sound, she refastened the belt into a loop with her left hand, then stopped. This next part had to be timed just right.

There was zero room for error. No second chances. If she failed to free herself and get out of her chair before he could react, she would die. And so would the others.

Not happening.

Ivy focused on the next series of movements. Planning everything carefully and breaking it down into the fewest steps required.

Grey still had his back to her as he reached into whatever was in the wagon bed. Laura was still sniffling quietly but she was now watching Ivy. So was Chad.

She shook her head at them in silent warning to stay quiet and not give her away. Then, shooting one final look at Grey to ensure his back was still to her, she bent her knees, lifted her booted feet high enough to catch in the bottom of the circle she'd made with the belt.

Now.

One quick shove with her legs and the tie around her left hand snapped.

After that, everything else seemed to happen in slow motion.

Alerted by the snap, Grey started to turn toward her as Ivy plunged her left hand down to reach under her pant leg and pull her knife. With one quick slice, she severed the tie holding her ankles together, them immediately arced the blade up to slice through the tie binding her right hand to the chair arm.

Free at last, she lunged from her chair, knife poised in her fist just as Grey faced her. His eyes widened in shock.

Then his hand went to the pocket on his jacket and withdrew something.

Her heart seized when she saw what was in his hand and realized her mistake. He must have a suicide vest on beneath his jacket—because he was holding what could only be a dead man's switch.

God, no…

There was no time to stop and think. She had to disarm him now or it was over. And she needed both hands to do it.

She dropped the knife and dove at him. Managed to clamp both hands around his right fist to hold his thumb down on the button.

Temporarily preventing him from detonating his vest and killing them all.

NINETEEN

Walker crept along the tunnel at a quick pace, flashlight aimed at the ground in front of him and the pistol Chloe had given him held in his left hand. He didn't know how she'd got it and didn't care.

Not when he was desperate to get to Ivy.

The instant they'd cleared enough rubble away for him to squeeze through the opening, he'd left the others to clear away more to make room for the specialized firearms team and first responders once they arrived.

Peering through that opening for those first few heartbeats, he'd been so afraid of finding Ivy buried under rock and either dead or dying. Instead, all he'd found was her flashlight. He was sure someone had taken her, and he was betting Grey. With her life in danger, every second counted.

He had to find her and get her out of here.

He had no idea how far he'd walked but he guessed well over half a mile before he saw light up ahead through the darkness, coming from around a slight bend in the tunnel. Faint, but enough to send a fresh surge of adrenaline punching through him.

He shoved his flashlight in his pants pocket and moved toward it as fast as he dared, double gripping the pistol, right index finger resting on the trigger guard. While he wanted to burst in there, drop Grey where he stood with a double tap to the chest and one to the head, he had to be cautious. He didn't know what Grey had set up or what he'd find waiting for him ahead.

Just then a scuffle broke out, followed by shouts of alarm. Walker broke into a run, came around another bend and saw that the tunnel opened up into a room of some sort.

But when he saw what was happening in it, his insides clenched in terror.

Ivy was wrestling around on the stone floor with Grey, both of them grappling for something in Grey's hand. And they both had explosives vests on.

"Ivy!" he yelled. The two other hostages were strapped to chairs, also in vests.

"He's got his thumb on a DMS!" she shouted back, face red with exertion as she twisted on the stone floor with Grey, both hands locked around the device he held.

Fuck. Walker shoved the weapon into the back of his pants and rushed toward her, unable to fire without endangering her or risking setting off the vests. Grey had this whole place wired to blow. One wrong move, and it would kill everyone in here.

"No!" she cried, the urgency in her voice freezing him in place.

He darted a quick look around him, afraid he'd missed a tripwire or something. Seeing nothing, he refocused on Ivy.

She was on her back now, legs locked around Grey's as they thrashed around. "Get the hostages out of here!"

No way. He was saving her first. He took a step toward her, picking the moment when he would pounce on top of Grey and take control of the trigger switch.

"Walker, get them out!" She grunted when Grey knocked her in the face with his shoulder, but didn't let go of his hand. "He's got this whole place rigged to a timer. They're just kids, get them out!"

His gaze shot past her for an instant to the device attached to the central pillar, and the various wires snaking out of it. He could see a digital timer on the top of it from where he stood, and it was counting down.

"Too late," Grey panted, trying to wrest his hand free from her. "All…gonna…die."

Walker looked back at Ivy as the magnitude of the situation sank in, his gut dropping like a rock. He so badly wanted to walk up and end this now by putting a bullet through Grey's head, but he couldn't. If they were going to have a prayer at dismantling this terror network, they needed to bring Grey in alive.

There was no way for Walker to take over now without risking detonating Grey's vest, and maybe all the other devices with it.

And Ivy knew *exactly* what would happen once he got the hostages clear. Knew that Grey would be even more enraged and unpredictable. That she felt responsible for all of this and was risking her life to try and buy enough time to give the hostages a chance.

And he knew that she was prepared to sacrifice herself to make it happen.

It gutted him. Especially after what he'd done and how he'd treated her last night. They never would have found Grey without her figuring out the final clue.

There was no fucking way he was leaving her.

Running footsteps echoed off the tunnel walls behind him before he could move. He glanced back in time to see Warwick, Chloe and Heath appear at the entrance to the room, all of them stopping short when they saw him standing poised halfway to Ivy.

"Grey's got a DMS," he said quickly, watching Grey's every move. Dammit, there had to be a way to subdue him without risking knocking Grey's or Ivy's hands off the trigger. "I don't know whether the vests are all linked somehow."

"Hurry," Ivy gritted out, sweat shining on her flushed face. "Get Chloe. She has to disarm the hostages' vests first."

"I'm right here." Chloe stepped out from behind Heath, took in the scene with a single sweeping glance and immediately started toward Laura while Warwick went to Chad.

Walker forced himself to leave Ivy for the moment and rushed past her and Grey, looking for something to subdue Grey with that wouldn't risk triggering his or Ivy's vests.

"Cloth," Ivy blurted, panting now.

"What cloth?" he asked, frantically searching in a pile of gear Grey must have brought earlier.

"Chloro—form." She grunted as Grey landed a punch to her face.

White-hot rage pulsed through him. For a heartbeat he almost dove at Grey but managed to lock his emotions down and continue his search, coming up with the cloth and the bottle of chloroform. It was almost empty.

Walker emptied the contents onto the cloth and hurried back to Ivy and Grey. Chloe, Heath and Warwick were still working on disarming the hostages' vests.

It was clear Ivy was tired. ALS may have weakened Grey, but he was juiced, probably on something, and putting up one hell of a fight. Walker needed to keep him still before he risked this next move.

"Hurry," she growled between clenched teeth. With a snarl, she twisted hard, wrenching Grey onto his back.

Walker seized his chance, dropping to his knees beside them

to clamp a hand over Grey's nose and mouth. "Night night, asshole."

Grey's eyes bulged, pure hatred on his face as he stared up at him, trying to thrash his way free. Walker didn't budge, his free arm coming down across the front of Grey's chest to pin him in place. "You got the switch pinned down?" he said to Ivy.

"Yeah," she gasped. He could feel her muscles shaking.

He kept his eyes on Grey's hand, clutched between Ivy's where she was clamping his thumb down on the trigger so hard her fingers were white.

Grey bucked weakly, his movements slowing. His eyes rolled back, muscles going slack as the anesthetic did its work.

The instant he went limp, Walker kept the cloth over Grey's face with his left hand and grabbed hold of Ivy's with his right, adding pressure to help her. "He's out."

Ivy groaned and dropped her head forward slightly, eyes closing in relief as she fought for breath. Walker got his first good look at her vest.

It was identical to Grey's. Different than the hostages' vests.

He studied the wires crisscrossing Ivy's torso, trying to figure out the best way to disarm it. He wanted it the hell off her so he could get her to safety.

"I think…" Ivy paused, dragged in a breath. "I think my vest might be linked to his."

Walker went cold all over. He looked up at her, an invisible anvil dropping onto the middle of his chest.

Grey had planned all this out. Had hoped Walker or someone else would step into the tunnel entrance so he could trap them, knock them out and strap them into this matching vest.

He glanced over at the timer, the numbers ticking down way too fast. Only thirty-something minutes remained. Not a lot of time to disarm everything, even for an expert like Chloe.

He was damn glad she was here. Without her, they'd be screwed. "What's the status on the response team?"

"Dunno," Warwick answered, still investigating Chad's vest. "They're calling in teams now but it'll take them a while to get organized and down here. With the amount of debris in the tunnel, who knows how long they'll be."

Dammit. "Chloe, what's the status on those vests?" He kept his hand locked around Ivy's, trying to figure out a way to take over and let her rest.

"Not too complicated," she answered, crouched down at Laura Hawes's feet. "They're not linked to anything else that I can see. Gonna take me a few minutes to kill the secondary and power source though."

"How long?"

"Six, seven minutes maybe."

That left precious little time to defuse Ivy's and Grey's vests, then the main device on the center pillar. And he didn't know how long Grey would stay under. The cloth was already drying under his hand, the chloroform evaporating. And the bottle was empty. "Hurry."

"Hurrying." She popped a small flashlight between her lips and pulled out a pair of wire cutters. "Heath, hold this flap out of the way for me."

Warwick came over and crouched down next to Walker. "Here," he said, ripping pieces off a roll of duct tape he'd found. "We'll clamp the DMS down with this."

"Good." Walker carefully shifted his grip around Ivy's hands, making sure Grey's thumb was still being pressed down hard on the button. She was tired, still catching her breath, her knuckles white from the strain of holding the DMS in place. Her hands had to be numb by now.

"I'm gonna slide my thumbs under yours and over his. As

soon as I do, let go and move back," he told her, simultaneously terrified for her and awed by her guts.

She should never have been in this position. He should have been the first into the tunnel. He should be the one in that vest right now instead of her.

"Ready?" His eyes remained locked on their combined hands as he willed her not to give up. *Hold on, sweetness. We'll get through this.*

"Yes." Her voice was steady.

"Hold still." He began slowly forcing his thumb between her fingers and Grey's thumb, careful not to jar anything. Grey was still unconscious but Walker doubted he'd stay that way for long. They had to be quick.

Squeezing Grey's lax wrist with one hand, he felt his way through the combined grips with his other until he found the spot where Grey's thumb was clamped over the trigger button.

Walker inhaled slowly, getting ready to make his move and never more aware that Grey was an explosives expert. He could have calibrated the trigger in any number of ways or made it sensitive enough to detonate the device at the slightest change in pressure. Grey was dangerous, but not stupid. Walker was playing the odds that it wasn't that sensitive.

Shifting his grip slightly, he angled Grey's hand around enough to slide his thumb into place. "Now," he bit out. Ivy hesitated only a second before letting go. Walker jammed his thumb down hard over Grey's, holding the button down tight.

He, Ivy and Warwick all let out a collective breath of relief when nothing happened. "Hurry," he said to Warwick, who had the strips of tape ready. "He could come around at any time." The chloroform would be nearly evaporated by now.

Warwick leaned in and made short work of taping Grey's thumb down, then wrapped his entire hand in duct tape so that he wouldn't have a prayer of moving any of his fingers when he regained consciousness. "Alright," he said.

Satisfied the trigger wouldn't move, Walker grabbed Ivy and pulled her away from Grey. "Chloe, what's your status?"

She was kneeling beside Chad now. Laura was leaning against the wall at the entrance to the room. "One last cut," Chloe said, snipping at another wire on Chad's vest. She quickly lifted it off him and pulled him from his chair.

"They're both pretty dehydrated," Heath said from beside her. "And in shock."

Walker glanced from Chad to Laura, decided there was no way in hell they were getting out of here on their own. "Get them back to the town hall," he told Heath as Chloe rushed over to kneel beside Ivy.

Heath shook his head, expression tightening. "I'm not leaving Chloe."

"We're running out of time and I need both her and Warwick here. *Go*."

"Go, Heath," Chloe said, studying Ivy's and Grey's vests.

It was clear Heath didn't like it, but he nodded and hurried over to wrap an arm around her from behind and press a kiss to the top of her head. "I'm coming straight back."

She nodded, still focused on her work. "I know. Love you."

"Love you too." He turned and went to Laura, bent and hoisted her over his shoulder. "Let's go," he said to Chad, and they disappeared into the darkness of the tunnel.

Chloe looked up at Ivy, gave her a smile. "You said you think both these are linked somehow?"

"Maybe."

"What about the main device? Did he say anything?"

"No."

Chloe got up and went to the main device, looking everything over with her expert eye while the seconds continued to count down. Under twenty minutes left now.

Walker kept his hand over Grey's nose and mouth and his other on Ivy's shoulder, needing to touch her. Hoping it gave her some small measure of comfort as both he and Warwick examined the vests, trying to find a solution to disarming them.

Chloe came back a few minutes later, and from the set look on her face it wasn't good news.

"What?" Ivy said.

"He's got an electronic device linking both your vests with the main device. So they all have to be disarmed individually before the timer runs out, and at the exact same moment…or everything goes off at once."

TWENTY

Ivy had only felt this level of fear once before in her life.

She'd lost consciousness several times when Tarasov's thugs had tried to beat her to death, but each time she surfaced, the terror forking through her was so intense it was all she could do not to scream.

Lying on the cold, wet pavement of the alley later, she'd only been aware of the single thought blaring in her mind.

I don't want to die.

The difference between then and now was, the first time she'd wanted to live out of a sense of vengeance. Now it was because she had so much to live for. And that made the fear and grief twisting inside her so much worse.

She didn't want to die. Not then, and certainly not now. Not when she'd finally been able to step out of the shadows to reunite with her sisters. Not now that she'd found Walker.

He might be mad as hell at her. Might even hate her a little. Yet here he was, risking his life by staying at her side as the minutes ticked past, each second measured on the digital timer only yards away.

His solid, steady presence penetrated the fear enough to

allow her to hold on while he, Warwick and Chloe all hunkered around her trying to find a way to kill the DMS on Grey's vest.

"Just gonna move you a bit more," he said, gently turning her onto her side so Chloe could get a better look at the wiring snaking up her ribs. He kept his hand on her shoulder, the warmth of it slowly seeping into her skin.

She closed her eyes, fought to focus inward and control her pulse and breathing. But no matter how hard she tried, her heart refused to obey, continuing to pound against her ribs with bruising force. All she could think about was the seconds ticking past, and that the others were risking their lives to try to save her.

It was insane, three people all risking their lives this way just to try and save one.

"Okay, I think I see what he's done," Chloe said, breaking the awful tension. "But I need to do a thorough examination of the main device first. Warwick, come with me."

Warwick jumped up and hurried over to the central column with her.

Walker squeezed Ivy's shoulder gently. "How you doing?"

She opened her eyes to look up at him. How was she doing? She was scared to death and her heart was breaking. She hated that he and the others were risking their lives for her. "Holding on."

"Good. It's gonna be okay. As soon as Chloe figures out the procedure, we'll stop all this and get you out of here."

Just then, Grey twitched and made a garbled sound.

Walker pulled the cloth away from Grey's face. "He's aspirating."

Moving fast, he released her and rolled Grey to his side. Without the chloroform being inhaled, Grey was regaining consciousness, but choking. They had to at least try to keep him alive so he could be prosecuted for all he'd done.

"What's happening?" Chloe asked.

"Probably his ALS. Weakens and makes his swallowing muscles spasm." Walker swept a finger in Grey's mouth, angled his jaw. "How much time left?" he demanded of Chloe.

"Just over six minutes."

Oh, shit…

Grey finally stopped choking. "Airway's clear," he said. "I'm gonna put him back out." He clamped the cloth back in place over Grey's nose and mouth, but it was anyone's guess if it would do any good at this point.

It seemed like an eternity before Grey's eyes rolled back and finally he went lax.

But it had cost them precious time they didn't have.

"How long now?" Walker asked.

"Almost five minutes."

"Let's go," Walker said to her, his tone low, urgent.

"Okay, on my count, you're going to cut the yellow wire running up the left side of the vest. Doesn't matter where, but we all have to cut at the exact same time. Got it?"

"Got it," he and Warwick answered.

"On three." She poised her wire cutters over a wire on the main device. "Ready? One. Two. *Three*."

Ivy flinched as Walker cut the wire on her vest. Expelled the breath she hadn't realized she'd been holding until now.

She looked up into Walker's face. He was completely focused on what he was doing while Chloe guided them through the next cut.

"One. Two. *Three*."

She flinched again. Couldn't control the shivers sweeping through her. Jolting her muscles and making her jaw twitch. "S-sorry," she whispered to Walker.

"You're fine. It's gonna be fine," he said, intent on his work.

"Black wire across the top now. Show me," Chloe said,

checking to make sure both men indicated the correct wire before turning back to her device. "Okay. Here we go."

Three cuts.

Four.

Five.

With each one, the stress continued to climb. She kept her eyes closed, all her energy focused on staying as still as possible.

"How m-many m-more?" she said in the next pause. She was so damn cold now. Her insides coated with ice.

"Three."

Did they even have enough time left?

She opened her eyes and grabbed Walker's arm, bringing his deep blue gaze to her. "Go," she whispered. "Just go. Go, all of you, it's okay."

"No," he said flatly. "It's almost over, Ivy. Just hang in there another minute and we'll have you free."

She shook her head, the fear taking hold now, breaking through her control. "You have Shae," she said in a tight voice. "You have to make it back to her."

"I will. With you."

Ivy opened her mouth to argue, sure she'd misheard or at least misunderstood what he'd just said, but Chloe's command for the next cut stopped her. So she clenched her jaw. Hung on through the next cut.

"Ninety-six seconds," Chloe said.

It was too much. "I'm not worth it," she blurted to Walker. "This is my fault, you know it is. Chloe, Warwick, please! Just go, all of you get out while you still—"

"I'm not going anywhere," Walker said, and it broke her that he was willing to die to save her—even after what she'd done.

"Sorry, babe, you're stuck with us," Chloe added. "Now be

quiet and let us work. On my mark, green wire. One. Two. *Three.*"

Snip.

Ivy jerked, pressed her lips hard together to bite back a sob.

"One more," Walker said, rubbing a hand up and down her arm. "Just one more and we're outta here."

"Last cut, red wire," Chloe announced. "Ready? One. Two. Three."

Snip.

Walker grabbed the front of the vest. Her eyes flew open as he ripped the Velcro straps apart and yanked the vest off her, tossing it aside.

Her heart lurched as she looked over at Chloe. Was that it? Was it over?

"Ah, shit," Chloe muttered, staring down at the device.

A split second later, a sharp beeping started.

"There's another fail-safe," Chloe blurted. "We've got thirty seconds. Move, move!" She leaped up and raced for the tunnel.

Ivy's heart constricted. *Oh my God.* They were *all* going to die because they'd stayed to help her.

Walker grabbed her, wrenched her to her feet. "Run!" he yelled, shoving her ahead of him.

They'd made it less than thirty yards and around a slight bend when a deafening explosion blasted through the air. A wall of hot air hit her in the back, punching through her chest.

Then she was airborne. Flying through the darkness.

She hit the ground hard on her stomach.

A split second later, a hard weight covered her back. Strong arms wrapping around her head as a hailstorm of debris and dust rained down on them.

TWENTY-ONE

Walker opened his eyes in the darkness, still on top of Ivy. His flashlight had rolled to the side of the tunnel, its shortened beam now shining up the rough stone wall. The air was full of dust but there was no wall of debris raining down on them and the rumbling from behind them had stopped.

He pushed up on his elbows, squinting down at Ivy. "You okay?" he asked, anxiously searching her face. Chloe and Warwick were stirring nearby.

She winced and shifted beneath him. "Yeah, I think so. You?"

"I'm good." Banged up and his head was ringing like a bell, but overall, damn lucky it wasn't a whole lot worse. They were all damn lucky.

Even Grey.

He'd been granted the quick death he didn't deserve. The universe had a fucking twisted sense of karma.

He eased off Ivy, bit back a groan as every bruise and sore muscle protested. Just as he got to his knees, running footsteps came from down the tunnel, a faint ray of light bobbing around off the walls.

"Chloe!" Heath yelled, his voice echoing from down the other end of the tunnel.

"Here," she called back wearily. "I'm okay. You guys all right?" she asked the rest of them as she rolled over and sat up.

"Aye," Warwick muttered, getting to his knees a few yards away from Walker and Ivy.

Heath came pounding up to them, his flashlight aimed at the ground so he wouldn't blind them. He dropped beside Chloe and grabbed her shoulder, stopping her from getting up. "Stay still," he ordered. "Let me look at you first."

"No, I'm good, I swear. The blast wave just knocked us over, that's all."

He ignored her, taking her face in his hands to peer into her eyes, intent on satisfying himself that she truly was okay.

Walker shifted, straddling Ivy, and grabbed the flashlight to check her out as well. There was blood on her lower lip and chin and it looked like she had a bruise forming on her left cheek.

He gently ran his thumb over her lip, a deep, black rage forming in his gut. "He hit you?"

"It doesn't matter. He's burning in hell now where he belongs." Then she curled her fingers around his wrists, staring up into his eyes. "You stayed," she whispered in a ragged voice, blinking fast. "You have Shae depending on you and you stayed with me, even though you hate me now. Why?"

His stomach clenched in shame. She'd really believed he would leave her partly because he'd been angry with her. Abandon her to her fate to save himself, just leave her sitting there waiting to die alone. Jesus.

"I would never have left you," he told her in a low voice, not caring if the others overheard. "And I don't hate you."

"You…don't?"

"No. I could never hate you." His feelings were pretty much

the extreme opposite of that. And there were so many other things he needed to say to her, but not here. When he told her everything that was weighing on his mind, he wanted them to be alone with no interruptions. "Can you get up?"

"Yes." She allowed him to pull her into a sitting position, then he went dead still when she wrapped her arms around his ribs and pressed her face to his chest.

Suppressing a groan of relief, Walker tucked his chin into the curve of her shoulder and held her tight, closing his eyes while his heart rate slowed.

That had been way too fucking close back there, several times over. The adrenaline whiplash was hitting him hard now, making him lightheaded and a little unsteady as his heart rate stabilized. So he knelt there and took the comfort Ivy offered, tried to give it back double as he held her to him.

"You guys hurt?" Heath asked as he started toward them.

"No," Walker answered.

"Good. Then how about we all get the hell out of here, huh?"

"Yep." He was looking forward to leaving this hellhole behind them forever.

Walker squeezed Ivy one last time before getting to his feet and pulling her up after him. He kept hold of her hand as he led her down the tunnel behind Heath, Chloe and Warwick. He'd come so close to losing her and now he didn't want to let her go.

The walk back down the remainder of the tunnel passed in a blur. About fifty yards from the base of the stone staircase that led up to the old mayor's office, they were met by the MI5 and FBI agents and Durham DCI.

"What the hell happened?" the male MI5 agent demanded, holding a pistol at his side.

"Grey's dead," Walker answered, leading Ivy toward the

stairs. "How bad's the damage above ground?" He wasn't sure how powerful the main device had been.

"No structural damage reported to the cathedral or other buildings around Palace Green as of yet, but we won't know the extent of it until we can get an engineering team in to do a full inspection. Are any of you hurt?"

"No." Although he still didn't know how that was possible.

The expected chaos was waiting for them when they stepped through the portrait hole and into the wood-paneled room. Various security personnel swarmed them. Walker waited until he'd gotten a good look at Ivy in the brightly lit room before allowing himself to relax.

She was pale, battered and bruised, but dammit, he'd never seen her more beautiful than right now. What she'd done, the incredible bravery she'd shown, floored and humbled him.

He had a lot to make up for with her, and he just wanted the rest of all this to be over with so he could do exactly that.

"Walker. Come with me." The MI5 agent grabbed his arm. He reluctantly let Ivy go, but not before he gave her a long, meaningful look. "We'll talk after this is all cleared up, yeah?"

She nodded, held his gaze while the female MI5 agent led her to the door and disappeared into the crowd of people standing out in the hallway. Walker exhaled wearily and glanced around.

Warwick, Heath and Chloe were all being corralled by different agents as well. It was standard procedure to split them up, interview them all individually to ensure everyone told the same story. But shit, all he wanted was to be alone with Ivy.

He'd hurt her badly last night. To the point where she thought he'd hated her guts and would leave her to die. He couldn't stop thinking about it. About what he could say or do to apologize and fix it.

Once the initial chaos settled down in the room, he went

with the male agent down a short flight of stairs, past a tactical team standing armed and ready—and far too late to be of any use to anyone.

Walker entered another, smaller room and the agent shut the door behind them. He locked down his personal feelings and mentally geared up for what was coming.

He knew the drill better than anyone, because he'd been in the agent's place before too many times to count. It would be hours more until he'd been interviewed by all the agencies involved and reported back to his own acting boss at the CIA.

A sudden wave of exhaustion hit him at the thought. Ivy was strong. In spite of everything she'd just been through, in spite of spending the past few hours thinking she would die, she would lock all that down and get through the rest of this process fine. He was proud of her for that too, but wished she didn't feel the need to be that tough all the time.

"Okay, Agent Walker, let's—"

"Just Walker," he said, sinking into a chair on the other side of the table from the agent.

By the time he'd relayed everything to him and everyone else tasked with interviewing him, and allowed a paramedic to check him over, he'd mentally moved on from all of it. All he could think about now was Ivy.

He needed to see her. Hold her. Tell her how sorry he was, and how much he cared about her.

When they finally released him and he stepped out into the marketplace a little before eleven that night, the sky was a deep, rich indigo and only a handful of emergency vehicles remained in the market square behind the police cordons. Somehow his phone had survived both explosions intact, so he texted Ivy right away.

I'm finished. Where are you?

Three dots appeared as she typed. *At the rental.*

Thank God. He didn't think he could have withstood having to wait any longer to see her.

I'm on my way.

He was desperate to get to her. Desperate to apologize and make amends. Desperate to get inside her again. Feel her surround him, let him in completely the way she had before everything had turned to shit between them.

Show her exactly how much she meant to him.

On the way, he quickly texted Donovan in case he'd heard anything about the situation through the grapevine. *I'm OK. Ivy too. Grey dead. Tell Shae I'm all right. Will call tomorrow. Give her a hug for me.*

Then he turned his phone off. He didn't want any interruptions with Ivy. Anything else could wait.

By the time he got across Old Elvet Bridge, turned up the cobbled alley and saw the turquoise-painted door at the end of it, his heart was pounding, the need to touch Ivy overpowering everything else.

Light shone through the curtains drawn across the cottage's front window in the living room. Before he could reach for the door handle, it opened. Ivy stood there dressed in a sweater and jeans, hair slightly damp and the scent of her shampoo trailing on the air.

"Hey," she said with a smile that was way too wary. "Everything go okay?"

Fuck this.

He walked straight in, shut the door with his foot and pulled her into his arms. "Yeah, everything's fine now." Now that he was holding her again and had the chance to fix this.

She seemed taken aback by his intensity, but she wrapped her arms around him and held him just as tight. Walker closed his eyes, breathing in her scent. He let her go when she pushed gently against his chest, looked into her eyes.

Her troubled eyes as she took a step away from him. "I just need to know if…"

"If what?"

"If you reported me," she said quietly.

He stared at her, his heart clenching as her words sank in.

Oh, goddamn it. On top of everything else she'd been through the past twenty-four hours, she'd been sitting in here alone wondering whether he'd turned her in for her role in Grey's capture in Moscow.

"*No*," he said in an anguished voice, cupping her face in his hands while his heart cracked in two. "No, sweetness, I would never… Oh, Christ, come here." He tugged her back toward him.

Relief flashed across her face, then her expression twisted and the strongest, deadliest and most capable woman he'd ever known buried her face in his chest and started to cry.

Walker wrapped around her and held her tight as her tears wet his shirt, his own eyes stinging. "I'm sorry. So sorry for what I said and what I did. I was a fucking idiot."

She sucked in a jerky breath, her shoulders shaking.

"Please say you'll forgive me. I know I don't deserve it after what I did, but—"

She slid her arms around him. Nodded.

He expelled a deep breath, feeling like he'd just escaped a death sentence.

TWENTY-TWO

Now that the dam inside her had cracked, Ivy couldn't control the tide of emotion pouring free. It embarrassed her but there was no stopping it. She'd reached her breaking point, and Walker had pushed her past it.

She hid her face against his solid chest, drinking in the feel of his strong arms around her, the solace and security they offered. For the past few hours, sitting here alone with her thoughts spinning around in her head, she'd braced for the worst. Finding out Walker did still care about her, that he had not only *forgiven* her but would protect her and keep her secret?

It broke her.

"Hey," he murmured, stroking the back of her head with one hand. "Don't cry, sweetness. Everything's okay now."

"S-sorry," she managed, horrified by the weakness she was showing. Back during training, she would have been locked in solitary confinement, deprived of food and sleep for such an unforgivable infraction. "I'm n-not usually...a crier."

"Well, it's been a bitch of a day."

She let out a watery laugh at his attempt at humor, managed to drag in a steadying breath and wipe her eyes before looking up at him. Her heart turned over at the look on his face. Admiration. Tenderness. Desire.

A burning, molten desire that sent a thrill shooting right down to her toes.

Walker's hand firmed around the back of her head as he dipped down to cover her lips with his. She sank into it, lost herself in the silken, seductive glide of his tongue against hers.

All the harrowing events of the past day fell away. There was nothing but this. No thought about what would happen tomorrow. Nothing but Walker and what he made her feel.

"Want you," he rasped out, his hold and kisses urgent, making her heart race.

What she was feeling went way past want. She needed him on a cellular level. Felt like she would die if she didn't get him on top of her and inside her in the next few minutes.

The bedroom down the hall from the kitchen was tainted with bad memories. She tugged him backward toward the stairs instead.

He paused at the foot of them to press her flat against the wall, pinning her there with his hips, the bulge of his erection trapped against her abdomen. *Yes. More. Hurry.*

But he didn't hurry. In fact, he slowed down, his tongue sliding between her lips to play with hers. Dragging across her lower lip before he caught it gently between his teeth, nipped then sucked on it, his unrelenting grip on her making her belly flip in the most delicious way.

Just when she was ready to rip his clothes off where he stood, he bent and scooped her up in his arms. She let out a startled laugh and wound her arms around his neck, but it died away the instant she saw the naked intensity on his face, read the unquenched need in his dark blue eyes.

In seconds, he had her up the winding staircase and into the other bedroom. He set her on her feet at the end of the bed and immediately began pulling off her shirt. She helped him, flinging it to the floor along with her bra and shoving his shirt off his broad shoulders while he undid her jeans.

When they were both naked, he pushed her flat on the bed and came down on top of her. She groaned and arched into him, reveling in his heat and weight. The freeing yet secure feel of him anchoring her to the bed as he kissed her again and again, as if he couldn't get enough.

She twined around him like a living vine, gasped when his dark head dipped and his mouth closed around an aching nipple. He flicked his tongue across it, sucking with a firm pressure that sent heat pouring between her legs.

As if he knew it, he stroked a hand down her side, over her hip and inward to her aching center. His skilled fingers stroked her slick folds, wrenching a soft groan from her before he found the hard, swollen knot of her clit. He stroked her with the exact right pressure and speed, drenching her in pleasure, his mouth now busy on her other breast.

"I'm close," she gasped out, aching for the feel of him sliding into her. The heat and fullness. The intimate connection of their bodies joined together. "Hurry."

"No."

She tugged at his hair, shuddered as his wicked fingers pushed her closer to the edge. "Walker…"

He released her breast, eased down her body until his face was between her legs and stroked his tongue across her clit.

She gasped. Closed her eyes. *Oh, God…*

His long fingers found her core. Slid just inside to tease the aching bundle of nerves there. Ivy whimpered as sensation suddenly sharpened and expanded. "Now, now," she demanded, setting her feet flat on the bed to give her more leverage.

Walker finally lifted his head. Stretched out on top of her to settle his hips between her splayed thighs and braced his weight on one forearm. Staring into her eyes, he reached down with one hand and guided himself into her.

Ivy's fingers curled into his shoulders. Holding tight. *Yes, yes, yes...*

He held there for another breathless moment before surging deep.

She cried out, eyes slamming shut, and dug her nails into his back. The sudden pressure, the incredible fullness at having him buried inside her formed a knot of emotion in her throat.

He murmured something to her that she didn't catch, but his soft, tender tone told her everything she needed to know as his lips skimmed across her closed eyelids. Her cheekbone. The edge of her jaw. All while pumping in and out of her in a steady, relentless rhythm, the pad of his thumb finding the side of her clit.

Oh God, oh God, oh God...

Orgasm rose sharp and fast at the edge of her consciousness. She wanted it. Craved it with every fiber of her being. But she also wanted more. Wanted them locked together in the most intimate human connection possible when she went over the edge and took him with her.

She pushed at his shoulder. "Let me on top." She wanted to be in control right now. Wanted to take him.

"Now?" His deep voice was like velvet against her ear.

"Yes." Her knees were bruised and scraped but she didn't care. She wanted this. Needed it.

Walker slid his hands beneath her then rolled and stretched out on his back, putting that long, powerful body on full display for her.

Ivy didn't know where to look first. Breathless, she draped herself over him, made a hungry sound as she nibbled her way down his neck, over his chest and down his stomach.

One hand curled around the hot, thick length of his erection while the other slid between her thighs to stroke her aching clit. His abs contracted as she stroked him, his blue eyes flaring hot like a match strike as he stared down the length of his body at her.

The need to tease him and draw this out took over suddenly.

She shimmied down low enough to take him in her mouth. Swirled her tongue around the flared head. Tasting. Teasing. Licking and sucking the hard length of his cock until his thighs tensed and his fingers bunched in her hair, his breathing turning ragged and a low, rough sound of pure need coming from him.

Only then did she slide up to straddle his hips and slowly ease down on him, watching his face the entire time.

Walker's hands flew to her hips, fingers digging into her flesh while she took him to the hilt. He made a deep, delicious sound of male pleasure and flexed his hips, adding to the heat and pressure between her thighs.

She quivered, stared into his eyes while she rocked, her right hand sliding between them to find her clit with a fingertip. She was so wet, so swollen and turned on, the instant she touched herself it magnified the pleasurable ache of where his thick length rubbed the hidden spot inside her.

Ivy gave a soft, plaintive moan as sensation shivered through her. Her head fell back, her entire body suffused in ecstasy.

"Oh, Christ, look at you," Walker rasped out, sliding one hand up to squeeze and play with her nipple.

She couldn't respond, utterly lost in him, in her pleasure as it built higher and higher, the feel of him moving inside her, the sound of his rapid breaths and the way he touched her pushing her over the edge.

The orgasm built, rippled through her in long, delicious waves that went on and on, prolonged with each rock of her hips. She moaned again, let out a satisfied sigh before forcing her heavy eyes open and planting both hands on his sculpted pecs.

"Your turn," she whispered, hungry to watch him as she made him shatter the way she just had.

Walker stared up at her, both hands holding her hips again as she worked him. She drank in every detail. Every tiny shift in his expression. The growing tension in his face and body. Watching the pleasure take hold of him until his jaw was rigid and low, almost inaudible groans came from his lips with every rocking glide.

He was beautiful. The most erotically gorgeous thing she'd ever seen as he let her take him. Then his eyes closed and he bucked beneath her as the climax hit with a rough moan of ecstasy.

Her heart swelled, filling her chest until she thought it might burst. And there was no way for her to deny or hide from it any longer.

She was in love with him. No matter what happened from this moment on, no matter what had happened before, she loved him. Always would.

In the sudden quiet that surrounded them, she stretched out on top of him to tease his lips with hers. Melting into a series of slow, lingering kisses that quickly had her getting hot and bothered all over again.

Walker made a rough sound and locked his arms around her, holding her tight with her face pressed to the side of his neck. She breathed him in and exhaled slowly, her entire body loosening.

He was right. It *had* been a bitch of a day. But somehow they had survived and it had ended in the most incredible way possible.

"I'm sorry for what I said last night," he murmured.

She shook her head. "I should have told you sooner. I

thought about it a thousand times. And I swear I wasn't targeting you or Grey in that op, I was trying to get—"

"I know."

She went still. "You do?"

He made a deep sound of confirmation, his big, warm hand gliding up and down the length of her back. It felt incredible. She never wanted him to stop. Never wanted to move again.

"I understand why you did what you did," he said in a low, quiet voice. "And to be honest, if it'd been me, I probably would've made the same call. There was no way you could've known what would happen after that. No one could've. And... I'm glad you told me."

"Really?" Because he sure hadn't been glad last night. Not that she blamed him. She'd known it would be like dropping a bomb on him and their burgeoning relationship.

"Mmhmm." He kissed the edge of her temple, his short beard catching her hair as he sighed. "And goddammit, I hate thinking of what happened to you after. And today."

"Don't think about it. I made it through. Because of you and the others."

His fingers trailed over her left hip. Lingered on the indentation of her mark. "What's this?"

"My Valkyrie brand." The Valkyrie symbol that marked her as one of the select few to make it through the program.

Walker stiffened then flipped her onto her side before she could say another word, reached across her to switch on the bedside lamp and study her mark. A dark scowl covered his face. "What the *hell*," he muttered in a tone she'd never heard from him before.

"It's the mark we got when we graduated from the program."

He looked up at her, still scowling. "Chloe said it was a *tat*."

She lifted a shoulder. "They used to use a tat before my

group came along. Then someone within the cadre decided to switch it to a brand."

He trailed his fingers almost reverently over scarred skin, as if he wished he could soothe the pain she'd felt when she'd gotten it. "Ivy, God," he breathed.

The brand was nothing compared to everything else she'd been through. And his reaction lit up the defensive part of her. "I'm proud of it. I consider it a badge of honor."

"It's brutal and barbaric, is what it is. Damn." He dipped down to kiss it, pressing his lips to the mark twice, three times. "It makes me crazy to think of what they did to you. To all of you."

"Then don't think about it."

He groaned and pulled her back on top of him, held her even tighter, as if he didn't ever want to let her go. She was more than okay with that, but afraid to hope for it. "Do you have any idea how amazing you are? How brave and smart and insanely talented you are? I'm in fucking awe of you, Ivy. Never imagined meeting anyone like you."

His praise simultaneously filled her with warmth and made her ache in places she hadn't known existed. "I never imagined meeting anyone like you either."

"But it's a good thing?" His hand was back at her hip now, rubbing her mark gently.

She grinned at the teasing edge to his voice. "Maybe. Haven't made up my mind yet."

He rolled her onto her back and came down on top of her, arms braced on either side of her head, his eyes serious. "Ever been to the Oregon Coast?"

She blinked up at him, insides tensing. Afraid to hope or read anything into what it might mean. "No."

"It's beautiful this time of year. Especially Crimson Point."

He dipped down to brush a tender kiss across her lips. "I'd love to show it to you."

Ivy realized belatedly that she was digging her nails into his shoulders. Realized with a start that she was afraid. Afraid to trust whatever was happening between them because it was so new.

Terrified of being vulnerable to a man again.

And yet she knew instinctively that Walker would never hurt her. Not on purpose.

He was everything she'd lacked in her life. Everything she'd secretly yearned for. Someone solid and dependable she could count on. Lean on.

A man she could entrust her secrets and her life to. That made him one in a billion.

So…maybe it was time to stop punishing herself and seize this chance at happiness.

Her heart was racing as if she'd just sprinted for a mile. "I'd love that. Tobias," she added with a smirk.

He growled and tightened his hold, crushing her to him as she laughed. "Walker," he corrected over her giggles. "Just Walker, even to you."

TWENTY-THREE

Warwick let the hot water pound down on his sore neck and shoulders in the shower of the flat he'd rented for his stay in Durham, his muscles aching. He hadn't arrived back until after midnight with all the interviews and paperwork, and had been so knackered he'd crashed hard as soon as he hit the bed.

What a hell of a day yesterday had been.

First the insane situation with Grey in the crypt, nearly getting his arse blown up again, then the aftermath with its numbing interviews and protocol from all the various security agencies involved in the investigation. He'd only had maybe three hours' sleep, with nothing to eat besides a coffee and a Greggs sausage roll since yesterday morning.

He dialed Walker's number and walked to the window overlooking the street. From here he could see the west side of the river and Framwellgate Bridge. The rain had stopped and there were patches of blue sky high above the twin towers of the cathedral.

Seeing the massive building still standing tall and proud on the peninsula sent a rush of pride through him. Very few people would ever know how close the city had come to losing it yesterday.

"Mornin'," he said when Walker answered. "I don't know about you, but I'm clammin' for some bait."

"You're...what?" Walker asked in his slower-cadenced drawl.

"Starvin'. You and the others eaten yet? I know a great place for brunch in town. Figure we deserve to all sit down to a proper meal together to celebrate before we go our separate ways."

He wasn't sure where he would go yet. Maybe up to Newcastle for old times' sake. Maybe to London or...hell, he didn't know. Try to forget everything for a while. Figure out what to do next. He sure as shite couldn't go back to just existing again the way he had before.

"Hell yeah, we do. Hang on a sec." Walker's muffled voice called out to someone, signaling he must have covered the bottom of his phone. "Ivy and I are in. Send me the details and I'll let Chloe and Heath know too."

"Right. Incoming." He ended the call, reserved a table at the place and sent the info to Walker.

He'd no sooner done that than he got a call from the MI5 agent in charge of the Grey investigation back at GCHQ. There had been friction between them from the get-go because he hadn't wanted Warwick on the taskforce. They hadn't spoken again until last night. "Mornin'."

"Good morning," the man said in his crisp, proper London accent. "Thought I'd let you know that the recovery team has reached the crypt. They're currently gathering up Grey's remains—what little is left of him, anyway. And the structural engineers just reported that their initial inspection shows there was no structural damage done to the cathedral or any other buildings around Palace Green."

"That's good news." He paused. Raised his eyebrows when the agent didn't say anything more, watching the people walking across Framwellgate bridge. "Somethin' else on your mind?"

"Yes. I, uh…just wanted to thank you again personally for your assistance in this case. And for the…" He drew a breath. "The outstanding courage you showed yesterday."

Would've been nicer without the pause, but he'd take it. He'd never gotten so much as a kiss my ass from either the military or the government when he'd been wounded. This was a welcome change. "My pleasure. That it?"

"Yes." He ended the call.

Once again, he'd been cut loose. At least this time he'd gotten a decent thank you for your service before they severed ties with him.

He tucked his phone away, put on his jacket and backpack and left the flat. There was still another twenty minutes before their reservation so he took his time on the way, strolling along the river for a bit and stopping to watch the water rushing over the weirs. The Riverwalk itself was busy this morning, full of people out enjoying coffees and pastries on the cool Sunday morning.

A subtle prickling at the back of his neck made him glance to his left. Two young men in hoodies had been staring at him. They quickly looked away and commenced a conversation.

He kept walking and the prickling faded. He mentally shook his head at himself.

Grey was dead. The job was done.

He was free to get on with his life. He didn't need to be paranoid anymore. There was no reason for anyone to be following him now.

Except for Grey's network.

He dismissed the thought and kept going, thinking about the new chapter he was about to begin in his life.

Except he didn't have a life anymore. Not really. And he couldn't shake the growing sense of dread his sudden lack of purpose posed.

Reaching the foot of Framwellgate Bridge, he glanced up at the castle looming above on the right. The cathedral bells began to toll from the top of the hill farther down the peninsula, calling everyone to mass, the melodic sound echoing on the morning air.

So strange to think that Grey had almost succeeded in destroying it along with more lives yesterday. Stranger still that only hours ago, he and the others had been fighting for their lives beneath it all.

No one outside of the agencies directly involved would ever know what they'd done in that tunnel yesterday. The public would only know that an undisclosed operation had taken place, the hostages freed and that Grey was dead.

They would be all the happier for their ignorance.

He passed a busker playing a fiddle at the top of the bridge and continued up the incline on Silver Street, pausing at the top at the marketplace. The area next to the Town Hall and St. Nic's was still cordoned off, its entrance guarded and police vehicles filling the square. Curious onlookers were standing around taking pictures and trying to figure out what was going on.

They'd missed all the fun by about twenty hours. And he would bet every cent of his military pension that officials would seal up the tunnel entrance for good once this was done, burying the legend of its existence forever along with what had really taken place inside yesterday.

The buzz about yesterday meant the town center was busier than usual this morning. He overheard several people he passed talking about whatever mysterious thing had happened. Felt that little niggling sensation at his nape again.

Glancing over his shoulder, he spotted the same two blokes from before. But they were engrossed in conversation, not seeming to be paying attention to him.

Unless they were trained to appear that way.

Stop. Let it go.

He moved through the throngs of slower-moving people up Saddler Street and up the hill to the restaurant, trying not to think of what would happen when he left Durham. The prickling disappeared again.

Since being wounded, he'd become somewhat of a recluse through his recovery. Today he had officially been cut loose again, all on his own. He was looking forward to spending another hour or two in the company of people he admired and who understood him before that happened.

He spotted the wooden sign hanging from a building up ahead on the left. A little hole-in-the-wall place he'd fancied trying. Inside, a hostess took him through the small reception area and past the narrow counter with its display case of freshly made cakes and pastries.

At the back, the restaurant opened up into a cozy brick courtyard with windows set into the far side that overlooked the east side of the river where the Hatfield rowing team was out practicing. Thought of Laura Hawes and Chad Clifford. He doubted either of them would be returning to uni anytime soon, but at least they were safe and would be reunited with their parents today.

Taking a seat at the private table reserved for their group, he studied the menu. Right away he picked out the bacon stottie. It had been ages since he'd had one.

"There he is."

He glanced up, smiled as Ivy came toward him with a bright

smile, Walker right behind her. Apart from a few bruises on her cheek and a swollen lip, she appeared to be recovered from her ordeal yesterday. He rose, pulled out a chair for her. "How you feelin'?"

"Great, thanks." She scooted her chair in and grabbed a menu. "So, what's good here?"

"Everything. Or so I'm told." He didn't react outwardly when Walker sat next to her and draped an arm across her shoulders. He'd figured something had shifted between them last night. "Should I offer me congratulations?"

"Rather you didn't," Ivy said, still looking at her menu.

He hid a grin, curious about her background. The things she had withstood yesterday and her bravery had amazed him. She was no ordinary analyst or intel expert. She was far, far more than that. "Fair enough." He leaned across the table and lowered his voice to a murmur. "Will you tell me about your training instead then?"

Her bright hazel gaze focused on him over top of the menu. "I think I might, actually. Someday." The hint of a smile creased the corners of her eyes.

He inclined his head and resigned himself to wait until she was ready. "Areet then. Someday. I'll hold you to that."

Chloe and Heath arrived just as the waitress took their drink orders. Chloe was in high form today, fairly bursting with energy, chattering away a mile a minute as she took a seat at the table.

Five seconds in, she noticed Walker's arm around Ivy and stopped dead, a big grin spreading across her face. "Well, all right!" She punched Walker in the shoulder. A solid punch that would have made a lesser man wince. "You be good to her, or you'll answer to me and the others."

Walker's lips twitched. "Nothing like being threatened first thing in the morning, hours after neutralizing another one." Everyone chuckled.

The server came back with their drinks and took their brunch orders. Warwick ordered the bacon stottie—

"What the heck's a stottie?" Chloe asked, looking at her menu.

"A kind of bread made here in the northeast. Big, flat round thing. Makes capital sandwiches."

She nodded in satisfaction. "I'll have one of those too then."

Warwick handed the server his menu. "With brown sauce, please, pet."

"Mine too," Chloe said. "Brown sauce is good, right?" she asked him after.

"Aye, you'll love it."

As soon as the server stepped away, Chloe jumped back into the conversation she'd started earlier about her sisters named Amber and Megan, relating a story. "Wait, so are you two sisters as well?" he asked, looking between her and Ivy. What were the odds that two sisters both had such a high level of training?

"Yep." Chloe beamed at her.

Big family. "How many of you are there?"

"Nine," Ivy said with a secretive grin. "We're a really interesting family. Maybe I'll tell you about us someday too."

There was plenty of laughter among the group as they had their brunch, but throughout it, Warwick was keenly aware of being the odd man out.

Heath and Chloe had a comfortable way about them that spoke of being together for a while. Whereas Ivy and Walker's chemistry was newer. More intense. Each moment of eye contact or a shared smile loaded with tension he would have to be blind not to pick up on.

There used to be someone who had looked at him that same way.

He shut down that thought before it could take hold. Nothing but pain could come of going there. That was all over now. That part of his life was done. Dead, really. He was nothing but a ghost now.

"Hey, anyone hear anything about the cathedral yet today?" Chloe asked. "Been wondering about the damage when that central pillar came down. Personally, I hope it flattened him to the thickness of a piece of paper," she said, lowering her voice.

"I got an update from GCHQ right before I came up here," Warwick said. "No structural damage. Crews are working now to secure everythin' and…clean up." There were only two other couples eating on the other side of the courtyard so he didn't say more, but everyone at his table would know perfectly well what he meant.

"I'm glad to hear that," Ivy said.

"I estimate that we mitigated the damage by at least sixty-percent by eliminating the four vests. Maybe as much as seventy-five," Chloe said, taking a sip of her latte. "Without that, it would have been a different story. Anyway, enough shop talk. What's everyone doing after this? Ivy?" She turned to her friend, propped her chin on her hand and stared at her with keen interest. "What's the plan for you now? Hmm?" She looked pointedly at Walker and back to her.

Ivy fought a smile and picked up her coffee. "Actually, I think I might go on a little holiday."

"That's fantastic!" Chloe straightened. "Good for you. Where?"

"Walker's invited me to go back to Crimson Point with him."

"Knew it!" Chloe crowed and swiveled around to punch Heath in the shoulder. Hard. "Told you. I totally called it."

"You totally did," Heath said without missing a beat as he forked up another bite of his meal.

Chloe turned to Warwick. "What about you?"

"Not sure yet." He still didn't want to think about it.

A ring tone went off. "Sorry. It's my daughter." Walker shifted to fish out his phone, smiled when he saw whatever message was there.

"All good?" Ivy asked.

He nodded. "She's back in Crimson Point and apparently at a book club meeting." He grinned as he watched the video, showed Ivy. "They're reading Jane Austen and all dressed up in Regency costumes."

"That's so cool. Can I see?" Chloe said.

Walker turned his phone around so she could see it. Warwick glanced at it too.

A young brunette woman around twenty or so had the camera pointed at herself. Must be Walker's daughter. She wore a plain white dress and had her hair done up like those period movies he'd seen on the telly.

"Hi, Dad. Glad to hear everything's okay over there now. Anyway, here's me at my first book club meeting. Anaya dragged me, but it wasn't really a hard sell after being under house arrest for the past week. Say hi, everyone!" She raised her phone and panned around the room behind her, showing the others.

Warwick froze, almost choked on his coffee when the camera caught a redhead near the back of the group. Without thinking, he shot out a hand and snatched the phone from Walker to reverse the video, the blood rushing in his ears.

His heart nearly stopped altogether when he paused on the woman. The lighting was shite and there were too many others crowded close to her for him to see her clearly, but…

He could never forget that face. No matter how many

concussions or comas he suffered, only death would ever erase that face from his memory.

Marley.

He stared in disbelief, his heart thudding painfully against his rib cage. And only then did he become aware of how quiet the others were as they all stared at him.

He thrust the phone back at Walker, raised his coffee cup with a slightly unsteady hand and took another sip, the hot brew suddenly tasteless in his mouth.

"What's wrong?" Ivy asked in concern.

"No, nothin'." The painful lump that had formed in the center of his chest expanded and rose up into his throat, making it difficult to swallow. He couldn't believe Marley was in Crimson Point of all places.

Stop. Let it go, he ordered himself, even as he knew it was impossible. He might just as well order himself to stop breathing.

He'd let her go long ago. For good reason.

She thought he was dead. Didn't know what had happened. Telling her now would only cause her more pain and he never wanted to hurt her again. Wanted her to be safe and happy, and that could never happen with him.

He'd told himself that it was for the best enough times over the past sixteen months that he'd eventually believed it. Or told himself he had. But seeing her now, even that low-quality, grainy image of her, and finding out she lived in the same town as Walker…

The awkward lapse he'd caused faded as the others began talking amongst themselves again. Warwick remained silent, too immersed in his thoughts to pay attention to what they were saying.

Chloe had asked him where he would go after this. Until two minutes ago, he hadn't known. Now he did.

The need to see Marley in person again was a living thing inside him, even if it would be from afar. Even if no good could come of it.

Even though this would only torture him more.

He had to see her. Just one more time, to satisfy himself that she was truly okay.

So he was going to Crimson Point, Oregon.

TWENTY-FOUR

"You swear you're both okay? Really?" Shae asked in a worried voice.

Walker shifted his phone higher and propped a shoulder against the wall as he stood looking out the window of the hotel room he and Ivy had spent the night in. Not that they'd slept much.

The bed behind him was rumpled, pillows everywhere and the duvet heaped on the floor. In front of him, the London skyline was silhouetted against a clear blue sky. A steady flow of traffic moved over Westminster Bridge, the parliament buildings and Elizabeth Tower standing on the opposite bank of the river.

"I swear, darlin'. Bit bruised is all. Ivy's okay. I'm taking care of her."

A loaded pause answered his words. "Like, personally? Alone?"

He smirked at the mingled shock and hope in his daughter's voice, but wasn't ready to just blurt out to Shae that they were involved now. They hadn't yet put a label on what they were, and hadn't talked about telling Shae yet.

"I'm saying I'm looking out for her to make sure she's okay."

"Oh." She sounded disappointed. "So…what happened yesterday? I've seen a couple things in the news online but it's all really vague, which I guess is to be expected. It said a domestic terrorist named Isaac Grey died in an explosion in Durham. Were you and Ivy both involved in any of it?"

"Yes. I can't tell you exactly what happened right now, but I'll share what I can, when I can."

"Okay." She gave an annoyed sigh. "I hate this part of your job too because I'm nosy, but I get it. Will you be coming home soon then?"

"In a few days."

"And you won't have to go back to working on anything related to this? It's over?"

She was worrying about him again. "All over," he promised. "I'll be back in Crimson Point and annoying you full time again by the end of the week."

"You don't annoy me," she said on a laugh. "Well, unless you lock me down like a prisoner or ask about my love life."

"Yeah, how's that part going, anyway? Any developments since I've been gone?"

"Daaaad. No."

Finn better step up and make a move soon before Shae got frustrated and made up her mind to move on. She was strong willed and stubborn when she made a decision. "Okay, well, I bet you're glad to have your freedom back. What've you been up to since you got home?"

"Yes to the freedom, and just the book thing and hanging out with a friend."

"Which friend?"

Her hesitation gave it away before she answered. "Finn."

Yep. *Thought so.* "Ah. That's good."

"Yeah? You like him?"

"You know I do."

"Good. What day are you coming home?"

"Probably gonna book a flight for three days from now." Enough time for him to wrap up meetings here at Thames House with MI5 and the Home Office, then pop up to the Cotswolds to see Kiyomi and Marcus.

It would also give him and Ivy an entire day alone together to decompress before they flew back to the States. They were also stopping in New York City to have dinner with Rycroft on the way home.

"Send me your flight info. Finn and I'll pick you up."

"You don't have to do that. I can—"

"No, we're coming," she said flatly, and he didn't have the heart to argue.

In the reflection in the window, he saw Ivy step out of the bathroom behind him, completely naked as she towel-dried her hair. He spun around to look at her, brain short-circuiting so much that he lost track of the conversation.

She was stunning. He wanted her all the damn time. Didn't think he'd ever be able to get enough of her.

"Dad. You still there?"

"Sorry, what?" he said, jerking his brain back into gear. Ivy raised her eyebrows at him in silent question.

Shae, he mouthed, and she smiled. A soft, endearing smile that did things to him inside. Things that made him want to press her down onto the rumpled bed and kiss her from the crown of her head to the soles of her feet, stopping to linger on the tender folds between her thighs on the way back up.

"Nothing. You sound distracted. Need to go?"

"No, I..." He held Ivy's gaze, hesitating.

As if reading his mind, Ivy's lips curved into a mischievous smile and she lifted a shoulder as if to say *go for it*.

He let out a breath. Chose his words with care. "Shae, listen, there's something I need to tell you. About Ivy."

"Okay," she said slowly. "What about her?"

"Well, the thing is—"

"Oh my God, are you guys *together*? Please tell me you're together." She sounded breathless with excitement.

Walker blinked, not expecting that reaction. But Jillian had been gone five years. Shae was all grown up now and he wouldn't lie to her about something this important. Not when he hadn't expected to feel this way again. Ever.

"Yes," he said. "I'm sorry to tell you like this. I wanted to wait until—"

"Are you *kidding* me? I'm freaking *thrilled*. Hey, Donovan!"

He stiffened in alarm. "Don's there?"

"Yeah, he and Anaya just came over a bit ago. Guys, guess what?"

He winced. "Sweetheart, maybe don't—"

"Dad and Ivy are together!" she said then laughed, her excitement and joy stamping out any annoyance he felt at having his personal business announced. An answering cheer rose in the background. "So when do I get to meet her? Where is she now?"

"She's right here." He held Ivy's gaze. Raised his eyebrows in question and received a hesitant nod. "You wanna talk to her?"

"Umm, yes please! No, better yet, I'll call you back on video. Hang on."

Oh, shit. He ended the call. "Shae's calling back on video," he blurted.

Ivy's eyes widened and she flew back into the bathroom, emerging seconds later tying the belt of a white hotel robe around her waist. She ran her hand through her hair just as

Walker's phone began to ring, the nervous gesture tugging at him.

"Hey," he answered, love and pride washing over him when he saw Shae's bright, happy face on camera.

"Hi. Love you, Dad, but I wanna see Ivy now. Please and thanks."

Chuckling, he hit the reverse camera to show Ivy standing across the room in her robe. She lifted a hand, put on a smile. "Hi, Shae."

"Hi! I'm so happy to see you and 'meet' you finally. Dad, hand her the phone, will you?"

He rounded the bed and gave it to Ivy with a reassuring smile. "Thank you," he whispered, quietly enough that only she could hear him.

"Oh, gosh, you're gorgeous," Shae said before Ivy could get out a single word. "I don't know how I pictured you exactly, but it wasn't this. Hi."

Ivy gave an uncomfortable laugh, pink flooding her cheeks. It was so damn adorable it was all Walker could do not to kiss her right then and there. The woman was tough as nails and deadly, yet a simple compliment made her blush and talking to his daughter made her nervous.

He stretched out on the bed, tucked a hand behind his head and watched as Ivy and Shae chatted. Well, mostly Shae chatted, but his daughter had a way about her that was completely disarming, and he could see it had already put Ivy more at ease.

"Where are you living now?" Shae asked a few minutes later just as Walker was about to intervene and take the phone back.

"Up in the Cotswolds right now, actually. Do you know where that is?"

"Yes, sort of, but I've never been there. Love to go someday though. So, when do I get to meet you in person do you think?"

Ivy hesitated a second and met Walker's gaze before looking back at the screen. "Actually, your dad asked if I wanted to come back with him to Crimson Point for a bit. Would you be okay with that?"

"Uh, *yes*. Oh my gosh, that would be amazing. And I know Donovan would love to see you again. You'll love Anaya, by the way. She's a sweetheart. And Callum and Nadia will be excited too."

"Great," Ivy said in clear relief. "I actually haven't been back to the US in a long time, so it'll be nice to be on home soil again." Walker didn't miss the poignant edge to her voice. He wanted to hug her.

"Really? How long?" Shae asked.

"Years and years."

"Well then, we'll have to make up for lost time. We'll show you all around. There are some really cool spots here, and everyone's really great. We'll introduce you to everyone—"

Recognizing the deer-in-the-headlights look on Ivy's face, Walker took his cue and plucked the phone from her hand. "How about we leave the social tour for after she's had a few days to decompress?" he said with a fond smile.

"Oh, yeah, of course! Whatever she wants. Oh, man, I'm so excited."

"Me too. Listen, we've gotta get going now, but I'll call you later once I know my flight details. Okay?"

"Sure. Nice to meet you, Ivy," she called out. "Love you, Dad."

"Love you too, darlin'. Bye."

He ended the call, blew out a breath and chuckled as he lowered the phone to his lap. Ivy still looked a little stunned. "You look more shell-shocked right now than you did in the tunnel the other night."

She laughed weakly and fiddled with the ends of her hair.

"I'm not used to socializing with strangers. Let alone my boyfriend's daughter."

"Boyfriend?" He felt like much more than that. He caught her waist with one hand and tugged her to him, pulling her down into his lap on the bed. She fit against him so perfectly, all warm and soft and cuddly and smelling edible. "You okay?"

"Yeah, that was just a bit of a surprise." She ran a finger along the edge of his beard, a gentle smile on her lips. "She's lovely, Walker. Really great."

"Yeah, she is." He understood that all this was overwhelming to her. But he was a package deal, and he was glad the initial introductions had been taken care of.

He shifted her to straddle him, the flash of her bare thighs and the shadowy center between them sending a rush of lust through him as she settled over his growing erection. Lifting a hand, he pushed the hair away from the side of her face and searched her eyes. "Is this moving too fast for you?"

She stared at him a moment. "Honestly? I have no clue. I don't know what normal is, so I have nothing to gauge it by."

He grinned and tugged her down to kiss her softly. "We can slow things down if you want." But he wasn't letting her go. "All I want is more time with you, for us to get to know each other more because I think we could be amazing together."

"I thought we were already pretty amazing together." She gave him a saucy smile.

"We are." Any more amazing and it would probably kill him. He eased his hand into the gap between the halves of the robe and pressed his palm flat between her breasts. Her heart rate was elevated, and not only because she was getting aroused. "I know you're scared, sweetness."

Her eyes widened in outrage, then she scoffed. "Scared? I'm not scared."

Yeah, she was. His Valkyrie was secretly terrified of what

was happening between them. Learning to fully trust him wasn't going to be fast or easy, especially after his epic fuckup the night before what had gone down in that crypt.

"It's okay. Because you're the bravest woman I know. You can handle this. Us. I know you can."

Ivy relaxed, her expression shifting to unguarded. Tender. Turning his heart upside down with it. "Will you help show me the ropes?" she murmured, reaching down to untie the knot in the belt of her robe.

"I'll do any damn thing you need me to," he answered, sliding one hand into the gap she made and tugging her down for a long, slow kiss with the other.

This woman already held his heart in her hands. He was going to win hers completely in turn.

TWENTY-FIVE

Ivy battled the nerves dancing around in the pit of her stomach as she and Walker came into the baggage claim area at Portland airport. So much had happened over the past week, she was still trying to process it all.

Grey. The argument with Walker. Then that terrible time in the tunnel and crypt. Briefings immediately after. Meetings. More meetings in the days that followed, in Durham, Cheltenham and London.

At least they'd been able to sneak up to Stow to visit Kiyomi and Marcus one more time for a few hours between the last of their meetings, and then spent all of yesterday alone together in London before flying out.

She'd needed that break with him, that time alone without any outside pressure or distractions. It had been heaven to sleep in together, lay there curled up in his arms and just…be.

They'd flown to New York on the way back and met up with Rycroft last night, then up early for the trek across the country. And any minute now, she would meet Walker's daughter.

Their convo on the video call had gone pretty well, she

thought, but she would always be somewhat socially awkward around people she didn't know really well, and she wanted Shae to like her. The good news was, any remaining threat against Shae had died along with Grey.

She could imagine Shae must have at least some misgivings about her and Walker being involved all of a sudden. She was the first woman he'd been with since Shae's mom had passed away, and now he was bringing her home to meet his daughter.

No pressure.

Breathe, Ivy. You got this.

As ever, her internal warning detectors were all working overtime as they always did in a crowded, public place. She was aware of everything going on around them. That part of her she couldn't shut off assessing and looking for possible threats. Beside her, Walker was watchful, but much more relaxed.

She was usually a master at compartmentalizing things, but this had been an overwhelming time and this whirlwind romance between her and Walker was moving a lot faster than she'd expected. She had no idea where it was going, was trying to just stay in the moment and not think too far ahead.

Afraid to hope it might last in case it all fell apart.

She reached her free hand up to grasp the pendant of the necklace Kiyomi had given her two Christmases ago. For strength.

For luck. Because damn, she was deep in unfamiliar territory and needed this to go well.

Walker glanced down at her, gave her a little smile that melted her insides as he squeezed her hand in reassurance. Part of her wished they were still back in their London hotel room bed. "Ready?"

"Yes." She hated that he knew she was nervous, uncomfortable with even him seeing that small weakness in her. She wasn't sure she would ever lose that part of herself, but so far

Walker was amazing with her. Patient and solid and so incredibly supportive and affectionate.

A tiny, frightened part of her she didn't want to acknowledge wanted to curl into him and beg him to never let her go.

"There's Shae," he said with pride, a gorgeous smile breaking over his handsome face as he gazed across the crowded space.

Ivy followed his line of sight and immediately picked out Shae waving excitedly from near the automatic doors, standing with a tall, dark-haired guy around her age. "I guess that's Finn?"

"Yep." He walked faster, pulling her along with him, only letting her hand go to engulf his daughter in a bear hug. "Hey, darlin'."

"Hi, Dad. Oh, it's so good to see you," Shae said, eyes closed as she squeezed him back.

The sight flooded Ivy with warmth. Watching the two of them, it was so clear that Walker and Shae adored each other.

A sudden memory flashed through her mind. Fleeting and fragmented. Of her own father hugging her when she was small. There was a Christmas tree in the corner of the room.

She snapped back to the present when Shae's green eyes flipped open to focus on her. She tensed.

"Ivy. Hi." Shae reached for her, smiling.

Pushing aside her awkwardness, Ivy stepped forward and accepted the embrace, resting her hands lightly on the back of Shae's leather jacket. "Hi." It was sweet of Shae to be so kind and to make her feel welcome.

Shae took hold of Ivy's shoulders and eased back, looking from her to Walker and back again with a huge grin. "I love everything about this."

One side of Walker's mouth kicked up, then he held out a hand to the young man. "Finn. Good to see you."

"Sir." Finn shook with him, then Ivy.

Ivy was definitely picking up on a subtle undercurrent between him and Shae, saw the secret grin Shae was trying to hide and the happiness shining in her eyes when Walker and Finn shook hands. Yep, there was absolutely something brewing between these two.

"You guys must be tired." Shae stepped to Ivy's side and wound an arm around her waist. "Come on. We're parked against the curb. I know you said to take it slow with Ivy, Dad, so Anaya and Donovan aren't coming over until tomorrow morning."

Walker shot Ivy a grin. "Good thinking, Shae."

"Right? I'm considerate that way."

Ivy trailed outside along with the others, still trying to adjust to her new reality. It felt so odd—but nice—to be accepted so easily and quickly. Whatever Walker, Donovan, Nadia and Callum had told Shae about her, it must have been good.

While Finn loaded their bags in the trunk of a purple MINI waiting at the curb, she and Walker got into the back. Shae sat in the front passenger seat while Finn drove them the two hours over to the coast.

At first, Ivy felt uncomfortable as hell being stuck in a vehicle with Walker's daughter and forced to make conversation, but pushed herself out of her comfort zone because she wanted to make a good impression.

Then Walker reached for her hand, his warm, strong fingers closing around hers. And when she glanced over at him, the proud smile he gave her filled up the empty place she'd been carrying around inside her since she was a child.

Every day she fell harder for him. Faster. That scared her too.

Finn didn't say much during the trip, mostly only answering when he was spoken to. He reminded her of Walker that way.

When they reached Crimson Point, Shae insisted they drive along the waterfront. The cute little shops and businesses they passed were decked out for Halloween, the windows filled with ghosts, spiders on webs and grinning jack-o-lanterns.

It looked like something out of a movie set, adding to the sense of suspended reality. Could this all be real?

They stopped at a café-slash-bookshop called Whale's Tale —clever name—and went in to grab treats and drinks. A pretty blonde named Poppy smiled and waved at them from the back. Walker told Ivy it was the owner, who was married to the town sheriff.

Finn drove them down the rest of Front Street after. Ivy gazed out at the rolling ocean. It was incredible. She couldn't wait to tell Kiyomi about this place.

A few minutes' drive up the hill, Finn turned into a quieter residential neighborhood and down a series of short streets to a slate-blue two-story house that reminded her of East Coast beach style, set back from the road. Finn and Walker grabbed the luggage while Shae hurried up the front walkway to let them in the door.

"Welcome," she said to Ivy, opening the door with a flourish and stepping aside.

"Thank you," Ivy murmured, walking in and looking around. The space was tidy and cozy with an unmistakable sense of warmth and peace about it. The bands around her chest that had been tightening on the drive here suddenly loosened.

Walker stepped in behind her. Set a hand on her waist, his fingers squeezing.

"Well, we're gonna let you two get settled. I've made reservations at the Italian place in town for six-thirty, so we'll meet you there." Shae hugged Walker, then Ivy before slipping out and shutting the front door.

Ivy turned to Walker in the sudden quiet, reeling a little.

He chuckled softly. "You made it."

She smiled back, feeling silly for being so off-kilter. "So where am I sleeping?"

His eyes darkened. "With me." He caught her hand and led her up the stairs to what was clearly the master bedroom.

It overlooked the backyard, and had a partial view of the sea from the windows across the room. A wide king-size bed dominated the room.

She looked up at him, felt that familiar swooping sensation low in her tummy. "Are you sure Shae won't be uncom—"

He put his arms around her waist and tugged her toward him. "You're sleeping with me in my bed," he said in a low voice that sent a shiver through her.

Then he closed the door, undressed her and took her to that wide bed, making her forget everything but him and the magic between them.

Shutting the rest of the world out and making her believe that maybe, just maybe, a happy ending might be possible for someone like her.

TWENTY-SIX

Two weeks later

Ivy finished drying the last pot at the sink and paused to look through the kitchen window into the backyard. Through a gap in the massive evergreens, a strip of green-gray ocean was visible down the hill in the distance. The wind had picked up a few hours ago, capping the waves with crests of white in the fading sunset as they rolled toward shore.

A gust of wind beat against the windows and moaned around the eaves. Inside, the house was cozy, quiet and peaceful. Shae was at class, and Walker was still at his office down near the waterfront. She wasn't exactly domestic but she'd wanted to have dinner ready when they both came home so she'd just thrown together a casserole recipe she'd found online that looked good.

Everything about this still felt surreal. Like she was dreaming. Or living someone else's life. Certainly not hers. She'd never known this level of peace before. Not even while living at the carriage house at Laidlaw Hall.

She felt like she could breathe here. Heal. Except she was due to leave in two days.

She didn't know how she would bear it.

Her phone rang. Kiyomi's name popped up on screen. "Well, hey there," she answered, anxious to talk to her bestie. The oven timer started dinging. She turned everything off but left the casserole in for now, focused on the conversation.

"Hey, yourself. I'm just here feeding your cat. He says hi." A familiar meow in the background made Ivy smile. "How's it going there?"

"Give my baby a hug from me. And honestly? It's been incredible." She'd braced for more awkwardness with Shae in the house while Ivy stayed with Walker in his room, but Shae had gone out of her way to make sure it wasn't weird at all. And thanks to her and Walker, Ivy already had a community of people here who seemed to like and accept her. A dozen people or so, nearly doubling her existing circle.

Kiyomi chuckled. "You sound shocked by that."

"I am. It's like I've stepped into a whole other world here." One different than any she'd lived in before. "And I'm just…a little shaken by it, I guess." She could be totally honest and open with Kiyomi. Didn't feel an ounce of embarrassment by telling her all of this. Every single one of her Valkyrie sisters had struggled to adjust after being emancipated with the death of The Architect.

"Why?"

She blew out a breath, struggled to put into words the secret fear she'd been carrying around ever since Walker had invited her to come here. "I don't want to ruin this."

She was still terrified she would. What the hell did she know about normalcy? Or relationships? "And I don't want to leave."

For as long as she could remember, even throughout all

those years when she'd tried to bury it, there had always been a secret longing inside her for safety and security. Probably a childhood wound that came from losing her parents so young and being put into the Valkyrie Program. Through everything she'd never lost the soul-deep craving for stability and a sense of belonging in the world.

Even with all her issues, from the small amount of therapy she'd done over the past two years, she knew that having those things was the only way she could ever be able to move on and truly leave the past behind her.

"Then don't," Kiyomi said.

Ivy quirked a brow. "Oh, well. Didn't realize it was that easy."

Kiyomi laughed softly. "It's not. Not for us, anyway. So I'm going to let you in on the secret to not ruining it."

"*Great*. Lay it on me."

"It's simple. And it's also maybe the hardest thing you've ever had to do."

Ivy waited, anxiety twisting deep inside. "Which is?"

"It's time to let go of who you were, and fully embrace who you've become."

She shook her head, bewildered. "Who have I become?" She had no clue.

"You're not Julia anymore. You're Ivy. Which means all the things that Julia used to fear and value don't mean shit now. Because that's all finished. You're free now, babe. Free to live and to love however and whoever you want. Isn't that amazing?"

Her throat tightened with a rush of emotion. She pressed her lips together for a moment, tears pricking the backs of her eyes. "It's terrifying," she whispered.

"I know, been there. But it gets easier fast if you let it. I promise."

"I'm trying. I swear I am." She wanted this so badly. Wanted to make Walker happy.

"I believe you. How's Walker?"

She went all mushy at the thought of him. "He's…everything," she admitted, fighting the stupid urge to cry. She'd never been so emotional in her life as she'd been the past few weeks. If she was being honest with herself, she'd lost her heart to him long ago.

"Aww. It makes me so happy to hear you say that."

Ivy laughed softly. "Feels weird to say it out loud." One of the things she loved most about him was how laid-back he was about most things.

She had full freedom here to come and go as she pleased. He placed no expectations on her whatsoever, hadn't tried to pin her down, force her into making any promises or commitments. "But…"

"But?"

"I can tell he wants more from me."

"Because he knows you're holding back," Kiyomi murmured.

Ivy sighed. "I don't know how to explain it, it's like he's cracked something open inside of me and I can't close it back up."

"I think that means he's your person, babe."

"Yeah." She thought it a thousand times a day. And yet she couldn't shake the fearful whisper at the back of her mind. "I keep thinking this can't be real. Like I'm waiting for the other shoe to drop."

"That's because you've been conditioned to expect it to drop."

She shook her head at herself, annoyed. "But I trust him and he's good to me. Why am I so damn afraid to say how I feel? What's wrong with me?"

"Nothing. It's going to take time to undo what was done to you, and for you to fully trust anyone again. Even him. And you also hate the feeling of uncertainty, the lack of control over any of this. But if I'm being brutally honest with you, there's never any guarantee that things will last. And the only thing you can control is yourself."

"You sound like that therapist you made me see."

"Do I? Good. Means I must've learned something from all my sessions with her. But boil it down for me. What's at the core of all this?"

Ivy rubbed at her forehead, her deepest insecurity taking hold. Kiyomi's pointed question forced her to look at the parts of herself she'd kept locked away her entire life. "I'm not sure I deserve a man as good as him," she admitted finally.

"Whoa, I'm gonna stop you right there, because that's ridiculous bullshit."

"No, really, I—"

"I understand how hard it is for you—for us—to let down our guards fully and let someone in to the deepest part of you. But the way I see it is, does Walker really deserve *you* and not the other way around. And based on what I know and what I've seen between you two… Yeah, Ivy, the man fucking deserves you. And you deserve him. That's the truth. All the others think so too, if that helps."

Ivy had to swallow the lump in her throat before she could respond, Kiyomi's words hitting her hard. "Yes." Her heart beat faster. Racing along with her thoughts. Walker had been so incredibly patient with her these past few weeks, never getting too serious or trying to push her into something she wasn't ready for.

She'd been a goddamn fool to hold back with him.

"Kiyomi?" she said. "I love you to death, but I gotta go right now." Without waiting for a response, she ended the call and went straight to the back door, grabbing her thin wallet and keys on the way out.

She had to see Walker. Right now, and tell him how she felt before she either burst or chickened out. She refused to be a coward any longer.

The last rosy rays of the sunset filtered through the broken clouds at the bottom of the hill as she got in the car they'd rented for her and set off toward town. Partway down the hill toward Front Street ten minutes later, she spotted Walker's SUV and her heart leapt with a combination of elation and terror, aware that she was standing on the precipice of something huge.

She flashed her high beams at him and cut into a pullout at the side of the road, was already out of her vehicle before he'd parked.

He opened his door and got out, his welcoming smile fading into a look of concern. "What's the matter? Is everything—"

She launched herself at him. Flung her arms around his neck and flattened her body against his, holding on tight while every cell in her body vibrated.

Walker caught her and gathered her to him, holding her in that solid grip she would never get enough of in a hundred lifetimes together. "Hey," he said softly. "What is it?"

"I love you," she told him. "I love you so much and I had to tell you."

He went dead still for a second, then peeled her away from him and held her by the shoulders to search her eyes. She'd never seen his expression so intense.

Then it softened. Turned impossibly tender while his stare seemed to burn straight into her soul. "Christ, I love you too. I've wanted to say it to you so many times, but—"

"Say it again."

He smiled. A smile so beautiful it brought a rush of tears to her eyes. "I love you, Ivy. Been in love with you ever since our first night in Durham."

She couldn't answer, certain her heart would explode at any moment. This feeling inside her was too huge. Surely she couldn't survive it.

Walker gently wiped the tears that fell with his thumbs. "Now you say it again."

"I love you," she whispered. It was easier now. Telling him made her feel truly free. Powerful.

He groaned and kissed her again and again. Hungry, desperate kisses, his hands gripping her hip, her hair.

"Then stay here with me," he rasped out against her lips. "With us. Shae would love it. I'd love it more." He pulled her tighter to him, his lips caressing hers. "Say you'll stay."

"Can I bring Mr. Whiskers here? He misses me." She missed him like crazy too, made Kiyomi and Marcus send her pictures and updates every day.

Walker laughed. "Yeah, you can bring Mr. Whiskers."

Ivy drew in a deep breath. She had no more excuses to hide behind. No more obstacles standing in her way...except herself.

The precipice was right beneath her now. She was standing on top of it, toes curled around the edge, staring down into the abyss below.

She couldn't see the bottom. Didn't know what lay there. There could be rocks waiting for her to smash against.

Or she might not ever land.

She gathered herself. Consciously and forcefully let go of the fears that had controlled her for too long. Allowed the strength of her love for him to give her the courage to propel forward into the unknown.

And jumped. Knowing that Walker would be there to catch her.

"I'll stay," she whispered, clinging hard to his solid frame.

He groaned in relief and triumph and Ivy felt a new surge of strength pour through her. A gut-deep certainty that she'd made the right call.

Against all odds, in spite of everything she'd done and everything that had happened to her, she had a brand-new life ahead of her now. It was the most unbelievable gift—one she'd never expected to be given.

All thanks to the incredible man holding her.

Then she remembered the casserole in the oven and tensed. By the time they got back it might be inedible. Not a great start to her domestic efforts. "Walker?"

"Hmm?"

"I'm pretty sure I burned our dinner."

TWENTY-SEVEN

Eight days later

"Warwick, you're here!" Ivy said, jumping up from her seat with a big smile. "I'm glad you accepted our invitation to come visit, it's so good to see you."

He grinned as he strode through the restaurant toward the table over by the huge picture windows, where Walker and Ivy were seated. He'd planned to make a trip here anyway, but their invitation gave him the perfect cover. "Good to be here." He hugged Ivy, shook with Walker and sat across from them, ready for a well-earned pint and a good burger after many long hours of travel.

"How was the drive down from Portland?" Ivy asked him.

"Brilliant. Just under two hours." He always did better with the time change coming west than he did going east. He'd slept for half of the flight from London to Seattle and felt completely refreshed by the time his connection touched down in Portland.

The sense that he was being watched or trailed had eased as soon as he'd driven away from the airport. He hoped it stayed that way, but he couldn't shake that uneasy feeling that something wasn't quite right. And lately he'd been having dreams and brief flashbacks about the Lake District op. As if his subconscious was trying to tell him something important.

As if the gaps in his memory from that period were hiding something dangerous.

"Welcome to Crimson Point," Walker said, silencing those unsettling thoughts.

"Thank you. From what I've seen so far, it's champion." The Oregon Coast was every bit as beautiful as he'd heard. "Not hard to understand why you took the job here."

"No. Shae loves it too, luckily." He signaled to someone over at the bar. Moments later, a server placed a cold pint in front of Warwick. "Cheers," Walker said, raising his own glass.

He grinned. Walker and Ivy seemed happy together. It was nice to see, if bittersweet since it made him think of how it had been with him and Marley. "Cheers."

"So, is this an actual holiday, or are you here for a job?" Ivy asked.

"Bit of both." He'd wanted to get away from the UK for a while. But the real reason was, he was here to do some secret recon on Marley. "You're back to work now, I'd wager," he said to Walker.

"Yeah, back at the office full time. And Ivy's been working for a nonprofit with one of her sisters and a friend here in Crimson Point."

"Really? That was fast," Warwick said.

"The foundation helps safeguard orphans in vulnerable spots around the world to protect them from trafficking. Anyway, no more work talk," Ivy insisted, and raised a knowing eyebrow at him. "Why are you really here?"

He bit back a smirk. "As you said, no more work talk."

She narrowed her eyes. "All right, fair enough." She passed him a menu. "The cheddar bacon burger is to die for."

The conversation was easy while they waited for their food and throughout dinner. The view from their table was incredible. Beyond the windows, the sky was nearly black except for the deep indigo ring around the full moon, its silvery rays shining on the rolling waves. He could hear the muted, rhythmic roar of it through the glass.

"Come stop by the house or the office for a visit before you leave town," Walker told him after another drink. "And think about what I said about applying for a job with us here. The company's growing constantly. We could use someone with your skill set and experience on our team."

"I appreciate that," he said. Crimson Point Security had a good reputation within the industry, and he both trusted and respected Walker. "But I don't think I'm ready to be tied down again just yet." Especially not with the eerie, intermittent feeling that he was being tracked somehow.

"Fair enough. Offer's there if you change your mind."

"I'll think about it." Maybe. Maybe not. In the meantime, he had other pressing matters to attend to. "Well, I won't keep you." He stood, tossed some bills on the table over their protests. "See you soon."

"Bye."

He walked through the bar and stepped outside, ready to go find the woman he'd just crossed the ocean for a glimpse of.

～

"I'M glad Warwick decided to come see us," Ivy said over the sound of the crashing surf as they walked north up the beach.

Walker tightened his fingers around hers. The wind had turned cold, gusting across the Pacific as it raced toward the coast and the restaurant was already a solid half-mile behind them now. "Me too. He's had a rough time since last June."

Chasing shadows while he hunted Grey across Europe and then the UK. Then finally finding him, only to be blown up by one of his bombs.

According to Rycroft and the other intel people Walker had spoken to over the past few weeks, Warwick shouldn't have survived his injuries. He'd been given a medical discharge and shown the door, only to be hauled back into service when they'd needed his insight on Grey. Where he'd narrowly escaped death a second time in the tunnel with them that final night, before being shown the door again.

Hell of a way to treat a decorated and elite soldier who'd served his country honorably for many years.

"He left pretty suddenly. Like he had somewhere to be. Why do you think he's really here?" Ivy said. "Amazing as you and I are, I don't believe for a second that he flew all this way to say hey to us and take off to Cali on a holiday."

"Must have to do with someone he saw in that video Shae sent." The way Warwick had reacted was beyond telling, no matter how hard he'd downplayed it.

"Exactly. Wonder who or what he saw?" She tucked a piece of windblown hair behind her ear, only for the wind to immediately tug it free.

"Not sure." With Grey gone, Warwick James was free. But alone.

Walker felt for the guy. Being that alone was no way to live.

"Oh, I see it!" Ivy said, looking straight ahead.

The lighthouse stood perched high atop the cliff overlooking the town, which was nestled into a small pocket in the coastline. It was no longer manned, but the swath of light it produced swept the bay faithfully each night, gilding the tops of the waves silver.

"That view never gets old." There was a little cove up ahead, a more sheltered beach dotted with large driftwood logs.

He led her to one, sat with her facing the ocean with the lighthouse in the background.

"It's just incredible." She closed her eyes and tipped her face back, her lips curving up in an expression of such contentment that he smiled too.

He'd asked her to stay, and she had. Mr. Whiskers had arrived at the airport in Portland last week and was now king of their castle, following Ivy around like a puppy and warming up to him and Shae more each day.

Seeing that look on Ivy's face now made Walker's whole chest tighten. He'd never imagined feeling this way again. Not this intense or deep.

It was different from how things had been with him and Jillian. She'd been warm and kind and outgoing, whereas he was more introverted. With her, things had been easy and relaxed.

Ivy was her polar opposite in so many ways. Mysterious and badass, yet sweet and thoughtful and sometimes almost shy in new situations. A constant study in contrasts that enthralled him.

Everything about her and their time together had been intense. Yet she'd fit seamlessly into his life here.

Every day she did or revealed something that amazed him. The other day, he'd come home from work to find that she'd fixed their hot water tank and installed the new light fixture Shae had been wanting for her room.

Shae hero-worshipped Ivy, and Ivy already had a huge soft spot and protectiveness with Shae. He was pretty sure Ivy would even tell Shae about parts of her past in time, a level of trust that she granted very few people.

He was completely hooked on her. Addicted even, and knew he'd never get tired of peeling back all her intricate layers to reveal the true essence of the woman beneath. He couldn't imagine his life without her. Didn't want to.

That's what he'd brought her here tonight to tell her.

Sliding his arm from around her, he went to one knee at her feet. Took her hand.

She opened her eyes, the moonlight revealing the startled look on her face when she saw him kneeling there. She sat absolutely still and didn't say a word. Looked almost a little afraid as she stared back at him.

He hid a smile. There was nothing for her to be afraid of anymore. "Ivy."

"What?" she half-whispered.

"I don't know how I lived without you for so long."

A tremulous smile tugged at her lips.

"All I do know is that we've both been alone for so long and I love you to death and never want to let you go." This was fast. They both knew it. But he'd also never been more certain of anything in his life.

He reached into his coat pocket and pulled out the velvet box he'd picked up after work last night. Opened it. "Will you marry me?"

She stared at him in shock for another moment, then her gaze dropped to the ring. The one he'd had custom made after getting Shae's approval on the design.

Ivy only ever wore two pieces of jewelry, and she treasured them both. One was a bracelet containing a single jet bead with a pink cherry blossom on it.

The other was a necklace with another jet bead. An ivy leaf sat in the center, with a ring of tiny cherry blossoms surrounding it.

The symbolism of the ivy was obvious. The cherry blossoms represented Kiyomi. Both pieces were cherished gifts from her. Physical symbols of their unbreakable bond as friends, sisters. Warriors.

Ivy had only known that kind of bond with a handful of people in her life. She had also known the pain and bitterness of betrayal. Walker had designed this ring as an enduring reminder that his commitment to her was as unbreakable as any of the Valkyries'.

"I had it made for you," he explained, giving her a moment to take it all in. The moonlight made the round solitaire diamond in the center sparkle and highlighted the white-gold band made up of tiny alternating ivy leaves and thistles. "Ivy leaves for you, and thistles for me because Walker is—"

"Scottish," she finished with a sniffle, biting her lower lip. Then her eyes lifted to his. "Oh my God, Walker…" The moonlight caught the shimmer of unshed tears. "You want to marry me?"

She sounded stunned by it. As if she couldn't fathom how he could possibly love her so much, let alone want to spend the rest of his life with her.

"More than anything." He reached out to slide his free hand beneath the back of her hair and cradle her nape, rubbing his thumb gently over her soft skin. He had no doubt at all that she loved him. Understood that her background made this a huge and scary step for her.

"It's okay, sweetness," he murmured. "Just say yes. Trust me to be here for you. Always."

Staring into his eyes, a wide, beautiful smile spread across her face. "Yes," she said in a shaky voice and flung her arms around him. "Yes, I'd love to marry you. As long as you're sure you know what you're doing. Valkyries aren't the easiest people to be in a relationship with, you know."

Walker chuckled. "I'm sure." He held her tight, smiling

against her windblown hair as a deep sense of peace and excitement flooded him.

Fate had unexpectedly given him this second chance at happiness with this incredible woman. He and Ivy already had a solid foundation beneath them. Together they were going to build a beautiful life on it.

TWENTY-EIGHT

Warwick drove slowly along the waterfront with his window cracked open, keeping an eye out for the little red sports car Marley drove. A strong, damp breeze was blowing off the water, pushing the waves onto shore with brute force. They crashed onto the beach with an audible thud, the exploding spray lit up by the moonlight. The air smelled of clean, cold seawater, the salty tang to it reminding him of home.

His former home. Because he didn't have one anymore.

Traffic was light. Most of the shops and businesses along the waterfront were closed now with the exception of a pub and the restaurants. He looked around one last time before pulling up the address he'd saved in his satnav and turned east up the hill, leaving the heart of Crimson Point in the rearview mirror.

There were only a few vehicles behind him on the road. Within a few blocks, the commercial area gave way to residential neighborhoods that thinned out more and more as he neared the highway at the top of the hill, tall forests of evergreens covering the rugged terrain. From there it was only a few miles north to his exit.

He drove to the center of another small town and parked in

front of the care home. Every window facing the street was lit. From his position, he could see some of the staff moving around inside the ground-floor rooms, tending to the elderly residents living there. But none of them had long, dark red hair.

He couldn't believe he was actually sitting out front of where Marley worked. When he'd first found out about it during his initial research after leaving Durham, it had surprised him. But really, it shouldn't have. Given her background, her innate drive to help others and her incredible management skills, this made perfect sense. Warwick could see her being happy here.

He needed Marley to be happy.

He pulled out a small pair of binoculars to take a better look, unconcerned about anyone seeing him where he was parked. Marley's car was nowhere in sight. She'd probably finished for the day while he was at dinner, but he'd wanted to come here anyway to see the place. Try to fill in some of the blanks about her life that he'd missed since he'd last seen her.

Satisfied she must have left for the night, he started the car and drove a ways south.

The back of his neck startled prickling.

He looked around him again, searching for any sign of danger. Thought he spotted a dark-colored car behind him that he'd seen behind him in town before dinner, but it was too far back to be sure. He sped up to go through an amber light and the car behind him stopped.

Relaxing, he kept going, concentrating on his destination. A condo building on the next block where, according to his research, Marley had lived until this past July.

One of her neighbors had turned out to be a member of Home Front. The neighbor had been one of the shooters involved in the Washington State concert mass shooting, and killed directly afterward.

Warwick wasn't sure whether the shooting and Marley finding new living arrangements were related, but she had moved out of the building less than two weeks after the attack.

He continued across town to a quieter area surrounded by parkland. Until a dark car similar to the one before showed up in his rearview again.

The warning buzz at his nape came back with a vengeance.

He automatically went into evasion mode, cutting a hard left and pulling a U-turn to speed back the other way.

The car kept coming at him in the other lane, about to pass him. He glimpsed two people up front as he drove by. Both male. Wearing ball caps. Neither glanced at him.

It put him on edge.

But the vehicle didn't swing around to follow him. Warwick turned right at the next street anyway. Waited. No headlights appeared behind him.

After a minute he continued on, circling back to the quiet street behind the park where the cottage Marley was renting stood. None of the cottages had driveways, only curb parking out front. Large red maple trees lined either side of the street, giving him a big area of shadow to park in between the puddles of light cast by the streetlamps.

A woman was walking a Golden retriever up the opposite sidewalk. He reached for the binoculars on the passenger seat. Stilled when headlights appeared behind him. This car was red, however. Not dark. It drove up and slowed close to him, allowing him to see the plate.

His heart gave a hard kick. *Marley*.

He slid down in his seat slightly. The car pulled past him and parallel parked in the empty spot three spaces ahead. Every muscle in his body pulled tight when the door opened and the dome light showed a glimpse of deep auburn hair.

Marley's long, lithe frame slid out of the car and straightened, adjusting the straps of a large bag over her shoulder with one hand and holding a mobile phone to her ear with the other. One look at that silhouette and his whole chest compressed.

Every muscle in his body pulled taut as she shut the door and rounded the bonnet of the car. She walked toward her place while she spoke to whoever it was on her mobile, locking her vehicle remotely behind her.

He stared, heart thudding in his ears as he watched her walk away. So close. Right there in front of him after all this time.

It took a superhuman act of will not to jump out and race after her. Call her name.

The only thing keeping him in his seat was the knowledge that she thought he was dead.

He didn't want to cause her any more pain than she'd already suffered. It would be selfish and cruel of him to let her see him now. She was safer without him, better off living half a world away.

But self-inflicted torture was still torture. It felt like his insides were being torn apart as he sat there and stared after her.

Look at me, the desperate part of him he couldn't crush willed her. *Please look at me.*

He told himself that if she looked his way, it was meant to be. That if she saw him, he didn't have to hide. Because if she did, there was no way in hell he could stop himself from going after her.

But she didn't look his way. Didn't so much as glance around her as she strode up the walkway with her sexy, confident gait he'd always loved and tossed her long red hair back over her shoulders as she neared the front steps.

I'm alive, he wanted to scream. *I'm right here.*

He shoved out a breath and dragged a hand over his face, unable to take his eyes off her. He was a right tosser for coming here. She'd moved on with her life, as he'd wanted her to.

Yet the crushing pressure in his chest made it almost impossible to breathe while he sat here spying on her like a damn stalker, the deep yearning inside him turning to something bordering desperation.

He'd come here just to see her from afar. To ensure she was okay.

He'd seen what he'd wanted. Now he needed to go.

He raised his hand to reach for the ignition. Ordered himself to turn the key.

Couldn't. Couldn't stop staring at Marley as she stopped on her front step and reached toward the lock on the door.

He prided himself on his strength and discipline. Both of character and his ability to withstand whatever life threw at him.

But he was only human. Even he had his breaking point.

And her name was Marley.

He reached for the door handle. Froze when headlights appeared in the rearview.

He glanced in his side mirror. Tensed when he saw that same dark car coming up the street. It suddenly accelerated hard.

His heart stuttered. *No…*

He glanced back at Marley, his brain screaming a warning. She was still on the call, her back to the road. She was still undoing the lock while the car's engine revved, tearing up the street toward them.

The passenger window was open. He thought he saw the muzzle of a weapon.

He yanked on the door handle just as the retriever he'd seen before suddenly darted into the street.

The dark car swerved with a squeal of tires while the dog's owner lunged for it. Warwick ducked as two shots ripped past him through the night.

The woman with the dog screamed and grabbed her pet. Panic punched through Warwick as he whipped his head around to look at Marley. She was crouched down on her front stoop.

The shooter's car took off with a squeal of tires. He got a partial plate before it ripped around the next corner and disappeared from view.

When he looked back at the house, Marley was gone. Escaped inside. But there were two bullet holes in her front window.

Without thinking he ripped open his door and ran toward her house. Was halfway to the front door before he realized what he was doing, raw protectiveness driving him.

This wasn't part of the plan but he wasn't stopping. He had to guard Marley. Make sure she was safe.

No matter what it cost him in the end.

—The End—

*read Warwick and Marley's story next in *Lethal Reprisal*!*

Dear reader,

Thank you for reading *Fatal Fallout*. If you'd like to stay in touch with me and be the first to learn about new releases you can:

- Join my newsletter at: http://kayleacross.com/v2/newsletter/
- Find me on Facebook: https://www.facebook.com/KayleaCrossAuthor/
- Follow me on Twitter: https://twitter.com/kayleacross
- Follow me on Instagram: https://www.instagram.com/kaylea_cross_author/

Also, please consider leaving a review at your favorite online book retailer. It helps other readers discover new books.

Happy reading,
Kaylea

LETHAL REPRISAL
CRIMSON POINT PROTECTORS SERIES

By Kaylea Cross
Copyright © 2023 Kaylea Cross

CHAPTER ONE

Marley carried one end of the long wedding gown bag up Everleigh's front walkway that her bestie had lined with cute ghosts and spiders, to the doorstep where two jack-o-lanterns stood guard. "This thing weighs a ton for its size."

They were cutting it close. Everleigh's Pararescueman fiancé Grady was due home from his shift at the hospital in about twenty minutes. They had to get the dress hidden before he arrived.

"It's because of all the beading and the train," Everleigh said brightly, her long, pale blond hair shining silver in the moonlight as she carried the top of the bag. "And that's also why it cost so much."

"Worth every penny of the price tag. It fits you like a glove and the second you put it on your whole face lit up. I knew within five seconds of seeing you in it that it was The Dress. We could have stopped right then and saved ourselves the next two hours."

"And denied us the mimosas and appetizers they served us later? No way." Everleigh unlocked the townhouse door and stepped inside the bright, clean space. "Still can't believe I don't need to have it altered."

"It was meant to be." Marley slipped her shoes off inside the door, feeling right at home. She and Everleigh had become fast friends about five minutes after Everleigh had moved into their former apartment building across town.

Turned out Everleigh had been through her own personal hell and Marley had instantly felt protective of her—even before their psycho neighbor and his terrorist buddies had committed the mass shooting at the concert in early July and nearly killed Ev in the process.

At least the bastard was dead.

"Where are we carting this thing to, anyway?" she asked, shelving those thoughts. Everleigh's strength and resiliency amazed her. Life had repeatedly kicked her friend down and each time Everleigh had gotten back up and carried on. Now she was about to marry the man of her dreams—an honest-to-God hero who had saved her life. Nobody deserved happiness more than they did.

She reminded herself of that every time thoughts of the upcoming wedding stabbed at her heart and made her think of what might have been.

"I carved out some space in the guest room closet this morning, just in case I found The Dress at my appointment," Everleigh said.

"Good thinking." They carried it upstairs and tucked it away in its secret hiding spot at the back of the closet, then carefully covered it up to make sure Grady wouldn't see it if he came in here looking for his Air National Guard dress uniform.

Marley moved that and some of his gear to the opposite side of the closet, just in case. "There," she said, standing back to study their efforts in satisfaction. "He won't notice a thing."

Everleigh grinned, her slate blue eyes sparkling with excitement. "Operation Wedding Gown complete."

She was so cute using military lingo. Being engaged to a PJ and bestie with a former Marine had rubbed off on her. "Yes ma'am." She pulled the closet doors shut. "When do you want to look for my bridesmaid's gown?" She'd taken a quick look at the boutique earlier but hadn't tried anything on because today had been about Everleigh.

"Um, that's *maid of honor* gown, but how does next Sunday work for you?"

"Works fine." Since her job title change and promotion at the senior's care home last month, she now worked regular business hours Monday to Friday and rarely had to go in on weekends anymore unless there was some kind of special event or emergency. She'd even been able to take part of the afternoon off today to spend with Everleigh. "Okay, bring it in." She held out her arms expectantly.

Everleigh flashed her a smile and walked into her embrace. Her friend was a tiny little thing compared to her. Though to be fair she was six feet tall, so most women were smaller than her. "Thanks for today. I love my dress."

"You're welcome and I'm glad. It's stunning on you. Grady's jaw's gonna hit the floor when he sees you in it." Marley gave her a squeeze and let go. "Speaking of, your man's gonna be home any time now, so go ahead and stay up here to get ready. I'll let myself out."

"Okay. You're the best, Mar."

"I know, I can't deny it," she teased and headed for the stairs.

Outside on the walkway she inhaled the cool evening air, taking a big breath of the sweet scent of fallen leaves mixed with damp cedar and pushing aside the sudden wave of aloneness at the thought of spending yet another night alone.

Nope. Chin up. Happy thoughts, count your blessings and all that.

She had a lot to be thankful for. Fall was her favorite season. In the Pacific Northwest it was different from back in Kentucky but she loved it just as much here. This place was finally starting to feel like home now.

Back in her car she drove north up the hills away from Crimson Point, the ocean a vast black expanse lit up by a swath of golden moonlight behind her, struggling against the weight of sadness she'd been fighting all day.

Just a few short months ago she'd been dreaming about picking a wedding dress of her own. Until she'd received the call that had blown her world apart yet again. She still hadn't recovered from it.

A call came in on the hands-free system just as she turned onto her street and her oldest brother Decker's name popped up on the display, saving her from getting sucked into the sadness and grief she was still struggling to process. "Hey there," she answered, glad to hear his voice.

"Hey. This a bad time?"

"Nope. Just got back from wedding dress shopping with Ev. You got your flights finalized yet?" She was both excited and nervous about his visit. It had been almost two years since she'd seen him in person and now that he was finally out of the Corps she was hopeful that they could heal the invisible rift that had stood between them for the past fifteen years and work on having the close relationship she'd always wanted with him.

"Yeah. I fly into Portland around fourteen-hundred-hours on Friday."

Two days from now. "Oh, that's perfect. I get off work at four, so I'll be home when you get there. We can pop down to the waterfront for dinner and I'll show you around."

She'd bought him the softest flannel sheets yesterday in

preparation, had already washed them and made up his bed in the guest room. Tomorrow she'd buy the groceries for his favorite meals and make him homemade biscuits and gravy the morning after he arrived.

She didn't cook much these days, didn't see the point in going to all the trouble when it was only her. It would be great to get back in the kitchen and turn out some home cooking for someone she loved again.

Unbidden, Warwick's face swam in her mind. His hard features softening in a sexy, knee-weakening smile as he came up behind her at the stove and wrapped his arms around her middle while she made the gravy in her grandmother's cast iron skillet.

"Something smells incredible," he murmured in that deep, delicious Geordie accent from Northern England.

"Sausage gravy."

"No." His lips skimmed the side of her neck. "It's definitely you, pet."

"Sounds good," Decker said, yanking her out of the memory.

"Great. Hang on, I'm just about to get out of the car, so if I lose you I'll call you back."

She quickly parked along the curb in front of her rental cottage she'd moved into in the summer, set against a forested park in a quiet neighborhood just a few miles from Crimson Point. It didn't have a view but the price of the rent was right and she had the whole place to herself. The properties on either side of her were rentals too, but with a different management company and the house to the east currently had sketchy tenants she'd steered clear of.

"Have you heard from the boys recently?" she asked, slinging the straps of her bag over her shoulder as she climbed out of the car. Their younger brothers. Identical twins who had caused their share of trouble when they were younger.

"Not for a few weeks. You?"

A middle-aged woman was walking her goofy Golden retriever up the opposite sidewalk. "I talked to them both a few days ago." She locked her car as she strode up the walkway to her front door where the porch light glowed in the darkness, making a mental note to pick up a few Halloween things and some candy in case any trick-or-treaters came next week. Maybe she could even talk Decker into carving a pumpkin or two with her. "Neither of them could get leave to come see you but they both said to say hi."

He grunted in acknowledgment. "You sure I won't be in the way staying at your place?"

It would be funny if it wasn't so sad. She snorted. "I'm sure." She had nothing going on in her personal life and no one knew about the tragedy that had rocked her world in June. Not her brothers. Not even Everleigh.

She was still too raw to talk about it, the pain too fresh. But life, in its own cruel way, kept moving on, and she'd been forced to move on with it. After months of feeling empty and lost she had finally accepted that he was gone. Had put a lot of effort into creating a life for herself here.

"I can still book a rental," Decker offered.

"No way, you're staying with me." Left to his own devices, Decker would revert to his solitary ways and she'd barely see him. They needed the time together. "Don't worry, I promise to give you your space." Time and distance hadn't done their relationship any favors. It was time for a new strategy and a fresh start, beginning with this long-anticipated visit.

"All right."

"Text me when you land so I know—"

"That my plane didn't crash," he said in a dry tone that

made her smile. "I already sent you my flight details, so you can track me yourself."

She entered the code into the lock on the door. "Thank you." She'd adopted a pseudo-mother role at the age of sixteen, had tried her best to be the glue that held the remains of their shattered family together. It was an integral part of who she was. "I'm really looking forward to seeing you, Deck."

A short pause followed. "Me too." He cleared his throat. "See you Friday."

"Yes. Safe tra—" She broke off and looked over her shoulder when a car suddenly raced up the street behind her. It swerved to miss the retriever that had somehow gotten away from its owner, and two gunshots cracked through the air.

She instinctively ducked, swallowed a cry when the bullets punched through her front window just feet to her left. *Jesus*.

"What was that?" Decker demanded in a taut voice. "Marley."

What the *hell*? Marley didn't answer, too busy scrambling inside. Heart pounding, she flung the door shut and went to her knees behind the narrow section of wall between the door and the ruined window.

"Marley, what—"

"I gotta go," she blurted and ended the call, waiting tensely in place.

She heard the car speed off and disappear down the street. She stayed where she was a few more seconds, listening for the rev of that engine to signal it had come back. When it didn't, she pushed out a breath eased into a crouch to pull the edge of the curtain aside and take a look outside.

There were two bullet holes about chest height through the window. Beyond her tidy front yard the street was quiet and still. She rose to her feet and dialed 911 to report it.

Gun violence was practically unheard of here. Yet some asshole had just driven by and taken shots at her for kicks?

She turned toward the kitchen. The call had just connected when her front door suddenly flew open behind her. She whirled around, a scream sticking in her throat as a man stepped inside and shut the door behind him.

Shock slammed into her, along with an icy wave of cold.

"911, what is your emergency?" a woman's disjointed voice said through the phone now dangling at Marley's side.

She stumbled back a step and dropped it with a thud on the hardwood floor in the heavy silence that throbbed in her ears.

Stared in disbelief as a sharp blade of agony sliced through her, certain she was looking at a ghost. Or dreaming.

Because Warwick James was standing in her living room.

End Excerpt

ABOUT THE AUTHOR

NY Times and USA Today Bestselling author Kaylea Cross writes edge-of-your-seat military romantic suspense. Her work has won many awards, including the Daphne du Maurier Award of Excellence, and has been nominated multiple times for the National Readers' Choice Awards. A Registered Massage Therapist by trade, Kaylea is also an avid gardener, artist, Civil War buff, Special Ops aficionado, belly dance enthusiast and former nationally-carded softball pitcher. She lives in Vancouver, BC with her husband and family.

You can visit Kaylea at www.kayleacross.com. If you would like to be notified of future releases, please join her newsletter:

http://kayleacross.com/v2/newsletter/

COMPLETE BOOKLIST

ROMANTIC SUSPENSE

Crimson Point Protectors Series
FALLING HARD (Travis and Kerrigan)
CORNERED (Brandon and Jaia)
SUDDEN IMPACT (Asher and Mia)
UNSANCTIONED (Callum and Nadia)
PROTECTIVE IMPULSE (Donovan and Anaya)
FINAL SHOT (Grady and Everleigh)
FATAL FALLOUT (Walker and Ivy)
LETHAL REPRISAL (Warwick and Marley)

Crimson Point Series
FRACTURED HONOR (Beckett and Sierra)
BURIED LIES (Noah and Poppy)
SHATTERED VOWS (Jase and Molly)
ROCKY GROUND (Aidan and Tiana)
BROKEN BONDS (ensemble)
DEADLY VALOR (Ryder and Danae)
DANGEROUS SURVIVOR (Boyd and Ember)

Kill Devil Hills Series
UNDERCURRENT (Bowie and Aspen)
SUBMERGED (Jared and Harper)

ADRIFT (Chase and Becca)

Rifle Creek Series
LETHAL EDGE (Tate and Nina)
LETHAL TEMPTATION (Mason and Avery)
LETHAL PROTECTOR (Braxton and Tala)

Vengeance Series
STEALING VENGEANCE (Tyler and Megan)
COVERT VENGEANCE (Jesse and Amber)
EXPLOSIVE VENGEANCE (Heath and Chloe)
TOXIC VENGEANCE (Zack and Eden)
BEAUTIFUL VENGEANCE (Marcus and Kiyomi)
TAKING VENGEANCE (ensemble)

DEA FAST Series
FALLING FAST (Jamie and Charlie)
FAST KILL (Logan and Taylor)
STAND FAST (Zaid and Jaliya)
STRIKE FAST (Reid and Tess)
FAST FURY (Kai and Abby)
FAST JUSTICE (Malcolm and Rowan)
FAST VENGEANCE (Brock and Victoria)

Colebrook Siblings Trilogy
BRODY'S VOW (Brody and Trinity)
WYATT'S STAND (Wyatt and Austen)
EASTON'S CLAIM (Easton and Piper)

Hostage Rescue Team Series
MARKED (Jake and Rachel)
TARGETED (Tucker and Celida)
HUNTED (Bauer and Zoe)
DISAVOWED (DeLuca and Briar)
AVENGED (Schroder and Taya)
EXPOSED (Ethan and Marisol)
SEIZED (Sawyer and Carmela)
WANTED (Bauer and Zoe)
BETRAYED (Bautista and Georgia)
RECLAIMED (Adam and Summer)
SHATTERED (Schroder and Taya)
GUARDED (DeLuca and Briar)

Titanium Security Series
IGNITED (Hunter and Khalia)
SINGED (Gage and Claire)
BURNED (Sean and Zahra)
EXTINGUISHED (Blake and Jordyn)
REKINDLED (Alex and Grace)
BLINDSIDED: A TITANIUM CHRISTMAST NOVELLA (ensemble)

Bagram Special Ops Series
DEADLY DESCENT (Cam and Devon)
TACTICAL STRIKE (Ryan and Candace)
LETHAL PURSUIT (Jackson and Maya)
DANGER CLOSE (Wade and Erin)

COLLATERAL DAMAGE (Liam and Honor)

NEVER SURRENDER (A MACKENZIE FAMILY NOVELLA) (ensemble)

Suspense Series

OUT OF HER LEAGUE (Rayne and Christa)

COVER OF DARKNESS (Dec and Bryn)

NO TURNING BACK (Ben and Samarra)

RELENTLESS (Rhys and Neveah)

ABSOLUTION (Luke and Emily)

SILENT NIGHT, DEADLY NIGHT (ensemble)

PARANORMAL ROMANCE

Empowered Series

DARKEST CARESS (Daegan and Olivia)

HISTORICAL ROMANCE

THE VACANT CHAIR (Justin and Brianna)

EROTIC ROMANCE (writing as *Callie Croix*)

DEACON'S TOUCH

DILLON'S CLAIM

NO HOLDS BARRED

TOUCH ME

LET ME IN

COVERT SEDUCTION